THICK AS THIEVES

AN ASTER VALLEY NOVEL

LUCY LENNOX

KEEP IN TOUCH WITH LUCY!

Join Lucy's Lair
Get Lucy's New Release Alerts
Like Lucy on Facebook
Follow Lucy on BookBub
Follow Lucy on Amazon
Follow Lucy on Instagram
Follow Lucy on Pinterest

Other books by Lucy:
Made Marian Series
Forever Wilde Series
Aster Valley Series
Twist of Fate Series with Sloane Kennedy
After Oscar Series with Molly Maddox
Licking Thicket Series with May Archer
Hostile Takeover
Virgin Flyer
Say You'll Be Nine

Visit Lucy's website at www.LucyLennox.com for a comprehensive list of titles, audio samples, freebies, suggested reading order, and more!

PROLOGUE
JULIAN

It wasn't the first time Parker had snuck into my house in the middle of the night, but it was the worst.

He was already crying, and his clothes were covered in dirt. I'd left the bathroom light on by accident, and when the sound of the window woke me up, there was enough light for me to make out the smudges on his sweatshirt and debris in his hair.

Parker Ellis was awkward at the age of fourteen—tall and scrawny, all elbows and knees—but he was *my* awkward.

"C'mere," I croaked, opening the covers so he could get warm. I was still half-asleep. Normally, I would have been annoyed at getting my bed dirty, but I could tell how upset he was.

As soon as he dove beneath the covers, I dropped the comforter and pulled him in close. He smelled like the cold night air and the dry leaves he'd probably had to wade through to get to my window. "What happened? What'd they do?"

Parker's parents were assholes. They'd been assholes the entire time I'd known him, but it hadn't been until the last two years of elementary school that he'd started sneaking over to my house when things got really bad.

In the beginning, it had been loud parties lasting late into the night. But then his dad had gotten a job with lots of travel. There was less partying, but there was also more neglect. Parker's mom had gone out with friends instead of having people over. She'd forget to get groceries or feed him dinner.

Once my parents had figured out what was happening, they'd given him an open invitation to come to our house for meals anytime. They also knew he spent the night often, but since they had a "no sleepovers on school nights" policy, they simply looked the other way when he snuck in on a weeknight.

This had been going on for years, but lately, it had gotten worse. Now that we were in middle school, his parents felt like Parker was old enough to be left home alone overnight, sometimes for weeks at a time. His mom had gotten jealous of his dad's travel and had insisted on joining him on his trips, leaving Parker on his own in a big empty house with no food and no one to help him with his homework or take him to and from after-school activities.

Watching Parker's parents treat him like shit was the first time I'd realized even a kid from a family with plenty of money could suffer from hunger and neglect. It wasn't quite enough for anyone to call Child Protective Services and risk putting him in the system, since he was surrounded by families like ours who would take him in and make sure he had what he needed, but it still sucked.

"I hate them," he growled, snuggling in closer to me for warmth. His skin was cold and prickly with goose bumps. "I hate them so fucking much."

We had an important math test tomorrow, and Parker had been over earlier that afternoon so my sister, Hazel, could help both of us with our review homework. He'd walked home right after dinner the way he usually did when he came home with me after school.

"What happened?" I asked again. I rubbed his back through his sweatshirt, trying to help him get warm. Hot tears landed on my neck, and his fingers gripped the thin cotton of my T-shirt.

"My key didn't work. I had to crawl around in the bushes to find that rock thing where we keep a hidden one, but that didn't work either." He sniffed and took a breath. "So I waited for Mom to get home, but she never came. And then I walked down to the gas station to use their phone to call her. She said she..." His hand clenched tighter, accidentally catching one of the few hairs on my chest. "She changed the locks because she didn't trust the house cleaners. But she forgot to tell me, and then... and then she left to go to Chicago with a friend at the last minute. She said not to break a window or I'd have to pay for it. But my English homework is in there, and all my clothes, and..."

I was so angry, I wanted to punch something. Parker didn't have any money. We were fourteen. Every dollar he made trying to mow people's lawns in summer and shovel snow in winter was spent on buying himself food or other things his parents neglected to provide for him, despite all the money they had.

"Did you talk to your dad?"

He shook his head. "How can he help? He's in Florida at a conference. I'm just so embarrassed. I'm sorry for coming over again. I tried to sleep on the chair on the front porch, but it's too cold without a blanket."

I pulled his face out of my neck and held him by the cheeks. "You listen to me, Parker Ellis," I hissed. "You never, ever need to sleep outside when I have a warm, safe place for you here. Okay? Don't you dare think you have to stay there alone when you can stay with me. My parents love you. They wouldn't want you to stay there by yourself, even if you had a key."

He sniffed again. "Yeah, I know. Okay."

I grumbled about his asshole parents while he nestled back against my shoulder.

"I like staying with you," Parker admitted softly a few minutes later. "Everything's better when I'm with you."

I let out a snort. "You just like the snacks my mom gets."

He pinched my side. "Yeah, so? I also like that I don't have to care about what I say and do when I'm with you. I can just be... regular me."

"Same. It's more fun when you're here. I wish you lived here all the time." And I meant it. Parker was my favorite person, and if I could have him with me every minute, my life would be just about perfect.

"Yeah."

"No matter what, we have each other, right?" I said. "No matter what, it's you and me, together."

"Always," Parker added with a nod.

He got out of bed, grabbed my math notebook and pen from my desk, and scribbled something on it before tearing off half of a page and handing it to me with a flourish.

You and me. Always.

"Remember what we learned in English? Once you make a pledge in writing and agree to it, it's pretty much law," he said before settling back down under the covers. "At least, it will be for us."

My dad had always implied he wanted me to get a law degree one day and join him in running our family's mining business. I definitely didn't know much about the law yet, but I was almost positive there was more to a contract than just writing it down. There were supposed to be signatures involved. And a judge, maybe.

But I didn't say any of that, because this promise was about something more important than laws; it was about friendship. And intention. And love.

After reading the words several times over with reverence, I put it on my bedside table. "I agree."

We got quiet again, but after a while, Parker started talking. This was normal for him. I called it the daily download. He needed to get *all* of the thoughts off his brain before he could fall asleep.

"What did Hazel mean when she said Erin was her best friend?"

"Huh?" I'd started to fall asleep again, so it took me a minute to try and figure out what he was asking.

"Tonight at dinner. She called Erin her best friend. It just seemed weird."

"It's not weird. They're close like we are."

He let out a snort. "Not like us. They're not best friends. They're..."

"Erin is Hazel's closest friend, and Hazel is Erin's. That's what it means, Parks. Best friends."

Parker sat up and peered down at me. "If they're best friends, then you and I are more than best friends. You're my... my..." He paused while trying to think up a word.

"Go on," I teased. "I'll wait. Pretty sure it's just called best friends."

Parker got an evil grin on his face. "You're my lil' Peanut."

"Oh, no you didn't. That nickname needs to *die*, Shortbread." I launched myself at him, pinching and wrestling and yanking his hair, all the while laughing and secretly coveting every moment of close contact with him.

When we finally pulled away from each other, both of us breathing heavily and me half-hard, I scrambled off the bed toward the bathroom. "Gotta pee."

I closed the door behind me and shoved my hand down my pajama pants to squeeze my dick. This had happened before. Both Parker and I had gotten hard around each other, but we'd ignored it or joked around about it.

We'd always been closer than most friends. When Parker first spent the night at my house in second grade, there had been a really bad thunderstorm. After a scary crack of thunder, Parker had scrambled from the other twin bed into mine, and we'd held hands until the flash of lightning lit up the entire room. We snuggled together, holding each other tight until the storm finally went away.

The next morning, Mom had found us tangled up together in my bed for the first of what had turned out to be many times. After that, it was easy being physically close to him. He was touch-starved anyway, according to my mom. So we all made a point of giving him lots of hugs, and I used every movie night as a chance to hold his hand or snuggle with him on the sofa.

When a birthday sleepover with six guys last year had resulted in us breaking both of my beds, my parents had replaced them with one queen-sized bed.

"You and Parker will just have to make do," Mom had said with a shrug. "You were already getting too tall for those little beds anyway."

We hadn't minded. The queen was plenty big for our two tall but scrawny bodies.

But lately, it was getting harder for me to sleep tangled up in him without wanting to touch him *that* way. I already knew I liked guys, but I also knew that telling Parker I liked him like that could make things really weird between us.

I didn't want that. I didn't want anything screwing up what we already had together.

As for who Parker was attracted to, I had no clue. He wasn't really into girls, and he wasn't really into guys. The person he seemed happiest spending time with was me... well, except when he was getting ski lessons from my dad or Mr. Rokas, Erin's dad, who coached the high school ski team. Maybe he was ski-sexual.

That thought was enough to make my boner quit. I walked back into the room laughing.

"What's so funny?" Parker asked. I couldn't see his face anymore since I'd turned off the bathroom light.

"I decided you're ski-sexual."

"What the fuck?" he asked. I could hear the grin on his face.

"Ski-sexual. I think you're in love with skiing and want to marry it."

I climbed back into bed but didn't reach for him. My boner was gone but not forgotten. It wouldn't take much for it to flare back to life.

Parker lay back and sighed. "If I could, I would. I love being out there. It's peaceful and quiet but also exciting, you know?"

"Yeah."

"What made you think about sex, though?" he asked. "Were you in there jacking off or something?"

I squeezed my eyes closed and wondered if this was the time to tell him I was gay. Parker wouldn't care about that, but I didn't know for sure if it would make him less likely to want to share a bed with me. Still... I couldn't keep such a big secret from him anymore.

"No, but... I kinda wanted to."

He turned over on his side and propped his head on his hand. "Why didn't you? You can, you know. I don't care."

I leaned over and turned the side lamp on its dimmest setting. I needed to see his face when I told him.

"I'm gay," I said.

He blinked and waited for me to say something else. When I didn't, he tilted his head. "I... know? I mean... I guess I didn't know if you liked girls *and* guys, but I know you like guys. I'm your best friend, Jules."

I blew out a breath. "And... you're okay with it?"

His face turned angry. "First of all, yes, of course I'm okay with it. But also? No one gets to *not* be okay with it. You don't need anyone's permission or approval to feel the way you do and like the things or guys you do. And if anyone gives you hell about it, I'll punch them in the fucking face."

I couldn't hold back a big relieved grin. "You're the best."

He leaned over and hugged me. "*You're* the best. No matter who you like. Just so long as you don't ever like anyone more than me. You can have a boyfriend, but you can't have another best friend. That job is mine. Forever. You just made a binding agreement." He nodded at the notebook paper on my nightstand.

I could tell he was teasing, but I still liked being claimed in that way.

"What about you?" I asked, trying to be brave enough to find out if there'd ever be a chance I could date my best friend.

"What do you mean? Like, who do I like?" He moved back over onto his own pillow.

"Yeah."

He screwed up his lips while he thought about it. "I think you're right. I'm ski-sexual. When Erin and Hazel mentioned their group of friends getting tickets to that concert thing, all I could think about was whether or not your dad would take us to the slopes instead. Do you think he will? Mr. Rokas said I'm almost ready to try the moguls."

The laugh that bubbled up was full of relief. I didn't need him to like me like that, as long as he didn't like anyone else that way either.

And he didn't. For two more years, he continued to prefer my dad's hand-me-down skis and soft, fresh powder to any kind of date with anyone of any gender, though most of the girls in our year and at least one guy had made a play for him.

But when we learned the homecoming committee had booked a popular local DJ sophomore year, I decided to finally ask Parker out. For real. As my date to the dance. I would tell him how I felt and ask him to give me a chance as more than best friends.

I kind of wanted to do the cheesy prom-posal idea but with something related to skiing. He'd gotten a coveted spot on the Evergreen High School team, and Coach Rokas said he had more potential than anyone he'd seen in a decade. Parker was already well on his way to making a name for himself in the state competitions.

As cheesy as it was, my poster would at least make him laugh. I'd spent all afternoon adding little drawings beside each ski word.

I would be snow board if I went to HoCo solo. I snow full well taking you would lift me up, so I'm asking icely if you'll be my date. If you say no, Alp be piste.

"What the heck is that?" Hazel asked, barging into my room uninvited.

I scrambled to hide the giant poster with a hoodie that had been on the floor by my feet. "Nothing. Get out. Jesus."

"Who are you asking... *oh*." She winced. "You were going to ask Parker, weren't you?"

I moved the poster behind me on the bed. "I *am* going to ask Parker. Yes. Not that it's any of your business."

Hazel took my hand, which wasn't something she did very often anymore. "Jules... Erin already asked Parker to the dance, and he said yes."

I stared at my sister in disbelief. "That's not possible. He would have told me."

"She only asked him today after you'd already left."

Parker didn't like Erin like that. I knew he didn't. At least... he'd never said anything about it to me if he did.

I was crushed.

"Maybe... maybe they're just going as friends," I said lamely.

Hazel squeezed my hand again. "I don't think so, Jules. She really likes him."

I looked at my sister while trying to stop myself from feeling so pathetic and disappointed. "I really like him, too," I admitted softly.

Hazel pulled me into a tight hug. "I know you do. And maybe one day you'll get your chance to tell him. But for now, let's think of some other cute guy you can ask. What about Toby Finley? Oooh! Or Sean Rollins. He's superhot and totally into guys."

In the end, I didn't end up taking anyone. And Parker and Erin became a thing, breaking up and getting back together so many times it made all of us shake our heads.

Over the years, I took comfort knowing I was still his person — still the first one he told when he got a killer scholarship and wasn't sure whether to take it, and the first person he called when he needed encouragement after a crushing loss on the slopes. I never doubted for a second that he was my person, too — the guy who rushed to my side when I was injured and sent me a joke every morning without fail during my most trying days in law school.

He was mine, and I was his.

You and me. Always.

Or so I thought.

But when Erin came back around for the billionth time with a much bigger proposal on her mind, everything changed.

Because Parker said yes to her again. Only this time, he agreed to marry her — to love her and put her first forever.

And I knew nothing would ever be the same again.

1

PARKER

Current Day (15 years later)

"Jules, you should totally come to Mexico with us," I said a little drunkenly. My arm rested along the back of Julian's chair, and I could see a spot he missed when shaving. My best friend was absent-minded at the best of times, but I could understand why he was especially distracted tonight. As my best man, he'd been put in charge of several important tasks, one of which was watching my sorry ass to make sure I got where I was supposed to go this weekend.

"Parker, Jesus," Erin snorted from my other side. Even though I wasn't looking at her, I knew she was rolling her eyes. I was very familiar with my girlfriend's—I mean fiancée's—eye-rolling voice.

"What? He should. That would kick ass. We'd have so much fun, the three of us, wouldn't we?" The more I thought about it, the more I liked the idea. Julian and I had been close for over twenty years. There was no one I wanted more on an all-inclusive vacation in the Caribbean.

Except Erin. Obviously.

Julian tried to shrug my arm off his shoulders and move away from me. The joke was on him. If I stopped leaning in his direction,

I'd fall face-first on the floor. "Pretty sure Erin wants the honeymoon to be just the two of you, big guy."

"That's not true," I corrected stubbornly, clinging tighter. "I overheard her inviting your boyfriend just a little while ago."

Julian attempted to move away again. "I keep telling you, he's not my boyfriend. Nolan doesn't believe in restrictive social constructs like monogamy," he muttered under his breath. But he frowned at the man on his other side anyway. "Wait. Nolan, why did Erin invite you on her honeymoon?"

"Huh?" Nolan shook back his sun-streaked blond hair like a golden retriever who'd heard his name called and grinned affably. "Oh, nah, dude. E didn't invite me. We were talking before dinner about how you two planned some adventure shit while you were in Mexico, like zip-lining and snorkeling, and I was telling her if she wanted real adventure, I could show her where to go outside the resort, like this kick-ass twenty-mile hike with a rope ladder you can take down into this underground cave complex—"

I wrinkled my nose. "But it's an *all-inclusive* resort," I repeated, wondering if maybe I was drunker than I thought. "Why would anyone want different adventures than the adventures that are... *included*?"

Before Erin said a word, I could still tell there was another good-natured eye roll pointed in my direction. "Because it's sometimes fun to step outside of our comfort zones, Parker. That's what life's about."

Julian stopped trying to squirm away and instead patted my leg reassuringly. "Or not. It'll be fine."

"Yeah, I mean, you gotta do what life's calling you to do," Nolan said with a kind of earnest passion. "You gotta live your truth. You've gotta find the life path that's meant for *you*. That's what I was telling E."

"Julian," I whispered loudly. "Is your not-boyfriend calling Erin 'E'? Is she letting him?"

Our friend Tiller snickered from across the table. "Ah, Parks. It's been years since you've overindulged. I forgot how much fun drunk Parker can be."

"Hey! I'm not drunk," I informed him.

"You're not sober," Julian's sister, Hazel, countered.

This was also true. But it had been way too long since our gang of childhood friends—Tiller, Erin, Hazel, Julian, and me—had been together, so I figured I had an excuse for getting a little bit tipsy.

Hazel was working for her dad in Denver and married to her job. Erin was working out of Denver, too, but on the road all the time as a buyer for Rokas Sports, her dad's flourishing local sporting goods chain. Tiller was busy being a famous football player in Houston while his friend Sam was busy managing construction on Tiller and Mikey's new ski resort in Aster Valley, which was where Julian was spending an annoying amount of his time, too, since he was doing lawyer stuff for Tiller. And meanwhile, I was a manager and ski instructor for Rokas Sports here in Vail. Since nothing made me happier than having all of us together, I was determined to enjoy it, even if being together meant sometimes tolerating other, more annoying people, like—

"Alcohol's a crutch for when a man hasn't examined his life, my dude," Nolan the philosopher pronounced, and I gritted my teeth.

"Excuse you. I have a great life," I informed him. "Awesome friends. Amazing best man." I pulled Julian more tightly against me. "Stable job. Sweet girlfriend."

"You mean fiancée," Hazel corrected. "Almost wife."

Oh. Right. My palms started to sweat a little bit. Or a lot.

"Whoa." Nolan's eyes widened, and he gave a full-body shudder. "Did anyone else just feel the atmosphere get, like, really heavy in here? Or was that just me?"

"Just you," Julian said firmly. "We're all very excited about tomorrow."

"It's supposed to be a beautiful day," Tiller's fiancé, Mikey, commented.

"And this hotel is killer," Sam's boyfriend, Truman, added.

"Erin's going to be a beautiful bride," Hazel chimed in.

"Wait," I demanded, rubbing my damp palms on my trouser leg, "what's tomorrow?" Suddenly, I felt a sharp pain in my side. "Ow! Erin, god. That hurt."

Now Julian was the one rolling his eyes at me.

"I was joking," I said, turning around to face my annoyed fiancée. "You know I would never forget my ski time with your dad and the guys. I'm looking forward to—*oof*! Stop elbowing me."

"Then stop trying to be funny when you're so bad at it," she teased. "Anyway, the girls want to meet at the bar to do a bachelorette nightcap thing we read about in a magazine, and then I'm going to head upstairs." She pushed her chair back. "See you at the altar, funny guy. I'll be the one in white."

She was beautiful even when she was annoyed with me. "Hey, stop," I said, pushing my own chair back and taking her hand in mine. "I'm just kidding. You know that, right? Nothing could excite me more than walking down the aisle toward you tomorrow on your father's arm."

Julian groaned behind me. "Can you ever be serious?"

The answer to that was no. Definitely not. Because I was completely full of shit. I was nervous, and the only way I knew to get through that was to make it all seem less important than it was. It was what I did. Julian's skin turned blotchy red when he was embarrassed or upset; I cracked stupid jokes.

I clenched my back teeth together. "Okay. I'm being serious. I love you."

That part was true. Erin had been one of my favorite people almost as long as Julian had been. We'd dated on and off for a decade starting in high school, and our relationship had always felt free and easy. We were never possessive and never demanded too much of each other, which was probably why we kept ending up together, no matter how many short, tumultuous relationships Erin had had in between over the years.

No lie, I'd been a little shocked when she'd popped the question almost out of the blue six months ago, but it had also been a strange kind of relief. Marrying her meant finally feeling secure and settled in the knowledge I'd never lose the people who'd come to mean the most to me in the world. That was what I kept reminding myself whenever I felt a rush of anxiety about the upcoming wedding... which was fairly often as the big day drew closer.

"Sweet dreams tonight. We're going to have an amazing time tomorrow. First, we get married, then we dance to our favorite band with all of our closest friends, and then we're off for a week in the sun. I can't wait."

I leaned in and kissed her, tasting the white wine she'd been sipping all night. An anxious part of me wanted to verify that she wasn't planning to drive herself anywhere after she'd been drinking, but I refrained. Erin hated when I "got on her case," and she was well aware that the memory of Julian being injured by a drunk driver still woke me up at night sometimes, which was why she'd agreed to have the wedding at a large resort hotel where no driving would be required.

It was the one concession I'd asked for in her dream wedding.

"Sounds good. I love you, too," Erin said. "Don't outshine my dad too badly on the moguls tomorrow, or he'll be in a bad mood the rest of the day."

"Pfft," I scoffed. "As if I can hold back the power of my talent. That's like asking Tiger Woods to throw a golf game to his accountant uncle. Besides, I tried deliberately losing to him once, and he didn't talk to me for a month."

"I heard that," Erin's father's voice boomed from somewhere behind me as Erin and Hazel walked out. "I'm nobody's accountant uncle."

I turned back to the man who'd been my first ski coach and mentor and was now my boss. I flashed him my signature smile. "Fine. It's like Tiger Woods throwing a golf game to his future father-in-law, who just so happens to also be great at the game. Only he's not engaged, so the metaphor doesn't work."

Rod clapped a hand on my shoulder and grinned at me. "Have I told you how happy I am to have you officially joining our family tomorrow?"

My stomach lurched with an odd combination of nerves, guilt, and affection. His opinion and approval had always mattered to me. I'd do anything to avoid disappointing him. "Yes, sir. Only about a thousand times. But it doesn't get old, so keep at it."

Erin's mom walked up. Lorraine looked beautiful in a deep blue jacket that made her hair look even blonder than it was. Erin had gotten the best of her parents' assets: her mother's head-turning looks and her father's business acumen. She'd followed her father into the family business and had a job as one of the buyers for the store. Everyone in town knew she—or more likely the two of us together—would eventually take over Rokas Sports from her father, but so far, Rod seemed happy at the helm, and I was even happier being able to continue teaching ski lessons before having to commit to the store full-time or worse, move to the main location in Denver.

Lorraine reached up to cup my cheek. "You know we love you, right?"

I'd had just enough to drink to make me irrationally emotional. "Yes, ma'am, although I'm not sure why."

"Because you keep Rod humble on the slopes," Julian's dad said, giving Rod a friendly nudge, while Julian's mom pressed a kiss to my cheek. "That, and you're a good man."

Lorraine dug the knife in extra deep and gave it a good twist. "Parker, I would love you no matter what. I need you to understand that, as much as Rod and I are thrilled about the wedding tomorrow, you have always been a member of this family in your own right, and you will continue to be one no matter what happens in the future."

I felt my chin wobble and my eyes smart. "I hate you," I whispered. "You're a cruel woman."

Julian's hand was a familiar weight on my lower back. I didn't even need to look to know it was him. He, more than anyone, knew how deeply I felt the words Erin's mother spoke. Both Erin's and Julian and Hazel's parents had taken over where my own had failed. The Thick and Rokas families had provided me with everything from shelter and food to love and support, not to mention the skiing experience that had earned me a college degree and a career path I loved. I didn't know what I'd do without either family in my life.

Lorraine leaned in and pressed a kiss to my cheek. "Put Rod in his place on the slopes tomorrow. It'll settle his nerves and give him something else to think about before he gives his baby girl away," she whispered into my ear.

I snorted. "Consider it done. Thank you for tonight. It was a gorgeous dinner."

She pulled back and gave me one more motherly look before turning to find her husband and making their way out of the hotel restaurant along with Julian's parents.

I turned around and realized Julian and I were practically the only ones left. The rehearsal dinner was over. The servers were already clearing up the rest of the dishes left on the tables. Mikey had pulled Tiller away by the hand with an obvious *fuck me* expression on his face, and Sam and Truman had already disappeared, probably for similar reasons.

"Where'd everyone go?" I asked. "It's too early for bed, and I could really use another drink—"

"Jules." Nolan slung an arm around Julian's shoulders and buried his nose in Julian's neck. "Parties make me horny. Let's go upstairs."

Ugh. I really did not like that guy.

Julian's jaw tensed, and he cleared his throat. "Not yet. I have a few more best-manly duties to get Parker ready."

"Can't you do that later? Some of us are already *ready*," Nolan purred, mouthing at Julian's skin and skating a hand over his chest.

I clenched my hands into fists.

"Nolan," Julian said, pulling away. "We talked about this, remember? This weekend is about the wedding. That's my priority."

Nolan's face fell almost comically. "Wait, you were serious about that? Does that mean no fucking tonight?"

Julian's neck turned splotchy red, which meant he was either really upset or really embarrassed. I *hated* seeing him that way. "I was serious," he confirmed.

"Ah, dude, are you still pissed about the monogamy thing? Because I really like you, Jules. I just like lots of other men and women, too. True respect in a relationship means giving your partner freedom to pursue their passions—"

I reached out and plucked Nolan's hand off Julian's shoulders, then pulled Julian slightly behind me. "I think what Julian's saying is that his passions are leading him down a different life path, Nolan. His path and your path? Two different paths."

"Parker," Julian warned.

"Go find your path, Nolan," I commanded. When the man stared at me uncomprehendingly, I grabbed him by the shoulders and faced him toward the door. "No, seriously, go now. Don't stop until you find it. In fact, I saw a couple of gorgeous women hanging at the bar earlier. One of them might be your path. Heck, *both* of them might be."

"Yeah? Sweet. But wait." Nolan frowned. "Jules and I are sharing a room."

"Roommates are social constructs, buddy. Pursue those passions. Run free!"

"Jules?" Nolan glanced back at Julian, then at me.

"Yeah, go ahead." Julian sounded resigned. "We'll catch up tomorrow."

"Solid." Nolan shrugged easily, like spending his evening with Julian or finding some random bar hookup was all the same to him, which pretty much confirmed my initial impression of the man.

Fucking idiot.

"Ass," Julian muttered, and I nodded as I watched Nolan leave, pleased that Jules and I were on the same wavelength, as usual.

"No judgment, babe, but he kinda is. You could do way better."

"Not him, Parker. You." Julian shoved past me more forcefully than necessary. "You're an ass."

"Me? What?" I grabbed his wrist, forcing him to turn and look at me. "I saved you from that guy. He was obnoxious. And rude. And overly familiar with you. And inattentive."

"Overly familiar? You sound like my nana. And how can he be overly familiar *and* inattentive?"

I opened my mouth, then shut it again. "I'm not sure, but he managed it."

Julian sighed and ran a hand through his hair, disturbing the product that had temporarily kept his chocolate-brown cowlick tamed. The little errant curl over his ear flipped up the way it always did, the way I always teased him about but secretly adored.

It made my buttoned-up bestie a little less perfect and a little more real.

"Well, that's just great. Really helpful."

I met Julian's eyes. His familiar faded blue irises looked exhausted and oddly sad. I wanted to pull the man into a hug and tell him everything was going to be okay. Maybe it was one of the reasons I'd suggested he join us on the Mexico trip in the first place. He looked like he could really use the time away. I knew he'd been helping Tiller with his new resort business, but I didn't realize it had taken that much out of him.

"I wasn't kidding earlier. You really should come away with us," I said softly. "You need a break."

His nostrils flared. "Crashing your honeymoon would be the opposite of a break. I'm going to Aster Valley for the week. I'll be fine."

"But—"

"Drop it. I'm going out for a drink, and apparently it won't be at the hotel bar."

"With me?" I asked hopefully.

Julian snorted. "Obviously. You're buying. It's the least you can do."

Hell yes.

I grinned at him and led him out of the restaurant. "You and me, Jules. Always. The way it should be."

We walked across the swanky hotel lobby to the gold-trimmed doors. The liveried doorman nodded and greeted us politely. "Need a car, gentlemen?"

"No, thanks. Where's a good place for a drink that's close enough to walk and doesn't cost an arm and a leg?" Julian asked.

The man's face creased into a genuine smile. "Bert's Brews, a block and a half that way. Tell them Jerome sent you."

I clapped him on the shoulder with a thanks and nudged Julian ahead of me into the freezing cold night air. Julian didn't need a recommendation since I lived here and he'd visited me plenty enough times to know where to go, but he had a knack for treating people well and engaging locals wherever he went.

The town of Vail sparkled with lights here and there despite the late hour. Even though it wasn't currently snowing, it was cold as balls.

"Fuck. Why didn't we stop for our coats?" Julian grumbled.

I put my arm around him. "I'll keep you warm, Peanut."

He shrugged me off and shoved me away. "Don't call me that, Shortbread."

"Fuck," I grumbled, forgetting that nicknames went both ways. Julian seemed in a pretty bad mood, so I stopped teasing him long enough for the silence to settle comfortably between us. Silence with Julian had always been comfortable. Being around him was, in some ways, like being alone, only... being alone with the best part of myself.

"Are you mad?" I ventured after a block or so.

Julian shrugged and looked up at the night sky. Despite predictions of an incoming snowstorm in the next couple of days, the sky was inky and clear. The stars were out in bucketloads. It reminded me of the nights we'd spent camping in his parents' backyard with our sleeping bags and flashlights.

"Not really," he said with a heavy sigh, as if he'd suddenly lost his never-ending patience with me. "Nolan and I weren't serious. But fuck... he's good in bed, and the man has a talented mouth."

I growled at him. He knew how much I hated hearing about him having sex with his boyfriends and hookups. I just... didn't like it. I hated thinking of him with someone like Nolan. Someone who didn't understand or deserve him.

"I still don't get the attraction. The guy sounds like a surfer. *Dude*."

"So?" Julian returned. "He's charming. He's fun. He's got a unique, interesting way of looking at the world."

Hmph. "What was about all his 'be free to pursue your passions' stuff?"

Julian shrugged. "What about it? He was honest about what he wanted from the beginning. And open relationships are very common."

"But they're not for you," I said confidently. "You're a one-guy guy."

I knew from previous conversations that Julian wasn't into open relationships himself. It was something we'd talked through several weeks ago when he'd first hooked up with Nolan. Julian was a serial monogamist. I wasn't sure the man knew how not to throw himself all in with one person. He was god's gift to whoever he was dating, too. A giver.

"Yeah," Julian said after a long, long pause. "Yeah, Parks, I'm a one-guy guy."

I nodded happily. "That's why I refrained from kicking his ass for abandoning you."

"Abandoning me? You told him to leave!"

"Yeah, but he went along with it." I shook my head, still unable to comprehend it. "Dumbass."

Julian shook his head with a kind of fond exasperation that made my chest warm. "Down, boy. No black eyes at Erin's fancy Valentine's Day wedding, especially on the groom. My sister would kill me since she's probably in charge of Erin's makeup."

His mention of the wedding brought all of my nerves back in full force. Thankfully, I'd been told many times over that having cold feet was very normal. I just had to suck it up. In twenty-four hours, it would all be over, and things could go back to normal.

"Then let's get you drunk," I suggested, pulling open the door to Bert's and gesturing Julian inside. "We can drown your sorrows over losing your, uh… talented friend and help drown my nerves."

"Erin would kick my ass if I let you start her wedding day hungover," he said, moving past me into the dim bar. It was exactly the kind of place we needed. Scuffed wood floors, red vinyl booths, and mismatched neon beer signs hung all over the place. It was doing a brisk business tonight, which I was grateful for. I wanted to lose myself in the buzz of the crowd noise and be able to talk to my best friend without worrying about who was listening.

After wandering toward the back, we found an empty booth and slid in, taking opposite sides the way we'd done a thousand times before. A young woman came by to take our drink orders and left as soon as we'd spouted off our favorite beers.

"Besides," Julian continued, "I don't have any sorrows to drown. I'd already decided to break things off with Nolan tomorrow before I left for Aster Valley." He hesitated before looking down at the beer mat the server had left and flicking it between his hands. "The only reason I hadn't was because I wanted him here as my plus-one. I didn't want to be single for the wedding."

His voice was so low, I could barely hear what he was saying. I reached across and used my finger to tilt up his chin. When those baby blues locked onto me, I felt the same warm surge of affection I'd always felt for him.

"Why the fuck not? You know nobody gives a shit except maybe your mom, and that's only because she wants little gay Jules babies since Hazel's too busy with her job to ever start a family."

He shoved my hand away. "Fuck you. You've been dating Erin on and off for a hundred years. You have no idea what it's like to go to a wedding as a single guy. It's the most depressing thing on Earth. Especially when your two best friends are the ones getting hitched and all the heteronormative bullshit is flowing more freely than the champagne."

His words made my stomach hurt. I never, ever wanted him to feel alone. Not when he had me. Not when he had Erin and Hazel and Tiller. We would always be his ride or die.

"I'm sorry," I said. "You're right. I don't know what it's like. But I do know that if all you wanted was a date for this weekend, I could've found you a much better guy than *Nolan*."

Julian snorted, and it took a little of the worry off my shoulders. "Like who?" he asked, leaning back and crossing his arms in front of his chest. He'd taken off his suit jacket and unbuttoned the top two buttons of his shirt. I could see the barest hint of the tattoo that adorned the left side of his chest and almost up to his throat. People were always surprised to learn my little geeky friend was secretly covered in some killer ink, but whenever his tank top revealed it at the gym, the gay guys were always all over him.

Drove me nuts. Only because it interfered with our workouts.

I snapped my fingers. "Layton from the gym."

Julian's jaw dropped. "Layton who's married to Rick and has two little kids?"

"Oh." I put some more thought into it. "I got it! Sex Pants from the coffee shop."

Julian laughed again and flushed pink in the cheeks. Bingo. I knew he'd had eyes for that guy.

"His name is Michael, and he makes a living doing OnlyFans stuff. I'm not sure that's for me."

I flashed a big smile for our server when she showed up with the beers. "Thanks a ton. Hey, you guys have anything like nachos this late?"

Julian groaned. "Seriously? It's after midnight. We had a full dinner."

I ignored him and batted my eyelashes at the server. She laughed and agreed to put an order in for us. I thanked her before looking back at Julian.

"What's the problem with selling fans? Since when are you a snob about a guy's job?"

Julian blinked at me. "Only... OnlyFans... the website? You know what? Never mind. Drink your beer and maybe stop flirting with the waitress since you're getting married tomorrow."

I took a long sip of my beer before wiping my mouth with the back of my hand. "You're very grumpy tonight. Maybe it's not too late to try and get Sex Pants out here from Denver."

Julian kicked my shin under the table, but he laughed.

And that was all I needed to finally let go of the nerves.

I was with Julian, and everything was going to be okay. Everything was always okay when I was with him. He would take care of everything like he always did.

2

JULIAN

If there was a record for how long you could carry a torch for the wrong person, I thought for sure I'd be appearing in the Guinness Book any day now.

Parker Ellis was the man everyone wanted. It had been that way my whole life. When we were seven, the tee ball coach wanted him on the team. "Julian, ask your friend Parker if his parents want to sign him up."

When we were thirteen, the girls playing chicken in the neighborhood pool all wanted him to be their partner because he was already taller than the rest of us. When we were sixteen, they wanted him between their legs for a different reason, and their parents wanted him cutting their lawns since he'd do it for cheap. When we were almost seventeen, our other best friend—Erin—wanted him to take her to homecoming "as a friend."

When we were eighteen, Colorado State wanted him on the ski team despite the fact he'd only been skiing for a few years with hand-me-down equipment from my dad's castoffs. It didn't matter, because they loved him. Everyone loved him.

Including me.

I glanced across the top of my beer bottle at his beautiful fucking face. He was seriously model pretty. Even though his parents had been complete and total losers unworthy of even a scrap of his attention, they'd gifted him with a square jaw, a cleft chin, and thick strawberry blond hair that never looked out of place. Despite starting off small, he was now several inches over six feet. He was also covered head to toe in freckles.

Freckles I'd spent an embarrassing amount of my life counting and daydreaming about licking.

"Are you even listening?" Parker asked.

"Mm-hm."

I wasn't. I was too busy feeling sorry for myself. I loved Erin, but she was getting everything I'd ever wanted tomorrow, and I wasn't sure how long I could keep it together before ugly crying, especially since Parker had just run off the one guaranteed distraction I'd had for the evening.

All I needed to do was hold out until I could get to the cabin on Sunday. It was the perfect place to spend a week mourning what I was never going to have so that by the time Parker and Erin got back from their honeymoon, I'd be ready to pack up all my unrequited love and foolish pining once and for all. Parker and Erin were a forever unit now. I was extraneous. So for my own sanity, I had to stop making my best friend the sun around which my entire life orbited.

But first, I was going to wallow. I'd already arranged for grocery delivery, kick-ass Wi-Fi for movie marathons, and even a nice dinner at Tiller and Mikey's lodge as soon as I'd finished crying.

"Why do you think Erin was talking to Nolan about our vacation?" Parker asked, reaching for a nacho from the giant tower on the plate between us. If he'd asked for a gourmet lemon peel cupcake, our waitress probably would have gone out of her way to make one for him. "Do you really think she wanted to make a big group thing out of it?"

Typical.

"I think she was making conversation with a guest at her rehearsal dinner. You know Erin. She loves meeting new people and finding out every single thing about them. I'm sure that's all it was." I reached out and took a small piece off the edge of the stack and popped it in my mouth.

Parker's eyebrows met in the middle. "She's been acting weird lately."

"So have you," I said without thinking. I could tell right away from the surprised look on his face Parker was going to turn this into a whole thing by asking me to elaborate. I tried to stop him by holding my hand up. "Don't."

"You can't just say that and not explain what you mean." He was stupidly cute when he pouted.

I shrugged and picked off another piece of chip. "I don't know. You just seem… squirrelly. Are you nervous or something? That's not like you. You're the steadiest person I know." That and his firm heterosexuality, of course.

He looked down at his beer bottle. "Maybe? I mean… I love Erin. Obviously. She's great."

I made a mental note to only accept marriage proposals from men who thought a little more of me than "great."

"But?"

"I dunno. Nothing really. The wedding came up really fast, didn't it?" His pleading eyes met mine, but for once, I wasn't sure what he needed from me.

It was true. Even though they'd had an on-again, off-again thing since the infamous "just friends" homecoming date, I'd never really expected them to end up together. Every time Erin broke up with a long-term boyfriend, she came crawling back to Parker like the relationship version of a security blanket. He usually went along with it, but I'd always figured it was because he loved feeling needed. I hadn't realized he was truly in love with her. But that all changed six months ago when Erin had suddenly suggested they get married and Parker had readily agreed.

She'd made an impassioned plea about wanting to settle down and start a family, have a big fun wedding like all her sorority sisters had already experienced. I'd worried about Parker agreeing so quickly when he'd never really expressed any interest in settling down with her forever and starting an actual family. He was amazing with the kids he taught in ski school, and I thought he'd make an incredible father, but after having shitty parents, he'd made it clear to me on several occasions that he didn't think he wanted all of the emotional baggage and pressure involved in raising his own children someday.

I got it. I didn't particularly want kids myself. Maybe I was selfish, but I wanted time with friends and the ability to throw myself into a career or a project. I liked knowing I could stay out late or go off on a weekend away with friends at the drop of a hat.

Considering how much Erin liked to travel and meet new people, I was surprised at her desire to settle down so soon.

But Parker was born to settle down, and if he really loved Erin, that explained his easy agreement. I'd do just about anything to make the love of my life happy.

Which was why I was sitting here in the first place instead of hiding under the covers of my hotel bed right now.

"You'll be fine," I said, because that's what you said to the groom the night before his wedding. "It's just cold feet, I'm sure. You hate being the center of attention, but that'll all be over tomorrow night."

"I worry about whether I'll be enough for Erin," Parker whispered. "You know? Fun enough. Exciting enough. What if I can't be what she needs?"

"Parker Ellis, you're the best man I know. You remember the winter we learned to ice-skate, and I was so in my head over it that I couldn't figure out how to push off? Who spent a whole Saturday, just the two of us, making up ridiculous dance moves to help me? Who texts me pictures of fun billboards and mating squirrels twenty times a day? Who is always ready to celebrate someone's birthday, or half-birthday, or quarter-birthday, anytime they need cheering up? You make every single day fun, Parker. You make regular life an adventure, and I..." Wow, I really needed to stop talking. "I think that's enough for anyone," I finished lamely.

"I kind of wish I was marrying you instead. Is that weird?" he asked with a nervous laugh.

I blinked up at him, batting down the hopeful idiotic butterflies that just took off en masse in my gut. "Yes. Yes, that's weird."

"I don't mean like that. Obviously."

"Obviously," I said with a sigh. And that was the problem. "Look, do you love Erin?"

"Of course I love her. I've always loved her."

Right. A fact I needed to remember.

"Then I think you two will figure things out." I picked at the label on my beer bottle. "I don't ever mind listening. But, you know, maybe you need to talk to *her* about this, not me. She's your life partner now. And she adores you. She would never want you to second-guess yourself around her."

Parker got that affectionate look on his face that he sometimes got when thinking about Erin. "You're right. She's an incredible person. She wouldn't want me to be nervous or scared. Besides, who wouldn't want to spend the rest of their lives with one of the best women on the planet?"

I dug my fingernails into my thigh through the suit pants. "Exactly."

"But even though Erin and I are getting married, you'll always be my best friend. My other half. When we're old and gray, it's still gonna be you and me, Jules. Always. That'll never change."

Except it would.

He started talking about the Mexican resort they were traveling to, how he wanted to do some stand-up paddleboarding and maybe try kitesurfing. I listened with half an ear. If I let myself pay too much attention to his descriptions of a sunny paradise in which he would be golden-skinned and half-naked, I would start my ugly cry exactly twenty-four hours too soon.

"We should probably head back," I said after the nachos were done and the server was bumping up her flirt factor a notch too high for my comfort. Not that she was flirting with *me*.

"Yep. You're skiing with us in the morning, right?"

I shrugged. "I always feel like a little fat potato next to you on moguls. I just bump along and hope for the best," I said without thinking. You would have thought I'd just kicked his puppy. Parker's face dropped.

"What? You're a beautiful skier. Are you kidding?"

"No, *you're* a beautiful skier. I'm the guy who chucks himself at the first mogul and hopes for the best. And ever since the accident, I tend to pull to the right no matter what I do."

It was a joke, but I should have known better. Parker still had a hang-up about the serious car accident I'd been in years ago.

"Not true. You have complete range of motion, and we both know it."

If I did, it was thanks to him and his dogged insistence on hauling my sorry ass to physical therapy for months.

We argued about it most of the walk back to the hotel until I finally agreed to meet him at stupid early o'clock for the run. My dad never passed up a chance to ski with Parker and Rod Rokas so he could brag to all his buddies that he still had the legs to keep up with champion skiers. Even though Parker didn't race anymore, he was still well-known on the slopes around here as one of the best, and my dad secretly preened when Parker gave Dad all the credit for introducing him to the sport.

With Parker here in Vail and Erin based out of Denver, I wasn't sure if they'd quite worked out what their "married with kids" life was going to look like, and I'd sure as hell never asked for details on how they planned to play house, but I hated thinking about him giving up the career he loved.

When we got to the elevator bank in the hotel, he turned to me. "You're staying with me, right?"

"Uh, no. Even if Nolan's there, the room has two beds." And I really needed some distance, because my ugly cry was looming closer and closer with every minute I spent thinking about Parker.

Parker clasped the back of my neck and forced me to meet his eyes. Every nerve in my body swarmed to take a hit off the feeling of that large warm hand. "I wouldn't put it past that asshat to bring his hookups back to your place. No, you'd better come sleep with me."

The man had no idea how his words affected me. "No, thanks. That asshat sucks dick like a pro. Wouldn't be my first foursome."

Parker's hand involuntarily squeezed my neck harder, not enough to be painful but enough to know he didn't like what I'd said. I didn't understand why it bugged him so much when I talked about these things, but I usually didn't push the issue, since I sure as heck didn't want to hear about his exploits with Erin. I couldn't say why I felt the need to push it tonight.

The elevator doors opened, and he guided me in before pushing the button for his floor. "Not negotiating this with you," he grumbled. "You're the best man. Consider this part of your duties. You know I can't sleep alone when I'm anxious or upset. You're lucky I'm not making you share the bed this time, since these beds are tiny. You can sleep in the second bed."

I wanted to lean into his big body and take comfort in him, but that wasn't my place. "Fine. But let me go to my room first and get my stuff so I don't have to get it in the morning."

"Fine." He reached out and pressed the button for my floor before I thought to do the same. I was impressed that he remembered it.

He reminded me of his hotel room number when I got off at my floor and told me he'd leave the door propped open in case he was in the shower. That was enough to convince me to give him plenty of time to get showered and covered up before I entered the room and sprung Parker wood.

As I rounded the corner toward my hotel room, I saw my sister coming away from Erin's room.

"Hey," I said in surprise. "You're up late. Everything okay?"

Hazel nodded. "Erin got kind of emotional while we were having our nightcap down in the bar earlier, and I wanted to check on her, but there's no answer. I'm guessing she's asleep. She's been exhausted for weeks from the wedding planning, and I don't think she's been sleeping very well the last few days."

"Is she sick?" I asked with concern. Erin's wedding plans meant everything to her. Her dream had always been to have a big fantasy wedding on Valentine's Day, and she and her mom had spent long hours putting it together on such short notice.

"No, I think it's just wedding jitters."

I smiled and told her Parker was having similar nerves. "I think if we'd stayed at the bar much longer, he would have tried to drink them away. I get it, though. I can't imagine making a lifelong commitment like that. It makes sense they're nervous."

Hazel squeezed my upper arm. "You'll find someone one day, and then it'll be you pacing the hotel room with cold feet."

Parker's smiling face popped into my head. "If you say so," I said. "I'm just glad it's not me this weekend, how about that?"

Instead of chuckling, she frowned. "You holding up okay?"

Hazel and I were close, not just because we were siblings but because we were friends. The six of us—Erin, Hazel, Tiller, Sam, Parker, and me—had been close for years, so it wasn't easy to hide my feelings from any of them. But, despite being Erin's best friend, Hazel also knew the truth about my feelings for Parker. She'd seen my face when I'd learned Erin had asked Parker to homecoming just hours before I'd planned to ask Parker to be my date instead. She'd also been with me two years later at a party when we'd accidentally spotted Erin and Parker half-naked and engaged in sexual shit I really wanted to scrub from my brain. I'd been tipsy enough to burst into tears and admit everything to her. The next day, I'd tried to walk it back by blaming it on the alcohol, but she knew me too well to believe it.

My nose stung in that way that warned me not to let this conversation happen unless I wanted the ugly cry to begin immediately. "Yep! Never better. So good."

"Liar," she murmured, pulling me into her arms for a hug. "You're going to get through this. I promise."

"Yep. Not sure how, though," I admitted into her familiar dark waves. "Being his best man was supposed to make things easier, but it's getting harder. Pretty sure I'm going to die of a broken heart." My voice broke, so I pressed my lips together and stopped saying anything at all. Eventually, she pulled away and wiped her own tears. She knew how torn up I was about this wedding, but she also knew that as long as Parker was straight, the best thing to help me get over my debilitating crush was to have him officially off-limits to me forever.

Besides, I wanted Parker and Erin to be happy. I did. I loved Erin. She was one of us. Like Parker, I'd been close to her for as long as I could remember. We'd been a pack. And packs stuck together even when there were obstacles to overcome.

Loving Erin while also wishing Parker would throw her over for me in some kind of fantastical grand gesture fit for a Disney princess movie was one such obstacle. And it made me feel guilty as hell.

I was a terrible person.

After attempting a reassuring smile that made Hazel's eyes widen in alarm, I kissed her cheek. "Gonna be fine. Eventually. G'night."

She sighed and headed down the hall as I made my way back to Nolan's room to grab my sleeping and ski stuff. Thankfully, he wasn't there. I grabbed my stuff and headed up to Parker's room.

When I got there, he was already showered and dressed in a thin old T-shirt from college and a pair of pajama pants that made his ass look like something I'd pay good money to squeeze if given the chance.

"Hey, took you long enough," he said. "Did Nolan give you a hard time?"

I wasn't about to tell him I'd been chatting with my sister about his bride having a particularly aggressive bout of cold feet, so I just shook my head. "Nope. Apparently Nolan found a welcoming path for the evening. I'm going to hop in the shower. I feel like I still smell like Aunt Tina's perfume. Did she hug you, too?"

It was a lame attempt at changing the subject, but it worked.

"Dude, someone needs to have a talk with that woman," Parker griped. "When is she going to realize that the reason your mom gives her a new perfume every year is in desperate hopes she'll stop using whatever the hell pickle juice that is. Remember when Hazel gave her a bag of free samples from the mall one time? Didn't make a difference."

I laughed and grabbed my sleep pants before heading into the bathroom. When I came back out, Parker was safely tucked in his bed and scrolling through his phone. His ski clothes were set out neatly on one of the tables, and he'd put two water bottles on the table between our beds. He was always thoughtful like that.

Erin was a lucky woman.

Parker put his phone on the table and stretched. I ignored his bulging biceps and adorably messy hair.

"Did I tell you what I got her as a wedding gift?" he asked with a grin.

"A ring?" I asked. Wasn't that what a husband bought for the wedding?

He flapped a hand in the air. "That, too, of course. No, I found out that Kygo is going to be at the same resort we're going to. He's doing some kind of VIP concert, and I managed to get tickets. Cost me an arm and a leg, but Erin's going to freak."

"Holy fuck. She is going to freak. How the hell did you manage that?"

He settled back under the covers and lay on his side to face me. "I called the concierge to arrange for a few special extras. I asked him to help me think of something huge that would really impress her. He set it all up."

Parker was a good man. I knew he wasn't necessarily an EDM fan, but that wouldn't have even crossed his mind when planning something wonderful for Erin.

"She's going to love it, Parks. Good job."

He smiled at my approval. I hated that he seemed to need it, but I was happy to give it. I knew he'd grown up with parents who were never proud of him or impressed by anything he did, so he'd always sought approval from others. As if he needed to make up for never getting it from the people who'd mattered the most.

He opened his mouth to tell me more. One of Parker's weird, adorable quirks that he hadn't outgrown since childhood was that when he was anxious, he couldn't seem to fall asleep without down-loading every single thought in his brain. He claimed it calmed him down. I wasn't sure what he did all the nights he slept alone.

But it occurred to me all of a sudden that this might be the last time I got to be the person to hear his nighttime rambles, since he'd be rooming with Erin until death did them part, and the pain of that nearly took my breath away.

"Go to bed, Parker. Tomorrow's a big day."

My chatterbox friend closed his mouth again and nodded before shooting me a wide grin. "Just think, once all this wedding shit is over, I get a whole week of hot sex at a luxury resort in the Caribbean."

I threw a pillow at his face. Fucker. The last thing I wanted to think about was him and Erin having a honeymoon fuckfest. And I didn't much care for the implication he wanted the "wedding shit" over with like it was a burden rather than something to savor and appreciate.

I closed my eyes and forced myself to think of other things, like how well stocked my little Aster Valley cabin was for the week ahead. While Parker and Erin were enjoying the exciting—sexual—celebration of having their whole glorious life ahead of them, I would be wallowing in my wallow hole with plenty of hard liquor and ice cream, trying very hard to forget the perfect day I was going to make sure they had.

It was fine. I was fine. Their wedding day was going to be *great*.

And it was.

Until everything turned to complete and utter shit and I ended up punching my best friend in the face.

3

PARKER

I was thankful for whoever's idea it had been to schedule an early morning run on the slopes. After a couple of hours of fresh air and fresher powder, I felt more relaxed and ready to meet Erin in front of our friends and family to say our vows. After all, wasn't marriage basically saying you wanted someone to be in your life forever? I wanted that with Erin, no doubt about it.

Julian, Hazel, and their dad had seemed to enjoy the morning as much as Rod and I had. A couple of my ski patrol buddies had blocked off a double black diamond run for us, and we spent a ton of time racing each other down the slope without having to worry about accidentally knocking anyone else over.

Hazel and Julian had both been skiing since they were practically toddlers, and growing up with money in Denver meant they'd had access to the best equipment and instructors money could buy, as well as having plenty of time on the slopes to improve. They were talented skiers. Rod had been my high school ski coach, something he still did out of passion for the sport, and his mentorship had turned my passion on the slopes into a college path and career. Being out on the slopes with him was always a good time.

After finishing the runs, we had lunch at the lodge halfway up the mountain before skiing the rest of the way down and making our way back to the resort.

We went our separate ways to shower and get dressed. The photographer had scheduled groomsmen photos as early as midafternoon, with my solo shots first up. Julian, Sam, Tiller, and two of my closest work friends would join us about half an hour later by the covered bridge for some outside group shots.

When I finished putting together all of the various pieces of the tux Erin had arranged for me, I glanced in the dressing mirror in my hotel room. I felt awkward and uncomfortable. There had been several times in my history with Erin's and Julian's families when I'd had to wear a monkey suit for various reasons, but I'd always felt like an imposter. This was no different. It wasn't that the fabric wasn't nice or the fit was wrong. Those things were perfect. Erin had selected the best of everything. It just... didn't feel like me.

I closed my eyes and took a deep breath. This was for Erin. For our future. To make memories we'd always be able to look back on. After tonight, I could change into my usual worn-in jeans and hoodie before boarding the plane to the islands and changing into board shorts and a tee. Perfect.

As soon as I turned to open my hotel room door, I saw the note.

It looked tiny on the carpet—a little cream envelope like a thank-you note or maybe a Valentine. I picked it up and recognized Erin's handwriting. I couldn't help but smile. Despite wanting a Valentine's Day wedding, Erin wasn't usually inclined to sentimental gestures, and I didn't expect them, which made it extra special that she'd taken the time to write me a note on our wedding day.

I let out another breath and knew everything was going to be okay. She was such a sweetheart and the woman I was closest to in the world.

I opened the envelope and pulled out the plain sheet of hotel stationery.

Dear Parker,

Do you remember back in college when I thought I wanted a career in fashion? I sewed you a pleather suit with faux fur trim for your birthday, and you actually wore it out to dinner, bless you. But then the pleather of the suit stuck to the pleather of the restaurant booth when you tried to get up, and the pants ripped apart at every single seam, and you stood there beside the table, wearing nothing but boxers and those weird scraps of fur around your ankles, laughing your ass off while we sang Happy Birthday. I remember you said, "So maybe your talent's not sewing, babe. You'll figure it out."

It's one of my favorite memories because that was you at your most Parker. It was me at my most Erin. And we haven't changed all that much since then, have we? You're still the king of stability, the guy who'll do anything to help and support a friend. I'm still the girl who's trying to figure her life out.

And for a minute there, Parks, I swear I thought I had. I thought, if I just have Parker, marry Parker, I can be calm and steady like Parker. But it turns out I'm no better at settling down than I am at sewing. And honestly? I'm tired of being calm and steady.

Last night, I was talking with a friend, and I realized that I've spent years trying to be someone I'm not. I want to try new things. I want the butterflies in my stomach that the heroines in my grandma's romance novels got. I don't want to be held back by my parents' expectations or repressive social constructs. I need to set myself on the right life path, expand my consciousness, and truly examine my life before I make any decisions.

I love you, Parker. I really love you.

And that's why I can't marry you.

I'm sorry that I'm doing this on what was supposed to be our wedding day. And I'm really sorry that I am too much of a coward to tell you or my parents about this in person, but I'm afraid if I see you, I'll remember how much I love you and think that's enough when it's not.

I want adventure. I want to find something I can't live without.

I want you to have that too.

Be happy. Please forgive me.

~Erin

I stared at it before reading it again. And again. I scrutinized the handwriting to make absolutely sure it wasn't some kind of wedding-day prank. Finally, I tried calling her, but it went to voicemail.

My hands shook as I texted her. She wanted adventure? That was what this was about? We'd been each other's first everything. First fumbling kiss during a spin-the-bottle party in middle school. First blow job after prom. First over-too-fast fuck in the back of my shitty pickup truck the following summer.

The only reason she hadn't been the first non-family member I'd said "I love you" to was because I'd already said it to Julian a million times by then. He'd been my best friend even longer than we'd known Erin and Tiller, so of course I'd told him I loved him first.

The thing was... I thought Erin and I had already had our adventures. Over the years, we'd gone on dates with other people—Erin way more than me—and tried new things. Hell, I'd even kissed Tiller one night after Julian had come out to me, as a kind of half-assed gay experiment, because I'd loved Julian Thick so much I'd wondered if maybe we could be more than just best friends, but I'd been terrified of fucking things up between us. (And it was a good thing I'd tried it on Tiller first because I'd felt absolutely nothing.) Sure, things with Erin weren't exciting, exactly, but they were easy. Comfortable. Good. I followed her lead and tried to make her happy.

And I thought I had.

I tried to call her again. When it went to voicemail, I sent a text.

Parker: *It's okay. I just want to make sure you're alright.*

After a few minutes, she responded.

Erin: *I'm so sorry. I'm so, so sorry.*

Parker: *If you want to sleep with other people, or whatever, we can talk about it.*

Erin: *That's not what this is about.*

Parker: *Plenty of people have an open relationship. At least... that's what Julian says.*

Erin: *That's not the kind of relationship you want, and I don't know that it's what I want either.*

She was right, of course. I wasn't a possessive or jealous person, but my parents had treated their marriage like a joke, and I had no interest in doing the same. To be honest, I hadn't even wanted a marriage at all until Erin had suggested how great it would be.

I sat on the end of the bed and thought about what to tell Erin. How did I feel about this? Was I angry? Betrayed? Confused?

Relieved.

I was overwhelmingly relieved, to the point of feeling almost giddy. Which, of course, made me feel like the worst person on Earth.

Why? Why was I relieved? I'd wanted to marry Erin. After she'd suggested it, I'd realized it would be the answer to all my hopes and dreams for a nice, stable life here in Colorado. We'd get married and be together, and nothing else would change. I'd still be part of her family, and we'd settle in Vail, close enough to Denver to still have Julian and Hazel in our lives.

I still wanted that. And I hated knowing that I wasn't enough for her. That I couldn't make her happy.

I sighed.

Parker: *Please tell me you're safe.*

I waited longer this time, so long that a text from the photographer came through. I realized I was late for the photoshoot. The photoshoot for a wedding that was no longer taking place.

Parker: *Does anyone else know? Hazel?*

Julian's sister was her closest confidante. Surely, she would have talked to her about this.

Thinking of Hazel made me think about Julian. He was going to be crushed. He was going to think I was brokenhearted, which meant he was going to feel guilty, even though he obviously had nothing to do with it.

Unless…

Parker: *Does Jules know?*

If Hazel knew, surely she'd told Julian.

Finally, she wrote back.

Erin: *I'm already back in Denver. No one knows. About any of it. I thought it wouldn't be fair to tell anyone before you and now… now I can't. Everyone will want answers and I don't have any yet. I'm sorry to put it all on you. I'm going out of town. I'll deal with things when I get back.*

My jaw tightened as little tendrils of anger began snaking their way in. She hadn't been acting herself last night. She had to have already been having second thoughts by then. How could she sit there next to me last night without saying anything?

Maybe for the same reason I hadn't said anything to her about my own serious misgivings.

Parker: *It's okay. I'll take care of it.*

I slipped the phone into my pocket and the letter into the bottom of my suitcase before turning to face the music.

After meeting the photographer in the lobby and explaining that the wedding was canceled, I asked to speak to the hotel event manager. I knew from emails I'd been copied on that her name was Sandy, and she would be able to help me with much of the rest of it.

She met me in the lobby and pulled me to the side where there was a little cluster of love seats next to a fireplace, but I was too keyed up to sit. I paced back and forth on the thick rug. As soon as I told Erin's parents, all hell was going to break loose, and I'd never be able to get through the rest of it.

"You excited about your big day?" she asked with a smile.

I ran my hand through my hair, upsetting all the gel I'd carefully applied to keep things just right for the photos. "Um, that's the thing I needed to talk to you about. The wedding is off. I need your help, ah… telling people and stuff. Like, I don't know how to get in touch with anyone. The band, the officiant, the cake people. The guests." I kind of squawked out that last part, thinking about how disappointed everyone would be and how everyone would grill me for an explanation.

Sandy stared at me for a moment before moving ahead like she had to deal with this sort of thing all the time. Hell, maybe she did. "Right, well, first things first, can I get you a nice, stiff drink from the bar? It's going to take me a little while to get us organized, and I think a drink is just what the doctor ordered. Why don't you follow me to the bar, and I'll grab my binder."

She led me through the archway into the darker hotel bar area. The place was mostly deserted as the wedding guests were probably busy showering, and the other guests were most likely still on the slopes.

The bartender looked up from slicing lemons. "Hiya, Sandy, what can I get for you and your guest?"

Sandy lifted a brow at me.

"Whiskey, neat. Any kind," I said, suddenly thinking Sandy was the smartest woman ever.

"Make it a double," Sandy added softly. "And it's on the house."

"It's not too late," I told her, trying to lighten the mood a little. I didn't want pity looks. "You and I could get hitched. I've got everything all ready to go. Just need a bride."

She laughed and squeezed my arm. "If I didn't already have a wildcat wife and two little girls at home, I might consider it. I'll be right back."

When the bartender slid the drink to me, I nodded my thanks and took a giant gulp. And then another.

By the time Sandy came back, I was on my second drink and feeling a smidge better. "Okay. How do we cancel this thing? Maybe we can donate the food to a local food kitchen or something?"

She pulled out her phone and started finger-typing. "First, we contact the band to cancel since they're coming from the farthest away. My assistant is already printing out signs to put on the doors to the ceremony venue for the guests. Obviously, it's too late to cancel the catering and the cake, but we can have the cake cut up and in boxes on a table at the ceremony venue for the guests to take away."

"Sounds like you're an expert on canceling weddings. I should have called you first thing," I said with a humorless laugh.

"What the hell is going on?" Julian's voice made me jump. I spun around and saw him standing there with Lorraine and Rod. Julian was a sight for sore eyes, but Erin's parents looked both excited and suspicious. It wasn't a good combination.

Maybe I'd had too much whiskey on a nervous stomach, or maybe it was just my need to make every tragedy a joke, but a laugh gurgled up before I could control it. "Can't you see? I'm canceling the wedding. Apparently it's way easier to jilt someone than I thought. Who knew?"

"You're what?" he asked, as if he'd truly not heard the words.

"I said I'm canceling the wedding. You should try it sometime. So exciting. Such an *'adventure.'* Think Erin would appreciate that?"

In hindsight, I wondered if I shouldn't have used the finger quotes. Something about what I'd said enraged my best friend. His face was full of fury, and in my whiskey-tipped haze, I actually thought he was angry on my behalf.

Until he punched me in the fucking face, and all hell broke loose.

Lorraine screamed, Rod raced over to "break it up," Sandy sighed and asked the bartender for ice, and that's when the entire bridal party came looking for the photographer.

Julian wasn't content with the one hit either. He followed it up with a shove to my shoulders while shouting something about me being an unfeeling asshole for succumbing to pre-wedding jitters and screwing over our friend. After the drinks I'd had and taking the shot to my face, I was fairly easy to shove. I took out two barstools on the way to the floor.

Julian landed on top of me and grabbed the lapels of my tux. His face was red, and his eyes were angry slits. "How fucking dare you, you chickenshit piece of shit."

"You said shit twice," I said, trying desperately to keep myself from bursting into tears and asking him to hold me. For some reason, I didn't think that would go over well.

When he pulled back his arm to punch me again, I reached out and grabbed his wrist. "Stop," I said. "You don't know what happened."

His eyes shifted between each of mine. "Fine. What happened? Because it looks to me like you jilted your best friend."

I let out a kind of laugh. "She's not my best friend. You're—"

This time, he kneed me in the junk.

And I really did start crying.

4

JULIAN

From the moment that I'd heard Parker and Erin were getting married, I'd fantasized about them calling it off.

But now that it had happened, I hated him for it.

What had started off as simple cold feet had turned into my... my *Parker*... walking away from his commitments. Now the rest of us were going to have to go through the whole process of watching them break up, only for them to decide next month or next week or next year that actually, no, they *did* want to get married after all, and then we—by which I meant *I*—would have to somehow find the mental fortitude to endure yet another bachelor party and write another best man toast, wishing the love of my life a lifetime of passion with someone who wasn't me.

If I'd stopped and thought about it, maybe I would have realized the truth sooner—that Parker had never walked away from a single commitment in his life. That he'd rather walk over hot coals than hurt anyone important to him, especially Erin.

But I didn't stop and think. I just took all my bitterness and rage and hopeless jealousy and threw it into making him hurt.

Even after I racked him, he had enough self-control to roll me over and pin my wrists to the floor, pressing my thighs down with one of his strong legs. I closed my eyes and reminded myself we were in a fight.

A fight.

"Fuck you," I spat. "Get off me. I need to go find Erin."

"She's not here," he said in a low voice. "Take a fucking breath."

"Don't tell me what to do, asshole."

He moved my wrists together so he could brush a lock of hair out of my eye with his free hand. "I didn't do this," he promised softly. "I didn't do this."

I stared into those familiar eyes, eyes that reminded me of the forests near Aster Valley because they captured every shade of green at once, and knew he was telling the truth.

"What happened?" I asked again. This time, reality set in. I remembered Parker worrying last night that Erin had been acting funny. I remembered my sister outside Erin's room with the same story of cold feet.

"She broke up with me. In a letter."

"Where is she?" I asked, yanking my wrists out of his grip and pushing him off me so I could go find her and talk some sense into her.

"Denver."

I got to my feet and froze. "What?"

He nodded without taking his eyes off me. "It's over, Jules. For real this time."

All at once, a flood of memories washed in. Parker spending the night after homecoming and telling me the date had been fine, but he didn't "like her like that." Parker calling me from college and telling me Erin had shown up unannounced and begged to go to a drinking party. He'd laughed and told me it was like corrupting a sister. Parker calling me from his first year of pro skiing and telling me he didn't know how to tell Erin he wanted to focus on his career instead of a relationship. Me calling Parker from grad school to ask why I hadn't heard from him in weeks and finding out it was because of his guilt over breaking up with her again.

At every turn, he'd been the one to resist their relationship.

So I'd just assumed he'd been the one to end it this time.

I looked around at Erin's and my parents' faces of shock, at Hazel and the other bridesmaids, who looked confused, and at the two other groomsmen, who'd made themselves comfortable with a beer at the bar.

"Fuck," I said.

Parker snorted. "I guess that's about right." He tentatively pressed fingers against his jaw where I'd landed the punch.

I batted his hand away and pulled him to his feet, then stepped in closer to investigate the damage. It was already looking red, and there was a smeared dab of blood from where his lip had split. I ignored the familiar scent of his cologne. "Dammit," I muttered. "I'm sorry. Let's get some ice on that."

"It's okay."

"None of this is okay," I said, turning to the bartender to ask for a bag of ice.

Meanwhile, Erin's dad stepped up. "What's going on?"

Before Parker could answer, I beat him to it. "Rod, Erin changed her mind about the wedding."

"What?" Rod looked between me and Parker before settling on Parker. "Did you talk to her? What did she say? Where is she?"

Parker sighed. "She broke up with me in a letter slipped under my door while I was showering. She wouldn't take my call, but I texted with her a little. She's back in Denver already."

"Did she say why?"

Erin's mom walked up next to Rod and leaned into his side. He slipped an arm around her and held her close. Hazel's arms were crossed, and her jaw tightened in a familiar expression of anger and hurt.

Clearly, Erin hadn't confided in her.

Parker reached for the ice I handed him and held it to his jaw. "Get one for your hand," he murmured at me before turning back to Erin's parents. "She said she wasn't ready to settle down and wanted time to..." He sighed. "I don't know. Try new things. Adventures. Something like that. I don't really remember much after the not getting married part."

"What does that mean?" Rod asked.

Parker shot me a pleading look, so I took over. "It means Parker just basically got left at the altar and shouldn't be the one explaining why. Maybe you should try calling Erin."

Lorraine didn't look nearly as surprised as everyone else when she stepped forward to give Parks a hug. "You're right, sweetie. I'm so sorry, Parker. But maybe this is for the best."

Rod shook his head. "She'll come around. Everyone gets nervous before the big day."

Parker hugged Lorraine back. "I don't think so." His jaw began to wobble, and his eyes filled up. When Lorraine pulled back, my own mom grabbed Parker to give him comfort. These two women were the closest things he had to a loving mother, and he loved my dad and Rod like fathers. Being comforted by the four of them would be both wonderful and excruciating for him.

I grabbed Parker away from my mom's tight grip and pulled him toward the hotel lobby and out of the bar.

"Mom and Dad, can you please deal with this while I get Parker out of here?" Even though I spoke to my parents, I met my sister's eyes. She'd know to take over, to get my parents on board with helping calm Rod and Lorraine down and help tell the guests.

Dad nodded. "Of course, son." He gave me a weak smile. "Take care of him."

I yanked Parker toward the elevator bank and up to his room, reaching into his jacket pocket for his key card when he seemed to have checked out for the moment.

When I finally got us into the room, he threw his tux jacket onto the bed and then turned and buried his face in my neck, hugging me tighter than he had since the day we'd buried his grandmother.

I held him while he cried, running my hands up and down the crisp cotton of his shirt. His body was big and warm and solid, and it reminded me how rare it was that I was the one comforting him. Usually, it was the other way around. He'd always been braver and stronger than I was. He'd always been the steady one.

"Maybe Rod's right," I said. "Maybe she'll come around."

He shook his head and pulled back, swiping at his face to brush away the evidence of his momentary lapse. "No. She's not in love with me, Jules. She doesn't want to settle down. Or to be held back by repressive social constructs." He rolled his eyes.

I narrowed mine, because something about that wording seemed extremely familiar. "Wait, did she say that? Literally that?"

Parker shrugged and nodded. "She said she and a friend were talking last night, and she realized she wants passion and adventure. She wants to expand her consciousness or something, and find the right..." He blinked at me in realization. "The right life path."

Both of us muttered at the same time, "*Nolan.*"

"I'm going to fucking kill him and bury him where he can't be found," I growled, pulling out my phone, though my vision was too hazed with red to even see the screen properly, let alone find his name. "And then I'm going to go have a talk with Erin about what friendship means, and what fucking *commitment* means, and how to not be an utter—"

"No, you're not," Parker said.

"No?" I snorted, jabbing blindly at the screen. "*Ha.* Watch me. This is the last time she's gonna fuck you over, Parker. Mark my words. Bad enough that she breaks up with you, then begs you to take her back a thousand times. Now she breaks up with you *on your wedding day* because she's taken advice from fucking Nolan, that... that..."

"Charming, fun guy with a unique way of looking at the world?" Parker suggested wryly.

I remembered saying those words the previous night, and an icy wave of guilt and anger swamped me. I'd been such a fool. "You're right. This is my fault. I brought him here, and he did this, and now I'm going to set it right. I will."

"You won't." Parker grabbed my phone from my hand and shoved it into his back pocket triumphantly, like he didn't realize that me having to manhandle him to get it out again was only *more* incentive for me to get it back. "This isn't your fault. And it's not Erin's fault. It's not even dumbass Nolan's fault—"

"The hell it's not!"

"It's my fault, Jules. No, hear me out," he insisted. "I was mad, too, at first. Hurt. But the truth is... Erin's right. And I should have had the balls to call it off before it landed on her. I knew we were rushing into things. I knew I wasn't what she needed. I should have been strong enough to tell her that."

"Not what she needed?" I demanded. "*You*, of all people? If intelligent, sexy, ginger Henry Cavill look-alikes with hearts made of pure gold don't do it for her, what the fuck does she want?"

I didn't even realize what I was saying until the words were out.

The edge of Parker's lip tweaked up. "You're biased. But whatever I'm paying you, double it."

I couldn't hold back the chuckle. "Fuck," I said, running fingers through my hair before taking off my own jacket and yanking at my bow tie. "This is fucked-up."

"Did I ever mention that I love the way you lose your lawyerly vocabulary when you're defending me?" He kicked off his shoes, pulling at pieces of his tux until he stood in the middle of the room in nothing but an undershirt and boxer briefs.

"That escalated quickly," I muttered under my breath.

He peeled off the undershirt.

Goddamn. My best friend had a six-pack from his job on the slopes, and even in the midst of this situation, I couldn't stop sneaking a glance at it.

I was a horrible person.

"Why are you naked?" I asked, resisting the urge to kick off my own shoes.

"Can't stand that fucking thing. I didn't want to wear one in the first place, and I'm sure as hell not wearing it one minute longer. Besides, I'm going to sleep, and I'm not waking up 'til July." He slid into the pristinely made bed, rucking the covers up and sprawling his big body out facedown across the crisp sheets.

I stared at him, unsure whether to let him hide in the bed or not. "Are you going to actually sleep, or are you going to fall into a mental spin cycle of self-doubt and guilt?"

His muffled voice spoke into the pillow. "Second one."

"That's what I thought. And I will allow you exactly one hour for wallowing. And then you're coming with me to Aster Valley, and you can wallow there in my wallow hole. I'm going to go downstairs and help sort out the bullshit. When I get back up here, we're packing and leaving."

"Mpfh."

"Don't do anything stupid," I warned.

He shot me the bird. I swiped his room key and headed back out.

Hazel and my parents were waiting for me in the lobby.

Hazel rushed over and wrapped her arms around me. "Is Parks okay?" she demanded. I saw the same helpless guilt on her face that I felt, like we should have foreseen this somehow and prevented it.

I shrugged. "For now. But you know how he is. The more serious the situation, the more he jokes." When this all finally hit him, though, he was going to be devastated.

It took longer than an hour to help sort everything out with the hotel and all the guests, but the woman in charge was amazing. She'd clearly had to do this exact thing for clients in the past, and it was obvious she knew how to handle it with professionalism and grace. When everything was finally sorted, and I was able to convince the Rokas and my parents not to try and make the drive home this late in the day, I went back upstairs to pack my stuff.

Nolan's stuff was gone, which was probably for the best since I was still feeling murdery and my knuckles were already bruised.

Once my bag was packed and I'd changed into more comfortable clothes for the drive, I rolled my suitcase to Parker's room and let myself in. He was dressed in well-worn sweats from one of his old sponsors, and I recognized the hoodie as one of the ones I'd stolen from him years ago.

"Hey. How'd you get that hoodie back? I thought it was in my closet at home."

He was sitting in a chair facing out the window to the slopes. His light hair was messy, his bare feet were propped on a small table, and his hands were tucked into the hoodie's kangaroo pocket.

"I had them send me a few more after you stole it. I figured if you liked it that much, you might want a replacement one day. But then I wore one and realized why you liked it so much, so fuck you on getting the spares."

We both knew he'd give me the literal clothes off his back if I wanted them. That was the kind of person Parker was. Besides, I'd been stealing his clothes for twenty years, and he'd never stopped me.

I walked over so I could look at his face. The bruise on his jaw was darker, but it was the tired eyes that stood out the most. He'd been thinking himself into a heavy state.

"Alright. Get your ass up. We're leaving."

"I'm just going to head home," he said without moving.

"Nope. You're coming with me to my cabin in Aster Valley. We're going to get drunk, watch all the Marvel movies in order, and do some cross-country skiing. If you're lucky, there'll be a couple decks of cards there, and I'll let you beat me at Spite and Malice."

Parker stared out the window. "I hate cross-country skiing," he muttered. "All that work and not a single moment of excitement."

I moved to the closet and pulled out his suitcase. If he didn't have the energy to pack himself, I'd do it for him. "Liar. You love anything that makes you sweat. Tell you what. If you come cross-country skiing with me, I'll make you my famous lasagne."

He swiveled his head and raised an eyebrow. "You know the pity party has reached full swing when Julian offers to tackle a multistep recipe."

"Desperate times." I reached for the tidy little stack of socks and underwear in his drawer and tried not to think too hard about how lucky that damned underwear was as I moved it to his suitcase.

"Make me those seven-layer bars, too, and we have a deal."

I narrowed my eyes at him. "You're not in a position of power in this negotiation."

"Fine. I'll just go back to my apartment. Alone. And cry. *Alone.*" He turned back to the window and sniffed. "So alone."

"Fucking jackass," I said under my breath. "Manipulating bastard, sugar pig, and also very bad at cards."

"I can hear you. And the only one of those that's accurate is the sugar thing."

I couldn't help but laugh. "Get your ass up, and let's go. I'm never going to find this place in the dark. It's over the mountain, and Aster Valley rolls up their welcome mats at sunset."

He stood up and stretched, exposing the strip of skin I'd come to think of as my own personal Valhalla. I focused back on the stack of T-shirts in my hand, making sure they were placed just so in the suitcase.

Parker came over and bumped me out of the way with his hip. "Go get the stuff in the bathroom. I don't want you perving on my panties."

"As if," I snapped. "Flatter yourself and your ugly-ass tighty-whities. Straight guys have the most boring underwear on the planet."

"Not true. I wear jocks for work. And they come in all kinds of *rainbow* colors."

Parker in a rainbow jock... Do not go there.

"Thank you for that lovely mental image, Parks. I'll try not to drool over the image of your hairy ass cheeks flapping in the winter wind as you teach some trophy wife how to snowplow."

I was pretty sure his ass cheeks were perfect like the rest of him was, but today was definitely not the day to think about them.

My job today was to distract him from the fact that Erin had just bulldozed his future and broken his fucking heart, leaving me to pick up the pieces and put him back together.

He finished packing his stuff before turning to me with a frown. "What's wrong with my ass?" He turned around this way and that to try and get a good look at it. "I don't have a good ass?"

"Focus. You can ask me about your ass again once we're on the road." I tossed his toiletries kit into his suitcase and reached for his tux.

I tucked all the pieces into the hanging bag and thrust both his and mine at his chest while I grabbed the rolling suitcases. "C'mon. If you're a good boy, I'll slip you one of Mom's Valium tablets in the car."

Parker sighed. "Christ, you're a good man. You know just what to say when shit goes sideways. Always have."

We managed to get to the parking garage with only three or four excruciatingly awkward conversations with bewildered wedding guests, and I gave Parker the promised pill. In typical Parker fashion, he started talking my ear off about utter nonsense before fading into a slurry, affectionate mess and finally nodding off.

When he fell asleep, his hand still rested on my leg from when he'd reached over to squeeze it while thanking me for being the "best best friend man, best man, I mean best friend, man" a guy could ever have.

"Just you and me," he murmured. "Always."

Fucking hell. This week was going to be excruciating, and now I was right back where I started.

In love with Parker Ellis who was suddenly and glaringly single again.

I was fucked.

5

PARKER

It wasn't the first time I'd slept halfway sprawled on top of Julian, but it was definitely the first time I'd done it in a vehicle. While he was driving.

"Well, hello," I mumbled, pushing off him. "Personal space much? God, you're handsy."

He didn't laugh at my joke. Instead, his nostrils flared, and his jaw tightened.

"Hey," I tried. "You okay? Sorry for dozing off on you."

"What? Yeah. Fine. No, it's... I can never remember how to get here, and the directions are in my phone, which is still in your back pocket." His jaw finally relaxed enough for him to shoot me a sheepish grin. "I didn't want to fondle you while you were unconscious."

I reached underneath my thigh and found it, typing his password in and pulling up the map app he used. I knew Julian well enough to know he'd already have the address entered into the system, and sure enough, it was right there.

I did a double take at the address. "Brokeback Ridge? This place is on Brokeback Ridge? Why, Julian James Thick, you dirty girl."

He sighed, but I could tell by the quirked-up corner of his mouth he thought it was funny, too. "Tiller and Mikey already gave me hell about it, even though Mikey was the one who helped me find it."

We talked about it as Julian continued to follow the directions through darkened curvy roads narrowed by passes from a snowplow. When we finally pulled into the barely marked driveway, I felt like we were about to drive off a cliff to our doom.

"I didn't sign on for any Thelma and Louise shit," I muttered, clutching the handle above my door as the SUV lurched over pits and bumps. I tried not to notice Julian's hands white-knuckling the steering wheel. When the headlights finally found the quaint little cabin, we both heaved a sigh of relief.

"There should be groceries in the kitchen," he said, turning off the ignition. "I hired a kid Tiller and Mikey recommended to stock it for my arrival."

"Even though you weren't supposed to arrive till tomorrow?"

He hopped out of the SUV quickly, waving his hand and mumbling something.

"What?" I asked.

"I went ahead and scheduled it for today. In case I wanted to get up here early or whatever."

He sounded strange when he said it, but I chalked it up to the general stress from the day.

My wedding day. The day I got left at the altar like the plot of a Julia Roberts rom-com. I wasn't sure where they got the "com" part of it because so far this felt much more like a drama or tragedy. Suddenly, the life I could picture ahead of me so easily was simply... gone. And in its place loomed a great big dark void. Everything in my life involved Erin. My best friend and hers were brother and sister. Her father was my boss. Her mother was the person who made soup for me when I came down with a cold.

I sighed and hopped out onto the snowy gravel drive. So much for the sweet relief of medical mood boosters. Other than a nice solid nap, that had been a bust. Before long, I'd be back in a downward spiral of guilt and second-guessing. Surely Erin hadn't decided she needed "adventure" out of nowhere. There was a reason, and it was my not being a good enough boyfriend. Fiancé. Whatever.

"Cut that shit out and help me with this stuff," Julian snapped from the back of the SUV. "Leave the skis. Let's just take in our suitcases for now."

After we got our stuff to the door and Julian entered the code on the cabin's numeric keypad, the front door unlocked. The cabin was as quaint on the inside as it was on the outside. Even though it was mostly one big open room with living, dining, and kitchen spaces all in one, it looked homey and inviting in the best way. The biggest feature in the space was the expansive stone fireplace already set for a real wood fire. I'd noticed a covered rack of wood on the front porch, which meant we wouldn't even need to traipse down into the snow to get more.

It was exactly the kind of place I could imagine spending a week in while licking my wounds. I let out a big breath and tried to get my shoulders to relax.

"This is nice. How long did you rent it for?"

Julian crinkled his forehead. "I bought it. It's mine."

I stared at him. "You bought a cabin in Aster Valley without telling me?"

He busied himself putting down our bags and fiddling with the thermostat on the wall. "I told you about it. It wasn't a secret."

It only took two strides for me to reach him. I grasped his arm and turned him to face me. "No you didn't. You didn't tell me you bought a place in Aster Valley. I would have remembered. I would have..." I stopped to try and figure out why it was bothering me so much. "I would have panicked."

Jules searched my eyes to see if I was joking. "Panicked."

"Yes. What does this mean? Are you moving here? Are you leaving Denver? Is this just a vacation place?"

Julian put a hand on my chest. "Calm down. Take a breath. You know I've been doing legal work for Tiller and Mikey's resort."

I nodded. "So you just need a place to crash when you're here, right?"

He hesitated, and I felt my heart rate spike.

Please tell me you're not leaving me, too.

Julian must have sensed where my head was because he patted

my chest reassuringly. "Babe. Aster Valley isn't that much farther from Vail than Denver is. It's just in a different direction."

"Yeah, but I'm always in Denver for…" I stopped. I only ever went to Denver anymore to see Erin unless there were family things scheduled with the Rokas and Thick families. "Oh. Fuck me."

I rolled my eyes and moved away from him, moving over to start a fire so I'd have something to do. There was crumpled newspaper, small bits of kindling, and split logs stacked perfectly in the grate. I reached for one of the long matches in a decorative thing nearby and struck it before poking it into the newspaper here and there.

"Who still gets a newspaper?" I muttered. "I mean, that's some vintage shit right there."

Julian came over to peer over my shoulder. I noticed the familiar scent of his hair gel. "They sell it in stacks at the store here. It's cheap."

"You know what we could use for a fire starter when this stuff runs out?" I asked. "My marriage license. I think I have it here somewhere. Might do us some good. Ball it up and shove it in the grate before putting a match to it."

Julian's warm hand came down to rest between my neck and my shoulder. He rubbed a strong thumb into the tight muscle there and worked through the worst of the tension spots. I tried not to groan in relief.

"I'm sorry," he said softly. "It sucks. I still can't believe she left. I could throttle her."

I stood up and moved to the sofa before dropping down on it and kicking my shoes off so I could put my feet up on the coffee table. "I'm telling you, she did the right thing, Jules. As much as it hurts, I want her to be happy." I wanted *me* to be happy, too.

Julian came over and sat on the other end of the sofa to face me, putting his arm along the back of the plump cushions. Now that I was calmer, I recognized his taste in the room along with a few of his personal effects. He had a way of decorating a place to make it both put together like a professional designer would but also make it homey and comfortable.

I pulled the soft blanket off the back of the sofa and tossed one end over his lap while pulling the other end over mine. He flicked it off his lap in annoyance.

"How can you say that? How can you tell me on the day you were prepared to promise your whole fucking life to her that you've changed your mind that easily?"

Julian's emotions were a volatile mix of anger and confusion, and I couldn't blame him. But I also didn't know how to explain to him that I'd never really felt that fairy-tale spark of romantic love with Erin that everyone said I should. That was her point.

"Can we not talk about this right now?" I suggested. "Not exactly in the mood for your lectures about doing right by her when *she* was the one who walked out on *me*."

His face fell. "You're right. I'm sorry. I just…"

"I know."

"I'm sorry," he said again.

I reached out and poked one of the fingers he had resting on the back of the sofa. "I know," I said again. I took a breath and tried smiling at him. "Please tell me you have some Little Dragon Chicken and Broccoli in that kitchen."

He rolled his eyes. "I wish. But there's stuff to make stir-fry if that's what you're in the mood for."

I couldn't imagine eating just yet, but I knew I needed to force myself to eat if I wanted to drink any more tonight. And I definitely wanted to drink some more tonight. "Yeah. Let's do that. I can show off my knife skills and do a little show for you."

He pushed off the sofa. "Not sure handing you a chef's knife is a good idea right now, Parks."

"Nonsense. I've had some whiskey and Valium. It'll be fine."

Julian chuckled as we made our way into the kitchen. The sound of it did more to relax me than the mini massage he'd given me or any of the chemicals I'd consumed. Maybe I wouldn't need to get drunk tonight. Maybe I just needed to spend some more time in my best friend's company without having to worry about what I said or did.

He'd always been my confidant, my good-luck charm, and my port in a storm. I was grateful he'd let me crash his vacation even though we both knew I'd probably be miserable company the whole time.

Once we'd gotten the rice started and settled into prepping the stir-fry, I asked him, "What was your plan here this week? Just ski?"

He shrugged. "Mostly."

There was something odd about the tone of his voice. I turned to look at him and realized he was holding something back. "Tell me."

He looked up in surprise. "Tell you what?"

"About this cabin. Why you're here in Aster Valley this week."

"Just for vacation, that's all. I wanted some time away. To... do some thinking."

Julian was definitely hedging. "Thinking about what? Work?"

"Mm. That, too," he said, going back to dicing the chicken. "Nap. Read. That kind of thing."

Now I knew he was lying. The man didn't do idle. "Knit? Basket weave? Maybe roll out some homemade pasta dough?"

He sighed and put down the knife before resting his palms on the counter on either side of the cutting board. "Of course not. I... I brought my cross-country skis, as you know, and I... I may have gotten around to arranging a hookup or something."

For some reason, that pissed me off. I knew that my visceral, negative reaction to hearing about him with other men was hypocritical and selfish. It made Julian tense, and that made me feel ashamed, but I couldn't help it.

"Are you serious? You were gonna invite guys out here to hook up? While you were *alone*?"

Julian set his jaw. "I generally don't invite an audience, Parker."

"I'm just saying, it's clear that you don't care much about your safety." I ripped the guts out of a bell pepper with more force than necessary. "Do you know the percentage of dating app hookups that end in *murder*?"

"No," he said darkly. "And neither do you."

The silence that descended between us was sharp and jarring. I wasn't sure why I could hear Tiller talk about Mikey all day and feel nothing but thrilled for him, or catch Sam pushing Truman up against the elevator wall at the hotel this weekend and think it was kinda hot, but the thought of Julian doing anything with another man made me feel like vomiting. No human alive was good enough for him as far as I was concerned.

"Just let me know when you need the place to yourself, and I'll go… out. Or whatever," I muttered after a while.

"Shut up, jackass." He focused on cutting onions into perfect thin strips. "I'm not having anyone over with you here."

"It's fine. Just because I got screwed over doesn't mean you have to go without." I added a little sniff for good measure since I was already feeling sorry for myself. I hadn't had sex in a very, very long time. Erin had read an article about abstaining for a month before the wedding to make the wedding night more special, but with her job in Denver and mine in Vail, it hadn't even been necessary to declare an abstinence pact.

Jules placed the frying pan down on the stove a little too hard. "Stop sulking. I hate it when you do that."

His bubble butt was calling my name, so I kicked him in it with my socked foot. "Feel sorry for me, bro."

"Don't call me that."

I kicked him again. "Feel sorry for me, Peanut."

"I hate you," he muttered, swirling some olive oil into the pan.

"You love me." I moved the piles of cut-up veggies over to his side of the kitchen before pressing a kiss to his cheek. "And thank god for that."

I moved over to the fridge and poked my head in to see what we had to drink. After grabbing a bottle of water for me and a beer for Jules, I cracked open both and handed him the beer bottle.

I studied his face as he began to throw the chicken into the pan. "So tell me what else. I know there's something you're holding back, or else you would have just stayed home and worked this week."

He huffed out a laugh. "I told you I'm going to be doing work for Mikey and Tiller, right? Well, it turns out I really like it, so I'm moving here permanently."

I blinked.

"You know my dad always wanted me to take over his mining company." He shook the pan firmly. "So that's what I always pictured myself doing. But when I started working there, I discovered it didn't make me happy. Working with Mikey and Tiller at the resort, though… it's new and exciting with so many different legal challenges. Later this week, we're meeting with some potential investors about financing a new property acquisition, which is going to involve a ton of negotiation. And there are liability issues, and vendor partnerships, and various on-mountain concessions to organize legally under the resort umbrella. It's…"

I stared at him, realizing exactly what had put that spark in his eye. I hadn't seen it since his college days. "It's what?"

Julian's teeth came out to bite into his plump bottom lip. "It's… it's fun, Parks. And it's… I don't even know how to describe it."

"It's yours," I said simply.

He blew out a breath. "Yeah. Yeah, it's mine. Every day is something new and exciting to learn about."

Julian and Hazel had both followed their dad into the family business. The successful mining company had been the center of their family for several generations. Jules had grown up knowing his dad would want him to take it over one day, so he'd gone off to college and followed it up with a joint business and law degree.

But he hated it.

He hated working for his family business while Hazel thrived in the role. I wasn't surprised Julian finally found something that excited him; I only worried about it being something that would require his relocating to a tiny town in the boonies.

There was no denying how happy it seemed to make him, though, so I would suppress my disappointment and support him.

"Jules, that's fantastic. Holy shit."

He held up a hand. "Don't get too excited. I'm not completely sure yet. That's why I didn't tell you before. You always get so excited, and I really need to be smart about this."

Okay, that stung a little, even though he was right. "I can be smart," I promised. "Besides, what's to know? It's a ski resort, which happens to be my specialty. Who knows more about skiing than anyone you know?"

"Rod Rokas?"

This time I swatted his ass with the kitchen towel, and he yelped. "Do I need to whip out my ski medals? My fucking World Cup title? My current resume overflowing with alpine awesomeness?"

Jules threw his head back and laughed. "You're the most modest person I know until the two of us are behind closed doors. Then it's all, 'World Cup' this and 'Olympic Team' that. Surprised your head can even fit in this tiny cabin."

We both knew that wasn't true. I rarely talked about the years I'd spent pursuing pro skiing because I'd actually hated them. It was why I'd used his car accident as an excuse to quit the team. Julian had been T-boned by a drunk driver one night in grad school on his way home from a study session. His parents and Hazel had been in Hawaii on vacation at the time, so I'd been the one to drop everything and fly out east to take care of him.

When he finished pushing food around in the pan, we served ourselves and took our plates back to the sofa in the living area. I threw another couple of logs into the fireplace and watched the wood take the flames as I sat back down to eat.

Being quiet with Julian felt natural and healing, as always. After a while, the sound of our cutlery clanking against the plates died down, and I took our empty dishes to the kitchen before returning to the sofa. This time, I lay down with my head in Julian's lap and felt his hand immediately go into my hair the way it always did. I stared at the fire while he gently sifted through my hair and lightly scratched my scalp. The faint headache I'd been fighting off for the past few hours receded a little.

"Think she's okay?" I asked softly after a while.

His fingers paused for a moment before continuing. "You should text her and ask."

Somehow, that didn't feel right. If she'd wanted my help, she'd have come to me instead of running away. "Nah. She needs to figure things out on her own."

He made a sound that didn't agree or disagree.

"Has Hazel texted you?" I asked after another few minutes.

I felt Julian shift as he reached over to the side table to grab his phone. After a few seconds, I felt his muscles tense.

He didn't say anything.

I rolled over onto my back to look up at him. "Dammit, Jules. What did she say?"

He didn't realize he was now cupping my cheek and brushing a thumb idly across the tender skin below my eye. The caress was soothing, but then again, he'd always had this effect on me. When I needed comfort, Julian was the first person I thought of. It had been that way as long as I could remember.

Julian sighed and met my eyes. "She said Erin decided to fly to Mexico."

I sat up so fast my head spun for a split-second. For some reason, a laugh bubbled up. "She went on our fucking honeymoon? By herself?"

Julian's pink ears were an instant giveaway. I laughed again. "Oh my god, she's planning to find someone to hook up with, isn't she? Well, that's an adventure alright."

"Parker, could you be serious for five seconds?"

"I am serious. She wants adventure, she's getting it." It still sucked that I couldn't be what she needed. I still felt adrift in all kinds of ways I didn't want to think about, but the relief I'd felt earlier was still there. Undeniable.

"Easy as that?" Jules demanded. "You're saying it doesn't bother you one bit? You don't even have any made-up statistics to quote about the percentage of all-inclusive-resort hookups that end in disaster?"

I snorted. "Not a single one." Surprisingly, the idea really didn't bother me. I felt zero jealousy when it came to Erin, which I suppose was yet another giant red flag I'd mistaken for a good omen.

I stood up and made my way to the kitchen, where I'd spotted an unusually large collection of brand-new liquor bottles stashed in the cabinet next to the fridge.

Julian bit his lower lip like he was struggling for patience and shook his head. "Don't worry about it, Parks. I'm sure it doesn't mean anything. She'll go have her fun and then come back with a clear head. You can do things differently next time. The two of you can go to Vegas or something."

"There won't be a next time, Jules. She and I are done."

"You say that every time, and yet..."

He was right. Erin and I were that annoying couple who broke up and got back together a thousand times over the years. Even I hated that about us.

"This time it's for real, though," I promised. "I'm done with women. From now on, it's just you and me, okay?"

I grabbed two short glasses and tossed a couple of ice cubes in each one before pouring generous amounts of Julian's fancy bourbon into each glass.

I tossed the first glass back and poured myself a second before bringing the glasses back to the sofa and handing one to Julian.

"You and me," Jules repeated slowly. "Do you remember that promise we made back when we were kids? You said when you wrote it down, it became law. I agreed to it."

"Heck, yeah." I nodded. "And it's still true. It's always been you and me —"

"It was," Julian corrected, staring down into his drink. "Then you and Erin got engaged. When you agreed to marry her, it became you and her. It voided our contract."

Normally, I loved it when Julian talked to me in his lawyer-speak, but today, I did not.

"What? No, it didn't!" I frowned. "Not really. Erin is... she's Erin. She's not you and me."

He snorted. "Brilliant insight, Shortbread. Keep drinking."

"No, seriously, Julian," I began, needing to convince him that I meant what I said. "I never —"

"It doesn't matter, Parker." Jules sounded weary, like all the drama of the day was catching up with him. "That promise was a long time ago. I barely remember it anymore." He threw back a healthy gulp. I noticed the way his throat moved as he swallowed. His dark evening stubble shifted as his Adam's apple moved under his skin.

Julian Thick was a beautiful man. That was nothing new. He was stopped regularly by men and women who did a double take when they saw his dark hair, square jaw, and defined cheekbones.

He'd even modeled in college on a lark. It wasn't like he'd needed the money; his family was obscenely wealthy. But he'd thought it was funny, and he'd had a crush on one of the photographers.

"I still have that picture of you," I said a little while later, completely out of the blue.

"You've had too much bourbon," he said with that kind of soft tone his voice got sometimes when he was buzzed.

"No, I mean the one you did for that magazine. The one without your shirt." I grinned at him. "The one with the nips."

Julian grinned back, rolling his head on the back of the sofa cushion, his earlier surly mood temporarily forgotten. "Jordan Pribble. Had an ass like a fucking vise. I remember that day. God, he was hot."

I stared at him. "You fucked him?"

He chuckled. "Yeah, I fucked him. Several times if I recall correctly. Sucked him off, too. He was—"

"Ugh," I said, interrupting him by holding up a hand. "Don't want the details, thanks."

"Fat like an eggplant," he finished deliberately. "Uncut. Nearly gagged me until I cried."

My heart rate tripped into a faster rhythm. "Stop."

I hated hearing this. Loathed it. But it was also doing funny things to my stomach. I stared at the shine of bourbon on his lips, at the way his blue eyes glinted with remembered heat, and felt like I was maybe catching a glimpse of a Julian Thick who wasn't my loyal friend but someone else's hot, aggressive lover.

I shivered despite the fire.

Julian chuckled darkly. "Fine. I'm going to bed. Good night, Parker."

He got all the way to the back hallway before I found my voice and called after him. "Stay. You can tell me about eggplant dick if you want."

"Go to sleep, Parks. There are blankets in that basket over there."

I got up and knocked my knee on the coffee table, cursing the pain as I stumbled toward the hallway after him. "No, really. I can handle it. Naked man dick. Tight man asshole. Blow jobs. Fingers. See? I'm cool."

I wasn't, really, but I wanted to be. For him.

He was standing in the bedroom, pulling off his sweater, when I walked in. The place looked larger than I expected, and I recognized the sheets and comforter.

"This is your bedding from home," I said stupidly.

Julian sighed and walked over to me. The familiar ink on his chest drew my eye the way it always did. He clasped my shoulders and met my eyes. He had gorgeous blue eyes. Sometimes dark with strong emotion and sometimes light with happiness.

"It's been a long, shitty day," he said softly. "Go to sleep." He leaned in and kissed me on the forehead like I was a sleepy child. I should have hated it. I should have shoved him off me, but I didn't. I wanted more of his familiar comfort.

I wanted more of him.

I cleared my throat. "Fine, then. We can go to sleep early, I guess. You want the left side?"

Julian paused and stared at me, his hands clenching and unclenching. "No. I... I want to sleep alone."

Alone? Since when? We'd shared a bed more times than I could count. Hell, I'd probably shared a bed more with him than even Erin at this point. And always, before we went to sleep, I talked about whatever random things floated into my brain, and Julian listened, until his replies faded to comforting half-formed murmurs and my eyes finally shut.

It was our routine. Our thing. For twenty years.

"But this isn't one of those dinky hotel beds like last night. It's plenty big enough for both of us."

Julian eyed me with an expression I couldn't read.

"Fine," I said, trying not to take it so personally. "If you need your space, I'll sleep in the guest room." I glanced back toward the living area. "Where is it?"

He turned toward the dresser to pull out a pair of flannel pajama bottoms. "No other bedroom. Just the one."

I stared at his bare back. "No... no other bedroom? What was your plan for when I came here to visit with Erin? Why the hell would you buy a one-bedroom place when you have friends?"

He didn't turn back to face me. "I'm a single guy. You were going to be married. Tiller and Mikey own a giant lodge down the road. Why did I need room for guests?"

Now I was truly angry. Since when did he not take me into consideration in his major life decisions? Had he truly thought he'd build a life here full-time and I'd... what? Sleep over at Mikey and Tiller's place, even though I came to see *him*?

"You should sleep on the sofa, Parks."

I stared at him in disbelief. But I wasn't going to beg to stay in here with him when he was sending me all kinds of messages that I was no longer the same priority in his life as I'd been before.

"Whatever," I said, making my way out to the living room and trying my best to hate-sleep.

It didn't work. Within three hours, I was sneaking into Julian's bed in hopes he wouldn't notice.

6

JULIAN

I woke up half-strangled by Parker's firm biceps. He was spooning the heck out of me, and his morning wood was riding a fine line between inappropriate and intoxicating as it pressed against one of my flannel-covered ass cheeks.

"Get off me," I grumbled, shoving him back. It was too dangerous to languish in his arms for even half a minute. I'd woken up to Parker's aggressive spooning many times before, and, honestly, it never got easier to resist.

He grabbed me again and pulled me close. "Stop fidgeting. I like this. You're warm. Erin never lets me spoon her."

I squeezed my eyes closed and tried not to grit my teeth at the mention of his... whatever she was to him right now. But my next inhale was full of the sleepy scent of him, which was exceptionally impossible to resist. "Have you ever heard of boundaries?"

"Uh-huh. But we don't have those. You knew I was going to wind up in your bed. I was upset. Besides, I don't even fit on that sofa out there."

His breath was warm as it hit the back of my ear. I cleared my throat and tried to clear my head. "Maybe you can stay at the lodge with Tiller and Mikey. Or at Truman's place with him and Sam."

He let out a soft snort, and his grip on me tightened. "Please. The last thing I need is Sam trying to distract me with some kind of DIY project or Mikey asking a lot of intrusive questions about my *feelings*."

I turned around to face him. His eyes were only half-open, and his hair was a ginger mess. Several of the freckles on his face were creased from the pillow. Parker Ellis was the sexiest man on the planet.

I moved back to put some space between us. I didn't want to talk about Erin and his relationship troubles, but it was necessary. I was the man's best friend, and he'd just been jilted. Someone had to be there for him for more than just cuddling. "How *are* you feeling?"

He pursed his lips together while he thought about it. "Hungry as fuck. What do we have planned today?" He moved away to sit up, stretching his golden muscles, which were too sexy to ever succumb to winter paleness like the rest of us did.

"Planned?" Was this when I was supposed to mention the pints of ice cream, liters of vodka, and gallons of self-pity I'd had prescheduled for the week? "I didn't exactly have an itinerary."

Parker walked over to the bedroom window and pushed the blinds open enough to look at the weather outside. "We should go cross-country skiing. I know you want to. Might as well knock it out right off. Stretch our legs. Get some outside time while it's sunny."

"Can we eat first?" I grumbled, rolling out of bed to wander to the bathroom. "I'm going to hop in the shower. There's a half-bath behind the kitchen you can use," I called over my shoulder.

When I finished showering, I dressed in warm underlayers for skiing and padded out to the kitchen in thick wool socks. Parker was on the phone with someone, so I moved past him to start breakfast. He stopped me with a hand on my arm and nodded toward two mugs on the counter.

He'd already made my coffee the way I liked it.

"Bless you," I mouthed at him before taking a sip.

It only took a few moments to realize he was talking to one of his asshole parents.

"I didn't call off the fucking wedding, Mom! Erin—" He clamped his jaws together. "No... no... I told you I... whatever. Fine... I... You weren't there! Why do you even care when you couldn't be bothered enough to—"

He closed his eyes and dropped his chin to his chest. I could see the slight wobble in his chin that warned of imminent disaster, so I grabbed the phone and hit the Off button before pocketing it. His parents had lost the right to upset him a very long time ago as far as I was concerned, and I had no qualms about protecting him from them, no matter how rude it might seem to others.

"Bacon or sausage?" I asked cheerily before opening the fridge door to pick one.

"Don't care," he said flatly before walking out of the room. I knew he was most likely going to shower so he could have an emotional reaction without witnesses. Sometimes I chased after him and forced my comfort on him in similar situations, but today I got the sense he needed time to himself.

I got busy cooking his favorites instead. By the time he came out in his snug long underwear, I was putting two plates with elaborate fried egg and sausage sandwiches on the kitchen table next to a couple of glasses of orange juice and ice water. I tried not to stare at the way his thermal layer clung to his muscles, and I sure as shit kept my eyes above his waist.

Mostly.

I busied myself getting us fresh mugs of coffee. "I forgot to text Tiller to ask him where we should go. Surely there are some good runs on their mountain. The ski resort isn't open to the general public this winter. It's only special access right now. I don't think the downhill operation is fully staffed yet."

Parker swallowed a bite of his sandwich. "It's not. He keeps begging me to come on board to run the ski school, but I told him I can't leave Rod and the program in Vail."

I knew Tiller and Mikey had approached him about joining the ski operations manager they'd hired, but we'd all known he'd never leave the Rokas family. "It's too bad, though. If I came on board full-time, think how great it would be if you were here, too."

I'd said it as a joke, as a throwaway comment. He'd never

consider leaving Rod and the future ideal plan of running their program with Erin. But Parker stopped eating and looked thoughtful.

"Now that Erin and I aren't together, maybe I could reconsider."

I almost choked on my coffee. How did I politely remind him that despite this temporary insanity on Erin's part, they were still going to end up together like always? Getting back together was what they did.

Thankfully, the doorbell rang before the conversation could continue.

Parker was closer to the door, so he got there first. A man's voice said, "Hey, cutie. Aren't *you* unexpected? My, my... look at those muscles. You sure know how to—"

"Excuse me." I yanked the door open more fully to reveal a man about our age with noticeably good looks and trendy clothes. "Can I help you?" I asked.

His eyes widened. "Oh, woah. I wasn't told there were going to be two of you. I don't do DP, but..." He eyed Parker up and down, taking his sweet time about it, before tossing me a more cursory glance. "There's always spit roasting, and I can see how that would be a happy solution to our little dilemma."

I stepped in front of Parker and growled at the inappropriate stranger. "What the fuck?"

He blinked at me. "I'm liking the angry vibe, but go easy on me, man. I thought one of you needed some tender loving care. I'm a lover, not a fighter."

I felt Parker's body brush against my back as his chin came to rest on my shoulder. "Are you a massage therapist? Because Julian could use—"

"You have the wrong house," I said quickly, elbowing Parker back from the open door. "Sorry. Have a nice day."

I closed the door and locked it before turning around to pretend like none of this had happened.

"Jules?"

"Need more coffee?" I asked.

"Uh, no? I have a full mug that you poured me like fifteen seconds ago."

"Then maybe drink it," I said before taking my seat and shoving the sandwich in my mouth.

"Hmm. You know, I thought the plan you mentioned yesterday was more... theoretical. But if you prearranged some... ah... male encounters this week..."

I choked around the solid mass in my throat before coughing out, "Male encounters?"

"Hookups. Grindr stuff."

I glared at him. "I didn't."

"That's okay. I can be cool with it. You know I understand, right?" His pained expression suggested he'd rather be coated with honey and left for the ants, but I appreciated the effort.

"I didn't. Jesus. I wasn't sure I'd feel like being..." *Vertical. Sober. Conscious.* "Social this week."

Parker went back to eating his breakfast, thank god.

After a few minutes, he spoke again. "Is that guy your type?"

I was too busy savoring my lukewarm coffee to answer.

"Because he's good-looking. And I know you like guys who are up for... whatever. I mean, I don't know what spit roasting is, but..."

I set the mug down carefully and rubbed my hands over my face. Last night, he'd clutched his pearls when I mentioned blow jobs. Now he wanted to know my thoughts and opinions on spit roasting? "Can we not talk about this, please?"

Parker pulled out his phone and tapped at it. I knew without asking he was googling things he was going to regret.

"Oh. *Ohhhhhh.* Well. Hm." He tilted his head this way and that as he looked at god-knew-what on the screen. "You're into that?"

"This is me not talking about it," I said before shoving the last bite of breakfast in my mouth.

"I hooked up with a girl one time who wanted to bring in a guy for a threesome. Maybe this is what she was thinking," he continued.

I tried to stay calm while picturing him naked with another man. Thankfully, the woman in my mental scenario was blurry and inconsequential.

"Did you do it?" I couldn't help but ask.

"No. Jesus. If I was going to have sex with a man, it wouldn't be some rando." He glanced up at me sheepishly. "No offense."

"None taken," I said. "Like I've told you a million times before, it's different with guys. Sex is more transactional sometimes. We fuck around for fun. I don't need a guy's resume to enjoy his body. Hell, I don't even need to know his name."

Parker made a low noise of disapproval in his throat. "So you would have fucked that guy at the door if I hadn't been here."

He said it like a fact rather than a question.

"Admit it," he added.

I pushed my chair back and grabbed my plate. "Yes, okay? He was gorgeous. If you hadn't been here, I'd have been dicking him down on the sofa by now. There, you happy?"

It wasn't true. Despite my big words, I wasn't one for jumping into sex without at least a conversation. But he didn't need to know that.

"No," Parker said. His cheeks were flushed red, and he couldn't seem to decide where to direct his gaze. "Not happy at all. I've never liked knowing you hook up with random strangers. It makes me fucking crazy, and you know it."

"Because you think it's dangerous."

"Exactly. You don't know that guy from Adam. He could be a serial killer. You need a weapon or something at the very least. Mace, like Hazel carries."

I set the plate down in the sink and turned back with a grin. "Thanks for worrying about me, babe. I'll stick to known quantities like Nolan from now on."

"Fuck off. I'm being serious." He brought his plate over and nudged me out of the way with his hip. As he began cleaning our dishes, he continued to lecture me. "You need to have me on speed dial with some kind of shortcut so I can come over and beat the guy to a bloody pulp."

"The guy. Meaning my serial killer Grindr hookup."

He nodded as if this was a completely rational conversation.

"Yeah. I already have you on my location app so I always know where you are. This way, when I get the call—"

"Can we go back to not talking about my sex life, please?"

"I'm trying to be a supportive friend."

I couldn't help but gawk at him. "Are you fucking kidding me right now? You are the one who doesn't want us to talk about my sex life. It makes you incredibly uncomfortable."

"Not true. *Clearly*, since I'm the one who brought it up."

Parker truly looked like he believed what he was saying, which was kind of funny. "You always get weird when I talk about sex with guys. Honestly, it's hypocritical."

He stuck his chin out defiantly. "I'm not homophobic, if that's what you're implying."

I blew out my cheeks. "I know that. Don't you think I know that? You don't have a problem when Sam and Tiller talk about their boyfriends. You don't have a problem when your friend what's-his-face from the ski school talks about his Grindr hookups. It's just me." I stared at him steadily. "But I don't get why."

He clenched his teeth and widened his nostrils. "I..." He paused. "I just don't think anyone you hook up with could possibly be good enough for you. You're the best person there is, and... and I don't want some asshole trying to use you for... sex or whatever... when there's so much more to you than... that."

It didn't really explain his problem with hearing about my hookups, but it was so damned sweet, I could hardly be mad at him after that.

"You're biased," I muttered, reaching for a dry kitchen towel so I could help him with the dishes.

"I'm not. Not when it comes to you."

I looked over at his earnest expression. He was such an affectionate soul. Parker Ellis loved harder than anyone I knew, and he was the most loyal friend in the world. It would kill him if anything happened to one of the people he considered family, including me. And maybe especially me. I'd been his closest confidant for over twenty years. I wasn't sure Erin even knew him as well as I did.

Just as I was feeling emotional and sentimental, my best friend had to go ahead and ruin it.

"But maybe you're right. Maybe I should be the one hooking up with strangers," Parker said. "Maybe that *would* be a good way to spend this week."

"Negative, Ghost Rider. Not happening."

He was back to his playful grin, the one with the dimple I sometimes fantasized about tonguing. "Maybe that could be one of those new experiences Erin was talking about. Flirt with a chick at the end of the bar... see where it leads... who knows, maybe I'll meet the future Mrs. Parker Ellis here in Aster Valley."

I couldn't hold back a laugh. Parker was definitely not a random hookup kind of guy. He would spend so much time talking to a woman and trying to get to know her, she'd most likely give up and try someone else before he even asked her back to his place. Leave it to Parker to think about his next serious relationship rather than having a random fuck to get over Erin. "What happened to your vow to swear off women and marriage? Or was that just the bourbon talking last night?"

He turned off the water and dried his hands before making his way over to the pile of ski clothes he'd laid on the end of the sofa. "Not the bourbon. I don't want to go through this shit again. It's exhausting."

Instead of interrogating him, I went to the bedroom to get my own clothes on. Once we'd loaded up the vehicle with our stuff, we followed the directions Tiller had sent. The cross-country trailhead was well marked by a freshly painted sign with the new Aster Valley Alpine Adventures logo Mikey and Tiller had selected for the ski resort.

We parked and unloaded our equipment. Within minutes, we were away from the parking area and surrounded by snow-covered trees. I thought about the many times we'd shared the muffled hush of a cross-country ski trail. The cold air pressed against my cheeks, but the sun warmed my head through my wool cap.

Parker led me through the trees the way he always did. He had an unusual talent for reading the trail and knowing the best ways to enjoy the run. I watched his elegant form like always, reveling in the strong, graceful movements his long legs made.

On the mountain at work, he wore bigger ski pants that formed a waterproof layer, but today he was wearing the tighter, formfitting pants we both had for cross-country treks. He still wore his red ski patrol parka, but it had rucked up enough in the back under his backpack to give me an incredible view of his muscular ass.

He had an incredible ass. Parker had complained that it was beefier than a skier's ass should be, but I'd never minded the extra. In fact, it had made an excellent resting place for my eyes for a long time now.

"Stop staring at my ass," he called back over his shoulder.

It seemed my eye-resting place wasn't as much of a secret as I'd hoped.

"Then stop doing so many squats," I replied. "That thing is too big to ignore."

"You calling me a fat-ass?"

I felt the cold air on my teeth as I grinned. "You complain about having junk in your trunk, and yet you do these insane squat challenges on social media. Don't you realize one thing leads to another?"

"I get paid to do those squat challenges. MaxRush sends me fat sponsorship payments as long as I keep posting about their protein shakes and showing off muscle mass to prove it works. In order to attract those sponsors, I have to stay in top shape and create fitness content."

"You're doing fine in the shape department," I muttered, watching the curved muscles of his hamstrings and calves bunch and stretch.

"You're in better condition than I thought," he teased, moving over to the side of the trail so I could catch up to him. "You said you've been working too much lately and having a hard time getting to the gym."

The trail left the trees and dumped us into a wide expansive meadow. I could see the little town of Aster Valley below and the shining silver curve of the river on the edge of town. It was beautiful.

"When I'm in Denver, Hazel forces me to go for a run during our lunch break. During the fall, we did Cherry Creek starting at the park, but once the weather got bad, she convinced me to get a Peloton bike."

As expected, he started laughing. "You hate exercise equipment. You claim it makes you feel like a hamster on a wheel."

"You're the exact same way. The difference is not all of us can ski outside all day. Some of us have to work for a living."

Parker's hand shot out and caught my upper arm, shoving me sideways into a deep snowdrift. Icy puffs of snow snuck down my collar and down my back as I struggled to right myself.

"Asshole! Fucking ass," I yelped.

When I finally extracted myself from the plume of powder, Parker tackled me back down again. Our skis were most likely still on the trail while the two of us wrestled in the deeper drift.

I grabbed handfuls of snow to shove under his clothes. "You of all people should know how dangerous hypothermia can be in the backcountry," I warned through short, panting breaths.

"Then stop doing that," he said with a laugh while he tried to shove my face in the snow. I wondered how many times we'd done this. All the years of fucking around on the slopes and on the hills near my house when we had a good snow. Hazel was the most violent snow-fighter, but Parker was a close second.

I grabbed his wrist and twisted his arm so I could shove him over onto his back. When I landed on top of him, our faces were inches apart. His cheeks were pink, and his eyes were bright. The white clouds of our exhales mingled and dissipated in the crisp morning air. Had a stranger come along in that moment and been told Parker had been jilted only the day before, they wouldn't have believed it.

I loved seeing him happy and playful, but when my body wanted to suddenly grind down against him with my hardening dick, I froze... and I realized just how long it had been since we'd wrestled in the snow.

Parker's eyes searched mine as the air between us stilled. All around us was the magical silence of a snowy mountain trail. I wanted to bottle this feeling and savor it, keep it close to my heart like a damned locket necklace from a fairy-tale story. Me and Parker alone in the snow.

Together. Just him and me.

I pulled off a glove with my teeth before reaching down to brush a chunk of ice away from one of his eyes.

Parker grabbed the back of my head and pulled my face down, pressing a firm kiss to my cheek and staying there for a beat.

"I love you," he murmured with his hot breath into my cool skin. It wasn't the first time he'd said the words, or even the hundredth, but it always felt like the first time. My heart erupted like a fire ant hill that had been kicked over. Stinging creepy-crawlies scattered everywhere, looking for cover.

Instead of saying the words back—words he already knew because I, too, had said them hundreds of times before—I grabbed a pinch of snow and shoved it in one of his ears before shoving away from him, snapping back into my skis, and hauling ass down the trail.

Because running away was the only way to keep from kissing him back.

Only, when I did it, it wouldn't be on the cheek.

7

PARKER

I loved the way I felt after a long, physical day outside. My muscles were comfortably tired, and my brain was no longer on overdrive. The bar Julian had brought us to looked like any old catchall tavern in small-town Colorado, all still decked out with pink hearts and cherubs for Valentine's Day. It seemed to function as a local hangout, bar and grill, and also made the best local brew, according to the table full of Aster Valley guys Tiller and Mikey had brought with them.

Tiller kept staring at me as if trying to assess how fragile I was, like I might be one Cupid decoration away from losing my shit and blubbering all over him about being left at the altar.

"Stop," I said before stealing a mozzarella stick from one of the platters in the center of the table and leaning back to put my arm on the back of Julian's chair. "I told you, I'm fine."

"No, I know. I just think... maybe you actually *do* need to take Erin's advice about trying something new. Having an adventure."

The first thing Tiller and Mikey had asked about when we'd sat down was what had really happened to call off the wedding. I'd explained Erin's note. By the time Sam and Truman had shown up and asked the same question, I'd been ready to scream. Thankfully, Julian had repeated the basics for them so I hadn't needed to.

"How so?" I asked. "I live a pretty adventurous life as it is. Besides, I don't particularly love adventure if they involve travel and shit. You know that about me."

Tiller nodded. "For one, you could take us up on the offer to move here and take over the ski school. It's one of the elements we didn't have in place in time for a full opening this winter. I'm not all that thrilled hiring just anyone to run it when one of my best friends is the best ski instructor in the state."

Their offer had been tempting. Hell, I could just imagine how fun it would be to live and work among my closest friends here in Aster Valley. But I couldn't imagine leaving Rod high and dry. When he'd offered me the management of the Vail store, complete with the ski-school contract, it had been a dream come true. I'd been able to quit competitive skiing but still spend most of my days doing what I loved.

"I don't know how I could ever leave Rod," I admitted. "But now, with everything that's happened…"

Julian's foot nudged my leg under the table. "He loves you, Parks. He'd understand."

Sam met my eye. "Just think about it. It's your future, not Rod's."

Thankfully, Julian knew I didn't have the mental energy to tackle more of this discussion tonight, so he changed the subject to an important finance meeting he, Tiller, and Sam had scheduled for Friday. As they talked about the logistics, I let my eyes wander around the crowded space.

I noticed a group of women at the bar giving our table the once-over with interest. I turned to Finn Heller, who was a friend of Tiller and Mikey's and also a famous actor. "Beware the fangirls," I teased with a tilt of my head toward his admirers.

He waved me off with a hand, but his partner, the slightly older sheriff, sighed. "This is my life now."

Before looking away from the ladies at the bar, I noticed a man near them. He was tall and good-looking in a rugged, fit kind of way, like someone from one of the outdoor fitness accounts Julian followed on social media. He wasn't looking at Finn. He was looking at Julian. With noticeable interest.

I forced myself to turn back to the conversation at hand. Which was a mistake.

Tiller tilted his head as he studied me. "Why don't I have any memories of you hooking up with girls when you visited me in Houston? I don't think you were with Erin most of those times, yet you never took any of the jersey chasers back to your room as far as I knew."

I shrugged. "I'm not really into hookups. I always worried about getting someone pregnant or hurting the woman's feelings somehow. Seemed easier just to... not."

I felt Julian's eyes on me, but I was determined to ignore him. He, too, assumed I was heartbroken over my breakup, and he'd misconstrue this little bit of information if given half a chance.

Tiller beat him to it. He leaned forward with a frown. "I always assumed it was because you were still in love with Erin, even when you were broken up."

"No," I said with a laugh. "Not at all. Believe me, it wasn't some kind of old-fashioned chivalry. And I did date other people during our breakups. Sometimes. But I'm just not wired for casual hookups." I shrugged. "Maybe that's Erin's point, though. Maybe I should try a random hookup and see if that's what I've been missing all this time."

It was a joke. The same one I'd used with Julian earlier. I had no interest in picking some woman up in this bar tonight, or ever. But unlike Julian, who knew not to take my nervous joking seriously and also knew hookups weren't my speed, these guys ran with it. Within moments, they were pushing me away from the table to go to the bar for another pitcher of beer. As soon as I saw the three attractive women sitting at the bar, I knew what my friends' motivation was.

"You're that guy," one of the women said as I approached the bar.

I looked behind myself to see if Finn had followed me, but he was still at the table.

"I mean, technically, I am a guy..." I said with a grin. "But I think you mean—"

"No, dude. You're a famous skier," she insisted, emphasizing her point with her index finger. Her nails were coated in Kelly green fingernail polish. "I remember you."

Her two friends leaned over to check me out now that their friend had claimed me someone worth recognizing.

"I'm a skier but not famous," I corrected. "I run the ski school in Vail."

"No, but... you race. Or you did at one time. I remember. You did this killer move the crowd went nuts over. A wicked twist hop thing on the moguls."

She was right. That was me. It had started out as me clowning around but had quickly become a signature move I did on runs where I could afford to lose time or points. "Did you by chance go to Colorado State?" I asked.

She snapped her fingers and pointed at me again. "That's it. Yes. But you went on to ski professionally, right?"

I nodded and set the empty pitcher on the bar, raising my hand to get the bartender's attention. "I did for a short time, but now I'm an instructor."

She smiled at me, flashing straight, white teeth in a pretty face. Her dark brown hair was pulled back in a long ponytail with loose wisps framing her face. She and her friends were definitely attractive, but it didn't do anything for me at all.

Maybe there was something wrong with me. Or maybe it was normal not to be attracted to anyone after being jilted so recently.

I made friendly conversation with the three of them while waiting for the beer refill, but when the bartender handed me the full pitcher, I gave my polite goodbyes and turned to go back to my friends. The man who'd been eying Julian stopped me.

He was a good-looking guy, maybe my height or a little taller, and his smile was friendly and a little hesitant. I hadn't realized before now that he seemed to have no interest in the three beautiful women sitting close to him at the bar.

"Hey. Look, I'm sorry to bother you, but do you mind if I ask about your friend? He's kind of gorgeous, and I'd like to buy him a drink."

"Finn?" I asked, deliberately being obtuse.

"Is that his name? The one in the Tom Ford sweater."

Normally, I wouldn't have known a Tom Ford *anything* from a hole in the wall, but in this case, Julian had lectured me about not getting near his Tom Ford with my "nasty lotion hands" after I'd helped myself to his fancy hand cream earlier. I'd made a joke about cream on my hands that he hadn't found remotely funny.

"Oh, no. That's Julian," I said, feeling my jaw tighten.

"Would you mind giving me an introduction?"

I felt a flapping panic in my chest. "Um... well..."

What the hell was wrong with me? Why shouldn't Julian enjoy a hookup the same way everyone was encouraging me to? Just because I didn't want to pick someone up didn't mean he couldn't. I needed to get over my selfish hang-up about Julian hooking up with other men —

Whoa, wait. *Other* men? Where had that come from? I meant with men, *period*.

Any men.

Because obviously he wasn't hooking up with *me*.

I swallowed hard.

The man sensed my hesitation. "Is he into guys?"

"Oh, yeah, totally. He's gay."

His face lit up. "And is he open to —"

"He's mine," I blurted, not knowing where the fuck that came from. "*Mine*, um... like... my man? So, no. No, he's not open to..."

The guilt clawed at me. This was wrong, unfair. And completely unacceptable. *Tell him you lied. Tell him Jules is available.*

I cleared my throat. "I mean... yes, he's available, but..."

The man held up both hands and took a step back. His face still held a friendly smile. "Hey, man. No worries. Sounds complicated. I didn't mean to —"

"No, it's fine," I said, scrambling. "I was kidding. I meant he was my *best* man. You see, I was supposed to get married last night. To a woman. But that's not important. Come on, I'll introduce you. He's really great. Truly."

He shook his head good-naturedly. "Nah, it's fine. Clearly I touched a nerve. I don't want to mess with that. Besides, I have an early day tomorrow. I'm just going to head out."

I wanted to slap myself. "He's sexy as fuck!" I said in desperation. If Jules found out I'd lost him a potential hookup, he'd be pissed. "He's got a great body. You would not believe the tattoos. *Hngh*. And look at his hair. It feels even better than it looks. He's also smart. An attorney! Top of his class in law school. And a great skier!"

The man walked away laughing, as if my panic wasn't important to him at all. I glanced over to the table where my friends were and found all of them staring at me. The look on Julian's face was terrifying. He was clearly livid.

"What did you just do?" he asked in a low voice that nevertheless carried through the sudden silence.

"What? Nothing. I was talking about someone else." I quickly slopped beer from the pitcher into a fresh glass and threw back a giant slug, nearly choking myself.

"Someone else who was top of his class in law school and whose hair you've touched," he said flatly.

Someone at the table added, "You do have lovely hair, Julian. I'd touch it."

"You don't know whose hair I've touched," I said with a sniff. "It's none of your business anyway."

"Were you trying to get me *laid*?" he hissed. "You found some random dude at the bar and tried convincing him to give me a shot?"

"What? No! It was the opposite."

Fuck.

I knew when Julian's eyes narrowed that much, trouble was coming.

"Explain." Jules had a certain tone he used sometimes with me that was bossy and demanding. It made me shudder.

"I just... well, he... you see," I began. "It started when I thought he was interested in Finn."

"Fucking Christ," the sheriff muttered, draping a possessive arm over Finn's shoulders that belied his easy tone. "You should have told him he could have him. The man doesn't know how to take out the trash or wash a dish."

"Hey!" Finn scoffed. "It's not my fault I've had housekeepers all these years."

"Ignore them," Julian said. "And tell me what happened."

"The guy was interested in you, and I said the wrong thing by accident. Then I tried to correct myself, but it was too late. And I feel bad because he seemed nice."

Tiller looked like he was enjoying this way too much. "What was the 'wrong thing' you said to turn the guy away?"

There wasn't a chance in hell I was going to admit to this table full of men that I'd accidentally given the guy the impression that I, of all people, was dating Julian. They'd never let me live it down.

I scrambled to think of an alternative, but in the meantime, I was pretty sure I looked like I was trying to concoct a bold-faced lie. I wasn't. I simply needed a meek-faced one.

My mouth opened and closed on a whole lot of nothing while Julian's eyes bored into me.

"I'm sorry," I breathed, reaching out to run fingers through his hair. It really did feel amazing to the touch. Nothing stressed me out more than Julian Thick being upset, and if he was upset at *me*? Worst thing ever.

"What did you say to him?" he asked.

"Okay, fine, but I really did just misspeak. I may have accidentally implied you were *mine*, when really—and you're gonna find this hilarious, just wait—I was trying to tell him you were my *best man*. Ha."

Tiller frowned. "Why'd you tell a random stranger Julian was your best man?"

I turned to him with a glare. "Can you please stop trying to 'help'?"

Mikey shoved back from the table where he'd been sitting quietly next to Tiller. He put a hand on my shoulder and leaned in to speak softly close to my ear. "Come outside. I need to talk to you."

I glanced up at him. I'd only known Mikey for a few years, but that had been long enough to convince me of his genuine care of others. Maybe he would have some advice on how to smooth things over with Julian.

I tried to ignore the fact that Julian still hadn't said a word and followed Mikey outside into the frigid night air. "What's up?"

He leaned back against the brick building and crossed his arms. "That's what I'm trying to figure out. This is at least the third time I've seen you cockblock your best friend in public."

I stared at him. "Are you kidding?"

He looked serious. "Not one bit. And here's the thing. I truly don't think you realize you're doing it."

"I'm not! I don't. Why would I?" Mikey wasn't as smart as I'd originally thought, which was a shame because Tiller was one of my closest friends, and he deserved a smart partner. "When have I ever cockblocked him?" *Except tonight*, I didn't add.

"When Tiller and I met you guys in Vegas for the bachelor thing and we ran into my friend Joey. I pointed Joey into the chair next to Julian, but you saw me do it and snaked the spot before Joey could sit in it."

"I needed a place to sit. I was the groom, for god's sake."

He eyed me. "Yes, and as the groom, you already had a spot at the head of the table, *which you'd already been sitting in all night.*"

I swallowed. "I didn't like that seat. It was too close to a speaker."

"And then there was the time you guys came here to see our new place and I tried introducing Julian to Truman."

"Truman was dating Sam!"

Mikey's lips curved in a smile. "Wrong. This was before Sam and Truman got together. You told Truman that Julian didn't like spicy food."

"He doesn't," I said, feeling smug. "That's the truth. Even one red pepper flake makes him sweat."

Mikey straightened up from the wall and stepped closer. I didn't like the knowing glint in his eye. "Let me tell you how the conversation went, Parker. I said, 'Julian, I've been looking forward to introducing you to Truman. The two of you have a lot in common. Truman owns a spice shop and—' That's when you interrupted to blurt, 'Jules doesn't like spicy food.'"

I felt my face heat despite the cold air outside. "He needed to know," I said stubbornly. "How could they possibly make a relationship work if—"

Mikey threw up his hands. "A relationship? Who said anything about a relationship? Jesus, Parker. Let the man get laid for once."

"I don't care if Jules gets laid."

"I think you do. I think you're jealous, and that's why you do the things you do."

"Jealous?" Wow. Yeah, I had definitely pegged Mikey wrong. "I'm concerned. I love him. I want to protect him. He's the most important person in my life, and he only deserves the very best. I don't want him to end up falling for someone who'll use him, or hurt him, or not give him what he needs."

"And has it occurred to you that that person might be *you*?"

"Huh?"

Mikey stepped forward and squeezed my arm. "Parker... you're giving Julian mixed messages." His voice was gentle, but his words were harsh.

"I don't understand what you mean."

He sighed and dropped his hand. "Never mind. Maybe you're not ready to hear it."

"No. Tell me what you mean because I know you don't mean what I think you mean. Julian isn't attracted to me like that."

He met my eyes. "You sure?"

"He's not."

He lifted an eyebrow. "Are you sure?" he asked more slowly.

I clamped my mouth shut and thought it through, grasping at any evidence to prove my point. "I wanted to share his bed last night like we always do, and he wanted me to sleep on the sofa. I mean, before I snuck in later."

Mikey's mouth opened in disbelief. "You're a fucking idiot," he said before moving away from me back toward the door to the restaurant.

I hurried after him. "Wait. Do you really think I've been sending him mixed signals? If so, I didn't mean to. We've been best friends forever."

Mikey spun around on his heel. "You touch him all the fucking time. Your face lights up when you see him. You spend half the time trying to make him laugh and the other half hanging on everything he says."

"Of course I do. He's my favorite person. We're best friends."

"I thought Erin was your favorite person?"

His question stopped me in my tracks. Why the hell would Erin be more important to me than Julian? How could he possibly think that?

"No," I said with a little laugh. "Not even close."

The words slithered around in the cold air between us, bringing some enlightenment to those of us who'd been utterly oblivious up till now.

"Oh," I said stupidly.

Mikey suddenly lurched at me and hugged me tight. His smaller body was lithe but strong as hell. "It's too bad you can't date him, isn't it?" he asked, pulling back and meeting my eyes. "Imagine how incredible that would be?"

For some reason, his words made my throat heavy as my eyes blinked away the dry night air. I didn't say anything, but it didn't matter. He'd already escaped back into the restaurant.

I stood there for a minute to calm my breathing. What exactly had just happened? We'd started the conversation with Mikey's implication Jules had feelings for me, but we'd ended it with the implication I was the one with the feelings.

When I finally made my way back into the warmth of the restaurant, I felt oddly removed from everyone else. The ladies at the bar tried to get my attention, but I only shot them the barest of smiles. Tiller asked me if I was okay, and I waved away his concern with a stupid joke.

But I couldn't stop thinking about what Mikey had said. It wasn't the first time I'd thought about Julian and me. In fact, years ago I'd wanted nothing more than to try a relationship with

Julian, but kissing Tiller had felt about as hot as kissing my own hand.

But then again...

I thought about the way I'd looked at Julian the night before. His stubbled jaw, his Adam's apple, his firm lips—

"Tiller!" I jumped to my feet. "Tiller, can I talk to you outside, please?"

Julian grabbed my hand and tugged me down so he could whisper in my ear, "Are we good?" His warm breath smelled like beer, and his skin smelled faintly like some kind of sexy cologne.

I wanted to let out a maniacal laugh. That was the question, wasn't it? I had no fucking clue if we were good or not. I felt like my life was a house of cards and someone had suddenly brought in a megaton turbine to blow it all to shit.

"Course we are," I said in a too-high voice. "Tiller? You coming?"

This time, I was smart enough to grab my coat. As soon as I got Tiller outside, I grabbed his arm and yanked him closer. "Kiss me!"

He reared back comically fast. "What? Did Mikey put you up to this? I'm going to kill him."

"No, I need... I need to test something. C'mon."

"That is 100 percent not happening. What the fuck is up with you tonight? Is this about Erin?"

I pinched the bridge of my nose. "Why does everyone think everything is about Erin? No. This has nothing to do with Erin."

"Oh, I dunno... maybe the jilting on Valentine's Day thing. That might be it. Silly me."

Two guys walked up and did a double take when they saw Tiller. One of them stopped to ask for an autograph and selfie, and I almost punched the guy to get him to go away.

I needed fewer famous friends.

"Listen," I hissed once they were gone. "It's about Julian. Remember when we kissed a long time ago?"

His shock was apparent. "You kissed Julian? How did I not know about this?"

"No, asshole. You and me. Remember when we kissed so I could see if I was into guys?"

"Oh, god, right." He let out a laugh before reining it in. "You're a terrible kisser."

I buried my face in my hands and yanked at my hair. I hated everyone.

"Fucking focus, okay? The reason I did it was because I was into Julian."

Tiller's expression was affectionate when he teased me. "Ouch."

I waved away his words. "I wanted to see if we could be more, but first, I had to know if I was going to freak out about kissing a guy."

"Classic gay panic panic. Panicking that you might panic. Continue."

"But I didn't feel anything. Nothing. Like... ew. Gross. Nothing at all."

Tiller looked all around us before focusing back on me. "Am I being filmed? Because I gotta tell you, this isn't at all what I was expecting when you asked me to come out here. And I'm not sure my ego can take many more hits. Are you sure Mikey didn't put you up to this? He's still a little miffed I broke his favorite serving platter."

I ignored him. "My point is, if I'd felt anything for you, I would have tried. But since I didn't, I decided not to risk fucking up what we had... *have* together. He's my person, you know?" My voice cracked a little, but I continued. "And the thought of upsetting him or of making him think we could have something great just to yank it away from him when it didn't work for me..."

"Would be bad," he finished gently.

"Would be devastating," I admitted. "I couldn't live without him, Tiller. You know that."

Tiller stepped forward and pulled me into his arms for a tight hug. The man was built like a pro wide receiver because that's exactly what he was. My muscles and bones groaned under the pressure.

When he pulled back, he kept his hands on my shoulders. "Is this the real reason you canceled the wedding?"

I shook my head. "No. Erin really did leave me a Dear Parker letter."

"Don't you think maybe what you're actually upset about is the thing with Erin, and you're using Julian's crush on you as an excuse?"

I had already opened my mouth to respond when his words caught up with both of us. "What?" I asked, feeling like I couldn't get enough breath to properly push the word out. "J-Julian has a...?"

Tiller's eyes were as big as fried eggs. "Nope! Nope. No, certainly not. And also, no fucking way. That was a mouth malfunction, was what that was. A typo but with my tongue. In fact, heh, I think you heard wrong. I said..."

I lifted an eyebrow, waiting.

Tiller shook his head. "Never mind what I said. Let's forget this whole thing ever happened, kind of like we did with that kiss."

"I have feelings for him, too," I said softly. "I just don't want to fuck things up between us."

"You were supposed to get married yesterday. To someone else." Tiller's voice carried a stern warning even though I knew it was given with love. "Don't do something stupid, Parker."

He was right. Of course he was. Maybe this was all some kind of weird boomerang emotional thing from being jilted.

"Yeah," I said, forcing a smile. "Yeah, you're right. I won't. I promise."

At the time I said it, I truly meant it. But the feelings only got stronger, like a flock of rabid bats trying to force themselves out of a crowded cave.

I kept the promise for exactly two days before releasing the bats into the wild.

8

JULIAN

Parker was being weirder than normal, but I chalked it up to the emotional turmoil of Erin's abandonment. We kept ourselves busy with outdoor pursuits, movie marathons, and an unhealthy number of naps in front of the fireplace, but Parker was quieter than usual. Sometimes I caught him staring at me with a funny look on his face, which I assumed meant he was lost in thought about Erin.

This morning, his weird quiet mood had turned crotchety. He was making us some BLT sandwiches when I walked up to steal a piece of bacon from the pile in front of him. He jumped a mile high and screeched. "Gah! Gimme space. Jesus."

I'd finally had enough. "What is wrong with you?"

"Nothing. Can't a man have some space?"

I couldn't help but smile at his hypocrisy. "Really? This coming from the man who literally almost put his hands down my shorts in bed this morning?"

His ears turned pink. "I told you already. I thought that was *my* dick."

"Mine is ten times larger than yours, hardly something you could mix up," I teased. Despite his mercurial moods, Parker had been good company this week. I'd enjoyed the chance to have him all to myself for once.

"N-no, n-not n-necessarily." The red blush had seeped from his ears to his neck. Parker rarely got embarrassed. That was more my style.

I stepped back and focused on his face. "What's going on? You know I don't care about you spooning me, right? I'm used to it by now."

He didn't say anything or look at me. Apparently, the sandwiches were way more interesting.

"Are you embarrassed you almost felt me up?" I joked. "Because I wouldn't have minded that. Feel free to make liberal use of my dick in the mornings if needed. I wouldn't want you to think I was an ungenerous host."

He still didn't say anything. His body radiated stress, but his focus remained on the food.

Was he offended? I'd been kidding. He and I had always been able to joke about anything before. But for some reason, today was different. My stomach twisted with worry.

"Parks? Is this your Erin shit coming out? Are you ready to talk about it yet?"

"I don't have Erin shit. And, no, I don't need to talk about it."

I took the hint and gave him even more room. After refilling my water bottle, I sat down at the kitchen table and watched Parker. He was dressed in soft gray joggers with a red ski patrol hoodie and thick wool socks. He'd taken a shower after we'd spent a couple of hours outside, shoveling snow off the long driveway, trying to fix a broken floodlight on the garage that Parker insisted needed to be in working order for security reasons, and hauling in more firewood. His damp hair stuck up in a messy arrangement, and yesterday's beard shadow gave his chin a golden-red glow in the light coming through the kitchen window.

I remembered him as an awkward preteen with a face full of acne and a big gap between his bottom front teeth. He'd loved listening to guitar ballads, watching competitive skiing on television, and chewing grape-flavored bubble gum. Despite having shitty, neglectful parents, he'd been the most optimistic middle schooler in history and had a joy of life that had kept me from sinking into my more pessimistic nature.

This man had been the most influential positive role model in my life, and now he was hurting. I wanted to help, but I didn't really know how.

When he set two plates down on the table, I murmured my thanks before digging in. The sandwich was amazing. We ate in companionable silence for a while until the doorbell rang. This time, I got up to answer. I was expecting an Amazon delivery of some things for the kitchen, but when I opened the door, it wasn't a delivery driver.

"Oh. Hi," I said, recognizing the man from the bar where he'd been talking to Parker. "Can I help you?"

"It's you," he said with a wide grin. "From the other night. This is a nice surprise." •

I felt Parker move up behind me. The man's smile dropped. "Oh. And you, too."

"What are you doing here?" Parker asked gruffly before moving around to face me. "Julian?"

I looked between the two of them. "I… have no idea what's going on."

The man stuck out his hand. "I'm Rocco Valentine. I had a date scheduled with…" He cleared his throat. "Jay Thick. I'm assuming that's a fake name."

Parker snorted. "Like you're one to talk. *Rocco Valentine*? Really? That's —"

I felt my face ignite. "No," I interrupted loudly. "I'm Julian Thick, but I didn't schedule a date with anyone."

Parker stepped back and set his jaw. "It's fine. You can go ahead."

I snapped my eyes to him. "Excuse me? Like I need your permission? I'm saying I never arranged anything. If I had, I wouldn't lie to you about it, and I sure as hell wouldn't lie to this man, who's obviously gone out of his way to show up here." I looked back at Rocco. "Sorry."

He was hot and fit, exactly the kind of guy I would have loved to have shown up at my door if Parker wasn't around, but Parker was around, and I was not about to kick him out so I could get some hot ass.

Eating a BLT with Parker trumped fucking a stranger any day of the week, even a sexy one like this guy.

Rocco looked from me to Parker for a beat before letting out a soft laugh and shaking his head. "Okay. See you later."

As he turned away, I reached out to grab his arm. "Wait. Who arranged this? Do you know?"

He shook his head. "I assumed it was you. The Grindr username was JThickAV. That's not you?"

"No. I'm…" I glanced at Parker before looking back at Rocco. "Not on there much."

Parker coughed out the word "Liar."

"Anyway," I said more firmly. "I'm so sorry your time was wasted. I think maybe a friend of ours arranged it to cheer me up or something. But it's not necessary. Good luck finding… some… other fun." I finished that stupidity with a toothy smile that most likely looked deranged.

"Yeah, no worries," he said, waving over his shoulder as he walked back out to his car. "Take care."

I closed the door and let out a breath. "Jesus. I'm going to kill Mikey."

"Awkward," Parker singsonged as he returned to the kitchen table. "Of all the guys in all the world, Mikey hooked you up with the guy who was asking about you at the bar."

"What do you mean?"

He swallowed another bite of his sandwich. "He was the one I was telling about you being my best man, remember?"

I remembered him yelling after the guy something about me having nice hair and a law degree. My best friend had a special talent for humiliating me in public with the best of intentions. "That was him?" I asked, only because I was seriously hoping I'd remembered wrong.

He nodded again. "He was staring at you all night. Then when I went to refill the beer pitcher, he asked if you were available. Which is really ballsy, when you stop to think about it, isn't it? I mean, just out of the blue, 'Your friend is gorgeous.' Who does that?"

I pushed the rest of my sandwich away. Something about this conversation was making my stomach uneasy. "If he was so interested, why did he leave without talking to me?"

Parker looked everywhere but at me. "I, ah... I told you, there was some confusion about you being my *man* versus my *best* man. I may have misspoken. It's all a blur."

I thought of the times Parker had interfered with guys I'd dated or guys who'd been interested in me. Of the way he'd *literally* shown Nolan the door the night of the rehearsal dinner. Of the way he couldn't stand to hear about me hooking up with anyone, ever.

"Did you warn him off?"

He stood up and took our plates to the sink even though he hadn't finished either. "No. I... well, I mean, he might have taken it that way? But it was an accident, I swear. And I tried to undo it, but he left."

"Whatever," I muttered, reaching for my buzzing phone. It was a text from my sister asking if I had time for a call. "I'm going to head outside to call Hazel."

He looked at me funny. His expression held a little bit of hurt that I felt the need to speak to my sister in private.

I didn't really care. I needed Hazel's advice, and since it was about my stupid best friend, it needed to happen out of his earshot.

"Yeah, fine." He reached over to crank up the wireless speaker next to the sink and turned on the faucet.

I put on my coat and scarf, stomped into my boots, and headed outside. The afternoon sun angled through the trees with a warm glow, and snow dripped from icicles along the eaves.

"Hey," I said when she answered.

"How's he holding up?" she asked in that hushed voice people used for funerals and cancer diagnoses.

I glanced back toward the house, where I could just make out Parker dancing at the kitchen sink while he did the dishes. "He's fine."

"Has he freaked out yet?"

"Not one single bit. But he is finally acting a little weird. After begging to sleep in the bed with me the first night, he insisted on sleeping on the sofa the past two nights."

"He's sleeping on that short thing?" she asked in surprise.

"Well, no. He tries to, and then he waits for me to fall asleep before sneaking back into the bed with me. I don't know why he doesn't just start off in the bed like a normal person. It's not like I don't see him there when we wake up, and I haven't called him out on it." Though, unlike the first day, the last two mornings, Parker had leaped out of bed and ran for the bathroom the second he woke up.

"That is weird. He even wants to sleep in your room at Mom and Dad's house when you guys stay there. He's never wanted to sleep in the guest room."

It was true, especially when he was upset about something and wanted to talk.

"Maybe he's still hurt that I didn't consult him before buying this house. Or because I told him I didn't want him sleeping in my bed the first night."

Hazel was silent for a moment. "You told him that, huh?"

"Didn't stop him from climbing in, but yeah. I'm trying to set boundaries," I said a little desperately, omitting the part where I'd nearly kissed him during our snow fight and the jealous display in front of the guy who'd shown up at the door. "Because we all know Parker and Erin will end up together eventually."

My tone begged for her to disagree, but she only sighed.

"How is Erin? Have you heard from her?"

"Yeah, she's... she says she ran into Nolan down there."

It took me a minute. "*My* Nolan?" I bleated.

"I didn't think you had feelings for him." I could tell by her voice she was worried.

"No, I don't. Not at all. But still... that seems... highly unusual."

Hazel's laugh was comfortingly familiar. "That's the understatement of the year. It's creepy. What's worse is I don't think she ran into him, Jules. I think she invited him to go with her. I think they're down there together."

An incredulous laugh burbled up. "This is unbelievable. It's like a reality television show. Why the hell would Erin take that asshat to Mexico?"

I spotted the broken security light still hanging by its wires on the corner of the garage. Screw it, I'd call someone else to fix it. The idea of Parker going back up on the ladder when there was this much ice on the eaves made me nervous.

"She said she was digging his open and easy vibe. He's supposedly all about trying new things and having adventures. He's helping her expand her consciousness. She likes that he calls her 'E' because —I kid you not—she says it makes her feel like a 'brand-new person.'"

I looked up at the deep blue sky. Erin was an idiot, plain and simple. Who gave up a lifetime of Parker Ellis for a throwaway week with Nolan? My brain couldn't even fathom it.

"Will Parker be upset?" Hazel asked.

"Well, for one, I'm not planning on telling him. For another, probably not. He keeps telling me Erin made the right choice because they wanted different things. When I asked what the hell that meant, he said she likes to travel and he doesn't. She likes to try things like skydiving and bungee jumping and he doesn't. He even said she'd been on one of those drug-induced 'journey' weekends and wanted him to come on the next one."

Hazel snickered. "Yeah, that was when she and I grew apart a little, to be honest. I think deep down, she hasn't figured out what she wants out of life. She's the queen of trying weird things and then freaking out and running back home to safety. Then it's like she recharges her batteries with Rod, Lorraine, and Parker before going back out to try something new."

The truth of her words struck me so suddenly, I sat down hard on the porch's wooden bench. "Fuck."

"But I thought this time was different. I really thought she was ready to settle down. Otherwise, why propose? Why talk Parker into the big wedding?" she continued.

"Why do you think she did it?" I felt weightless with nerves. When Parker learned this, that he'd essentially been used all these years as a safe place to land, he'd be devastated. He deserved more than this. He deserved to be someone's everything. Someone's permanent home, not just a temporary landing pad.

Hazel let out a frustrated breath. "Honestly, it sounds awful, but I think it was FOMO. All her friends have gotten married lately, and she was sick of being the bridesmaid. The one who couldn't commit. But also, her parents were pressuring her to stop stringing Parker along. You know how much Rod and Lorraine care about him."

I stood up again to pace down the front walk. When I turned back, I noticed Parker singing into a butter knife like it was a microphone.

I loved him so much it made me dizzy.

"Then why didn't she follow through with it?" I asked myself more than anything.

"Maybe Nolan reminded her commitment wasn't really what she wanted. Jules... you need to tell him. You need to make sure he doesn't hear it from someone else."

"Fuck," I said again.

I'd do anything to protect his heart, but Hazel was right. I needed to tell him. It had been bad enough thinking Nolan had triggered all of this in the first place and that Erin might have gone along with the wedding if it hadn't been for Mr. Open Sexfest sitting at the rehearsal dinner swapping stories of fun in the sun with no restrictions. It was so much worse thinking that she'd taken him on *Parker's* honeymoon. Remembering how Parker had put in so much effort to make the trip special for Erin made me want to throw something... specifically Nolan.

A faint voice in the back of my head reminded me no one could lure another person away from a wedding they truly wanted, but that voice was pretty damned dim at the moment. My guilt was much, much louder.

"Hazel, I gotta go."

I went back inside and prepared to tell him the truth.

Parker turned around and grinned. "I think we should pay

Mikey back by sending random hookups to the Lodge. Tiller will…"
He must have seen something on my face because his grin faded.
"What's wrong? Is Hazel okay?"

I reached for his hand and pulled him over to the sofa. "Yeah,
she's fine. Everyone is fine. Listen…" How the hell was I supposed
to tell him his ex-fiancée was this selfish?

"I told you Erin went to Mexico," I began.

Parker's eyebrows came together. "Yeah?"

"She didn't go alone. She went with Nolan."

He looked crestfallen. "Oh shit."

I squeezed the hand I still held. "I'm sorry."

"Wait. What? Why are you sorry? *I'm* sorry. I know you said you
didn't have feelings for him but…"

I stared at him. "Parks. I don't give a shit about Nolan. I told you
he and I weren't a thing. This is about Erin. She went on your
honeymoon with someone else."

He looked down at where he now held my hand between both of
his. His thumb rubbed gently across the back of my hand enough to
almost distract me from the conversation. *Almost.* "He's probably a
good fit for her right now. I bet they're out there climbing a Mayan
ruin and reveling in their freedom, opening their minds or whatever.
I'm sure they'll have fun together." He shrugged and looked back up
at me.

I yanked my hand out of his grip and stood up to pace. "Fun?
Fun? Didn't you hear what I said? She's with Nolan. Probably
sleeping with Nolan. On your honeymoon."

Parker tilted his head at me. "Yeah… you told me. So?"

I flapped my arms up and down like a deranged chicken. "Are
you kidding? Your fiancée —"

"*Ex*-fiancée," he interrupted from the sofa.

I glared at him. "*Ex*-fiancée is sleeping with him. How is this
okay with you? How is *any* of this okay with you?"

Parker shrugged. "I don't know. Just is."

"It can't be. You're repressing, or —"

"I'm not."

I shook my head. "You haven't processed —"

"I have."

"Then for fuck's sake, explain how you didn't even want me sharing a room *platonically* with the guy the night before the wedding ago, and now you're perfectly calm at the fact that he ran off with your fiancée!"

"Because she's not you, damn it!" he exploded, nostrils flared, then blinked as what he'd said caught up to him. He didn't back down, though. "She's not you," he repeated softly. "And once again, she's my *ex*-fiancée, Jules."

"For now."

"Forever."

"And what does that even mean," I whispered, almost afraid to look at him. "She's not me?"

Parker stood up and grabbed my hands to hold them down by my side. He suddenly seemed so close. Uncomfortably close. *Intimately* close.

I sucked in a breath.

Meanwhile, Parker looked as calm and unruffled and confident as I'd ever seen him. "It means she's not the person I obsess about when they're gone. She's not the person I want to run to when I have something cool to share." His eyes pinned me with an intensity that made my stomach drop to the floor. "And she's not the person I want so fucking badly to kiss right now."

What. The. Ever-loving. Fuck. Was happening.

I stepped backward and nearly fell over a side table. I turned to grab it before it fell, and then I scrambled to right the few items that had fallen over. "Nope. Nope, you didn't just say that. Stop doing this. You're saying things you don't mean. You're upset. Understandably so. You were left at the altar. On Valentine's Day. That has to cut deep. So... so, yeah. That's all this is." I turned back and glared at him. "Confusion."

Parker stepped close again, that sexy little smile playing at the corner of his mouth. "I'm not confused. Not anymore."

My breathing came fast and jagged. "Well, I sure as fuck am. This is ridiculous. This... this week was supposed to be... not about this," I said frantically, running my hand palm out in a circle between us to indicate everything encompassing the two of us. "This week was supposed to be... supposed to be..."

He leaned in until our noses almost touched. Almost.

"Supposed to be?" he asked in a low, breathy voice that made my balls ache.

"Supposed to be me moving on from you."

9

PARKER

My dick was hard.

My dick was hard for my best friend, and my heart felt like it was going to skyrocket out of my chest. I wanted him so fucking much. It was like someone had popped the cork on a bottle of champagne I'd spent twenty years inadvertently shaking.

For the past two days, I'd been staring at a bunch of troubling puzzle pieces, trying to make them make sense. I couldn't be gay, since I still had zero desire to kiss Tiller, or the guy at the bar, or any other man I'd ever met. But then, why had I been subconsciously cockblocking my best friend for years? And why was the idea of Julian having a crush on me so damn thrilling and satisfying? And why was my cock suddenly malfunctioning every time Julian grinned or stretched or spoke or *breathed*, like it was a radio permanently tuned to the Horny Channel?

I'd been subtly trying to avoid Julian—well, as much as it was possible to avoid someone you couldn't resist sneaking into bed with every damn night, anyway—because I didn't want to talk to him about any of this until I was a hundred percent sure what it all meant. I was done making half-hearted promises and getting swept up by the tide like I had with Erin. Julian was too important for anything else.

But then Julian had been standing in front of me, yelling at me, looking so desperate and angry and concerned and loving and *mine*, and suddenly, all those puzzle pieces fell into place like *click click click*, and the picture became perfectly, amazingly clear.

Of course I hadn't felt a spark with Tiller. Because I wasn't *in love* with Tiller. Just like I wasn't *in love* with Erin... which was why I could never have been the partner she needed, no matter how hard I tried.

Julian was all I could think of.

He always had been.

His body, his smile, his infernal ability to both get under my skin and also be the ultimate comfort.

His words took a minute to sink in.

Supposed to be me moving on from you.

"You don't get to move on from me," I growled in a low voice. I was trying my hardest not to yell at him, not to grab him and shake him the way he'd shaken me just by being himself lately.

"You don't seem surprised that I had feelings for you." Julian's eyes flared. "Oh, god, please don't tell me you've known all along—"

I shook my head. "Mikey mentioned it at the bar the other night. He wanted me to stop giving you mixed signals, but I hadn't known I was. I hadn't known I *could*. I didn't know my own mind. But you know I'd never hurt you—"

"But you have," he whispered, his voice raw and small in a way that Julian's voice should never be. "You didn't mean to, but..."

My chest felt tight, and it became harder to pull in air. The thought of hurting him was excruciating.

"Talk to me," I pleaded. "I can't fix it unless you tell me."

"You can't fix it *at all*. It's ancient history, and none of it is your fault. Like, did you know that I was going to ask you to homecoming the same day Erin did? Yeah." He nodded when I grimaced. "I made you a poster. A whole big prom-posal thing, with puns and glitter—"

"But you went on a whole rant about prom-posals," I reminded him. "You told me they were elitist, and exclusionary, and heteronormative. I figured it was because no one had given you one. That's why I did that whole stupid fake prom-posal thing at the Rockies game—"

"I know. But what was I supposed to tell you?" he said tiredly. "That I had glitter under my nails for two weeks because she got to you first? That I cried myself to sleep? What good would that have done, Parks?"

"I would have been more careful, at least! I wouldn't have, I dunno, kissed you as much. Or slept in your bed. Or snuggled up on your couch when we watched movies."

Julian huffed out a breath. "Don't you get it? I didn't want you to stop doing any of those things. I told myself that was all I'd ever get of you. I tried to convince myself that was enough. For more than a *decade*, Parker. And I swore to myself that it was going to end this week. This—" He waved a hand at the cabin around us. "—this was my wallowing hole. The place where my unrequited crush was going to end once and for all."

I met his gaze squarely, my mind a tangle of heartbreak for what I'd put him through, fear that it might be too late, and a tentative, cautious hope that he and I might transform our friendship into something even more precious.

"It's not unrequited. It's you and me, Jules. Always."

I could see the rapid up and down of his chest. Jules was as riled up as I was, and I knew him well enough to know it wasn't all anger.

"Don't do this," he begged. "You don't know what you're doing."

I moved even closer until one of my legs was between his. The warmth of his thigh against mine made the hair stand up on my legs. "What if I do?"

"You're just upset about Er—"

"Don't do that, Jules. Don't tell me what I'm feeling. I can assure you the only person I'm thinking about right now is in this room."

I noticed a slight tremor in Julian's body, and I was torn between soothing him and provoking him further.

"Is this you being weird about Rocco?" Jules asked with a slight desperate tone to his voice.

"Who's Rocco?"

Julian's hands clutched the front of my hoodie. I wasn't sure if he was trying to keep me from moving away or moving closer.

"The guy. The Grindr guy," he said. "Because you get weird when I want to hook up with guys."

Yeah. Yeah I did. And I'd been so fucking blind about what that meant.

"You don't want to hook up with him," I said, mostly to convince myself. "You sent him away."

"Maybe I shouldn't have," he said, lifting his chin. "Maybe I should have invited him..." The movement of his chin brought our noses together in the lightest brush of skin on skin. Julian's breath hitched.

"No." My voice sounded strange in my ears. "No you shouldn't have."

Jules finally pushed me away, shoving me hard. Now he was legit angry. "Damn you, Parker. Why now, huh? Why now, when I'd finally started reconciling myself to the fact that you were never going to love me? When I'd finally decided to move on and find someone who could be *mine*?"

"Because you have someone who's yours already," I corrected, stalking across the room after him. "Me. And I do love you."

"That's not what I mean, and you know it. I want someone who... who sneaks into my room at night to do more than cuddle." His chin was firm and defiant, and I noticed his hands were balled in fists at his side.

I stepped closer. "I can do that." I smiled fiercely. "I very much *want* to do that."

Julian's eyes widened. "No you can't. You're straight, remember?"

"No," I said without any doubt.

Now the wide eyes were almost comical. He swallowed and backed into the rough-hewn log wall behind him. "What are you talking about? What the hell's gotten into you?"

I resisted making a joke. Nerves were starting to sneak in, and the easiest thing to do would have been joking it all away.

"I love you," I said in a voice I wasn't proud of. It sounded almost as terrified as I felt.

"I know that."

"No. I mean… I… I…"

"Oh, god, Parks. Don't say anything you can't take back."

He was right. For Julian and me, there would be no on-again off-again. There would be no breaking up and getting back together.

To me, nothing had ever sounded so right.

But I understood that Julian would be harder to convince.

"Don't tell me what I mean. I've wanted to kiss you for a very, very long time."

His jaw clenched. "You want to know what it's like to kiss a dude? Fine. I'm calling your bluff so you can get this fucking whatever-it-is off your mind once and for all."

He grabbed the front of my hoodie again and twisted me around until my back was the one pressed against the rough wooden wall. Julian's other hand shot out and gripped me around the throat, pinning me in place, and within a fraction of a second, his lips were on mine.

After a beat of shock, I realized this was it. I was kissing Julian Thick, my best friend, my confidant, the most important human in my life.

And he tasted like everything I'd ever wanted.

I let out a feral sob and reached for the back of his head to keep him from pulling away. Our mouths devoured each other. A loud rushing sound filled my ears, and it almost, almost, drowned out the sound of Julian's sexy-as-fuck whimper.

His kiss lit me up everywhere in a way I'd never in a million years even fantasized about. My brain oozed into a puddle of useless slop, and my body sang with the need for more. The harsh rasp of his beard scruff, the strong clasp of his fingers on my throat, and the insistent erection pressing against my groin were new sensations.

And they were breathtaking.

"Please," I begged when he moved his lips off mine. "Don't fucking stop."

Julian's lips quickly moved to my cheek, my jawline, my ear.

"Not stopping."

His teeth grazed my earlobe, and I wondered if I would have sunk to the ground if he hadn't still been holding onto me.

I grabbed his shoulders, his ass, the back of his thighs, anywhere I could reach to both feel him and also keep him trapped in the cage of my arms. If he suddenly pulled away and stopped all this, I would freak out.

I yanked at his shirt until I could ruck it up enough to get my hands underneath and feel the warm skin of his back. I wanted to slide my fingers down inside the waistband of his pants, but I didn't dare. At any minute, he was going to decide this was a mistake and call a halt to everything that was delicious and thrilling.

So I savored every minute of it while it lasted. When he moved his kisses down my neck and into the collar of my sweatshirt, I sank my fingers into his hair and whispered words of encouragement. As soon as I realized the bulky hoodie was keeping him from being able to reach the places that would feel the best, I scrambled to remove it and toss it aside.

Julian's eyes were dazed as he took his fill of my bare chest. The combination of his glassy eyes, flushed face, and messed-up hair was the sexiest fucking thing ever.

I reached for his shirt and pulled it up over his head before wrapping my arms around him again and bringing our bare chests together. It felt amazing. Weird and different, but hot as fuck.

He was tall and strong. His flat chest had hair on it, and I wanted to rub my hands across it to feel the dips and swells of his muscles. Instead, I grabbed his face in my hands and kissed him again until I couldn't breathe. I didn't care. He was the best kisser on the fucking planet, and I needed more.

There would never be enough. I could kiss him every minute for the rest of my life, and it wouldn't be enough.

"What're we doing?" he gasped between kisses. "Parks. This…" I kissed him again to shut him up, and then I reached my hand down to feel his cock through his pants. If he was going to put a stop to this, I wanted to know what he felt like first.

His groan went all the way down to my dick, and the way he

pressed his shaft into my hand, almost against his will, was intoxicating.

"Want this," I murmured against his lips. "Want you."

"You don't," he said back, arching into me again. "You can't."

I grabbed his hand and yanked it to my own dick, forcing him to feel how hard I was for him. "Tell me I don't want this," I growled against his cheek. "Tell me I'm holding your hard cock in my hand and thinking about anyone other than you."

He whimpered again, as if fighting with himself, but then he must have come to a decision. Suddenly, he was the aggressor again, ripping the front of his jeans open and moving my hand inside before shoving his own down my pants.

As soon as I felt the smooth warmth of the skin of his cock, I felt my skin prickle. This was strange but good. So fucking good. Had I ever been this turned on by anyone? If so, it had been obliterated from my memory by this moment.

When I felt his grip around my own shaft, my legs wobbled, and I let out a cry of relief. "Don't stop," I begged again.

I humped into his hand erratically, trying my best to give him as much pleasure as he was giving me.

"Just like that," he urged. "Oh fuck, fuck."

"More," I gasped. "What do I do? Tell me what to do." I felt panic rising up in my chest. I wanted everything with him, and I wanted it right fucking now.

Jules yanked down my pants and underwear before stepping closer to me until I was shoved hard against the wall again. When he brought our bare dicks together in his grip, I stared down at them in shock. How could something so simple feel this good?

He was right. He was bigger than me. Not by ten times, of course, but the thick head of his cock towered above mine in a way that made my heart pound even more. It was ruddy and engorged, shiny and damp at the tip, and hot against my skin.

Watching us slide against each other made my head spin. "Gonna come," I squeaked. "Jules, gonna come."

He grabbed the side of my face with his free hand and held our faces together cheek-to-cheek. His breath puffed out against my ear.

"Come all over me," he grunted. "Want to feel your hot spunk all over my hand."

Oh god.

His words were all it took. I squeezed my eyes closed as the waves of my climax crested, and I thrust even harder in his grip. I turned my face into his and opened my mouth to taste his skin as I came.

When his grunted curse hit my ears, I opened my eyes and looked down just in time to see him come. It covered his hand and my stomach, getting caught in the hair below my belly button and dripping down into my pubic hair. I reached down without thinking and spread it against my skin.

"Fuck," Julian said, gasping for breath. "Fuck. Fuck."

Instead of exclamations of pleasure, his words sounded like regret. I glanced up at his face and saw it all there.

Regret, horror, sorrow.

I knew before he moved an inch that he was going to run.

"Don't," I warned in the split second before he shoved away from me. He stumbled to the kitchen, yanking up his pants and scrambling to wash his hands in the sink before grabbing his coat and car keys. "Jules, don't you dare leave," I shouted, trying to pull up my own pants so I could grab him and make him stay.

He held up a hand and turned tear-filled eyes at me. "Please. Please let me go. I just need... I just need to think, okay?"

I shook my head and held my hands out. "Please stay here and think with me. Please."

He bit his lip before choking out the word "Can't."

And then he was gone.

I stared after him, torn between forcing the issue and letting him have the time he needed to process what had just happened between us. When his SUV pulled out of the driveway, I realized it was too late anyway. He was gone, and I was left here without a vehicle.

I shuffled back to the bedroom and crawled between the sheets. At least here I could smell him and remember what it was like to hold him in my arms and connect with him on a whole new level, even if that one stolen moment was all I would ever get of him.

10

JULIAN

The ride across the mountain to Rockley Lodge was a blur. When I got to Tiller and Mikey's place, I stormed through the front door and made my way directly to the kitchen.

This wasn't the first time I'd cried in Mikey's big, beautiful kitchen, and I was fairly sure it wouldn't be the last.

"What the fuck?" Tiller said as soon as he saw me barreling toward him. Sam and Truman were already there at the kitchen island, and both stood up quickly as if ready to respond to an emergency.

And it was an emergency.

"I kissed him," I howled through sucking breaths. I could barely see through my tears, and I felt like I couldn't get enough oxygen. "I fucked up and I called his bluff and I kissed him and then... and then... oh my god."

Tiller held me in a tight hug, shushing me and running strong hands up and down my back. "It's okay. Slow down and catch your breath." I felt him turn his head away. "Mikey, what's happening?"

"It sounds like they fucked."

I choked and sputtered, accidentally inhaling a string hanging from Tiller's Riggers hoodie. "No, Jesus. Well, maybe. Kind of? Not really."

"Clear as mud," Sam said, sitting back down at the counter and reaching for a snack from a tray of appetizers. I remembered we were supposed to join them for dinner later because Mikey wanted to test recipes for a new cookbook of his.

I pushed off Tiller and swiped at my eyes. "I ruined everything. He's going to hate me. He was supposed—" I hiccuped. "—supposed to get married a few days ago, and I kissed him and..."

Mikey leaned forward with nosey eyeballs. "And...?"

"We... we..." I made a vaguely obscene gesture at the front of my pants.

Sam nodded solemnly. "They made martinis in one of those fancy shakers."

I blinked at him and shook my head. He held up a finger. "Wait. No. They... shook a cup of dice before throwing them in a rowdy game of Yahtzee."

Truman leaned around Sam's wide form. Regrettably, I had to admit his teasing grin was kind of endearing. "I think they tossed birdseed out for the pigeons."

Mikey studied me. "I still think they fucked."

I closed my eyes and took a deep breath. "I hate all of you."

Tiller reached out and put his arm around me, pulling me close to his side and dropping a kiss on my head. "We love you. And so does Parker. Even if you touched his... martini shaker, I'm pretty sure you two can work it out and get past it."

"How?" I asked, moving away from Tiller's embrace to help myself to a glass of white wine. "How do you just get past seducing your straight best friend?"

"I don't know if he's totally straight," Tiller said. "You know he tried kissing me years ago."

The wine soured in my gut. "That was a joke. A prank."

"Not exactly. He had feelings for you, Jules, but he didn't know if he could be what you needed, and he didn't want to fuck things up between you two. So he tried it on with me first."

Mikey turned his judgy squint on his husband. "And?"

"And nothing." He laughed as if it was no big deal. As if it wasn't the biggest deal. "I didn't pass muster. I let down the entire male gender. Apparently the experience was enough to turn him off men forever."

"Until today," Mikey added with a little bit of smug satisfaction.

I blew out a breath and collapsed on a barstool. "He's confused. He doesn't know what he wants."

Tiller eyed me. "You sure about that? Because I can't imagine he'd let himself go there if he wasn't sure."

Sam stood up to get another beer out of the fridge. "Presumably he got hard, yeah?"

My face heated. Even thinking about Parker getting hard for me made my stomach squirm. "Yeah, but who doesn't get hard when someone rubs them off?"

All the men in the room gave various reactions, but Mikey's giggle was the most obnoxious. "Straight guys don't let you rub them off, Jules. They shove you away."

"Parker would never shove me away," I huffed. "He's too nice. He cares about me too much to hurt my feelings."

"But I think that's Tiller's point. Wouldn't Parker have thought about that before he let anything happen?" Truman finished eating something wrapped in bacon before sliding the tray my way. "I don't understand why you two don't just get together. You love him. He's said a million times he loves you. Why not try?"

I buried my face in my hands. *It's not that easy*, I wanted to say.

Tiller answered for me. "They have a lot of history. They've been best friends for a very long time, and I get why Julian's scared that changing things would mess that up."

Truman thought about it for a minute. "But isn't it already messed up?"

Mikey nudged the plate of appetizers closer to me until I took one and popped it in my mouth. The salty flavor of the bacon reminded me of the BLTs we'd had for lunch. I tried not to let the thought get me down. There had to be a global rule about not crying when eating bacon.

Tiller continued. "When Parker was six, he didn't have anything to eat for lunch and was too embarrassed to ask for a free school sand-wich. Julian figured it out and passed him half of his own sandwich."

"It was peanut butter crackers," I muttered, reaching for another bite. Inside the bacon were water chestnuts, and they were surpris-ingly addictive.

Tiller ignored me. "It happened more than once, so they ended up sitting together at lunch and becoming friends. Then one day when a couple of guys were bullying Jules, Parker defended him and got into trouble with the school and his parents."

I remembered the red welt on Parker's arm from where one guy had clipped him with a backpack strap while swinging it wildly at him.

"Julian's parents were so grateful there was someone bigger to help defend Jules that they encouraged Jules to invite Parker over to the house to have pizza and play video games."

I lifted my head up and met his eyes. "You're leaving out the part where you came over to play games, too."

Tiller shook his head. "Not that time. I didn't start coming over until fifth grade. When Harbo Morris asked me to find out whether Hazel liked him or not."

I let out a snort. "That's a name from the past."

"Anyway," Tiller continued. "By then, you two were thick as thieves, did everything together, and practically lived in each other's pockets."

It was true. But we'd still welcomed Tiller into our crew and then Erin a year later when she and Hazel became tight.

Sam interrupted. "Your parents love him. Tiller says they treat him like a second son."

I scraped my upper lip with my teeth. "They learned pretty quickly that his own parents were shit."

Tiller reached over to squeeze my shoulder. "Total shit. They weren't even poor, is the thing. Just incredibly, horribly neglectful. They both had jobs that took precedence over Parker's welfare. But instead of hiring someone else to care for him in their place, they simply forgot about him."

I slumped again with my chin on my hand. "That's putting it mildly."

Tiller glanced at Mikey. "It's one of the reasons I wanted to retire sooner rather than later. I don't want to focus on my career to the detriment of my family and personal happiness."

Mikey's smile was so tender and affectionate, it made my chest tighten. I wanted that. I'd always wanted it. But the problem was... I'd always wanted it with one specific person.

And he was off-limits. At least... he always had been. If Parker was no longer off-limits, what did that mean for our future?

Tiller was still talking. "Then Jules was in a really bad car accident after college, and you would have thought Parker's heart was being torn out of his chest. I will never forget the sound he made when he got that phone call." He shuddered. "To this day, Parker is insane about drunk driving."

I'd never heard this before. "He made a sound?"

"He made us swear never to tell you, but it's been long enough now it probably doesn't matter," Tiller continued.

It mattered. It mattered to me a great deal. "I knew he was upset..."

Tiller rubbed his chin. "Jules... he was... he was traumatized. When the doctor told him you were in critical condition, the blood drained from his face so quickly, I thought he was going to pass out. When he got off the phone, he made a sound that made the hairs stick up all over my body. I thought for sure someone had died. Then he bolted." He let out a humorless laugh. "He was barefoot. We had to run after him and drag him back in. We'd been kicking back drinking a few beers and playing video games when the call came in. I was in town during the off-season, so we'd all gotten together a few nights in a row."

Mikey reached across the counter to refill my wineglass. "I remember it, too. You called me that night to ask if I thought he should fly out there, too, even though you were supposed to be reporting back to Houston for team commitments."

I took a sip of wine and let the cool, sweet flavor sit on my tongue for a beat before swallowing it. "I remember waking up and seeing Parker there. He was holding my hand. Looked like shit."

This was too much. I didn't want to relive the injuries I'd sustained and the long recovery I'd had to endure afterward. And I didn't need more evidence of how much Parker loved me because I already knew. I knew I was the most important person in his life—even more important than Erin.

I'd always known he wasn't head over heels in love with her, and I'd had the sense he didn't tell her nearly as much as he told me, but I'd still thought... I'd still expected things would change once they were married. It was why I'd planned on coming here and wallowing this week.

I glanced up at my friends, the one who'd been with me for years and the ones who'd become close more recently. They were good men, the best. "Not to sound cheesy, but there's a difference between loving someone and being in love with them. Parker sees me as his safety net. I worry he's grasping at me right now out of fear. Losing Erin would make him feel like he might lose Rod and Lorraine. If there's one thing Parker craves, it's stability and family. He's probably terrified, and he's clinging to me out of fear, not love."

I could tell Tiller was really thinking about what I'd said. He pursed his lips in hesitation before speaking. "I don't think that's what this is."

"I know him better than you, Tiller," I said, suddenly feeling exhausted. "He sees me as his family. He was hurt by Erin's rejection, and he's seeking comfort from his family."

I felt the intense stares from all the guys in the room, but it was Sam who said what they were all obviously thinking. "Comfort. Right. So you're saying the two of you were hugging and talking about your feelings when the ejaculate just sort of... happened?"

He was twisting my words around. "We're friends! How can you go from close friends to sex partners?"

Tiller and Mikey exchanged a look before Mikey said, "Pretty easily, actually."

"No, that's different. You two were at least both gay to begin with," I countered. "Maybe I just need to reassure him I'm not going anywhere. Maybe then he'll stop panicking and doing... weird things."

Truman looked confused. "I thought you said you kissed him? Who initiated the sexual stuff?"

I winced and looked down into my wineglass. Why had I thought kissing him would be a good idea?

In the middle of my awkward guilt moment, the telltale *brrup* sound of a Grindr notification rang out. I snapped my head up to look at Mikey, who was busy fumbling for his phone.

Tiller tapped his chin. "I may have a bad memory, but isn't that..."

Mikey flashed him a guilty grimace. "It's not what you think!"

Tiller huffed out a laugh. "Oh, I think it's exactly what I think. Michael Kincaid Vining, what the fuck did you do?"

Mikey's eyes snuck to me before landing back on Tiller. "Nothing." He tapped at his phone before sliding it back in his pocket.

"He's been sending Grindr hookups to the cabin," I said. "Which has made things even more awkward with Parker, so thanks for that, *friend*."

Tiller sighed. Sam laughed, and Truman tried to hide a grin. Mikey began apologizing. "I actually arranged those before I knew Parker was staying with you. Remember how you thought you were going to be wallowing this week?"

"I can manage my own dick, Mikey," I said.

Sam made an *mmpfh* noise, calling bullshit on my lie. I ignored him.

"Besides," I continued, "Parker *is* staying with me, so please stop."

"That's just it," he exclaimed. "I tried! But for some reason, I can't get into the app. It keeps sending me notifications, but it won't let me access my messages or cancel the account."

I reached for the tray of appetizers and popped several more in my mouth. At least I was in Mikey's kitchen, where eating my feelings was especially decadent.

After swallowing another sip of wine, I rested my head on the counter. I needed to go home and talk to Parker.

And I would.

Just not yet.

11

PARKER

I couldn't get to sleep, mostly because it was midafternoon but also because my dick got hard every time I replayed the encounter with Julian in the living room.

And I couldn't stop replaying it.

Watching Julian respond to my touch, my kiss, my staggered breaths had been hotter than anything I'd ever experienced. What was it about hooking up with him that had made it so much more exciting? Was it that I'd never done any of this with a man before? Or the adrenaline spike of fear from changing the dynamic with my best friend? Or was it simply because he was the most attractive and enticing human I knew?

Maybe all three.

Thinking of Jules as hot wasn't new. I'd always known he was attractive and sexy. I just hadn't let myself imagine kissing him or touching him, not since I'd tried it on with Tiller and thought sex wouldn't be good with a guy.

That seemed so naive and silly now, given how explosive it had been once I'd gotten my hands on the *right* guy.

I wasn't sure what that meant about my sexuality—maybe I was bi, or pan, or a billion other things I'd never really investigated. And maybe I was supposed to care more about figuring out *which* thing, like it would be more legitimate if I put a label on it. But it was really hard to get all worked up over any of that when being with Julian felt like Christmas and the Fourth of July and summer vacation had all come at once.

Being as close to Julian Thick as possible was the only thing I'd ever wanted, even when I thought we could only be friends. And now that I knew I could possibly have him in all the ways—that he could be my best friend *and* I could make his eyes roll back in his head with pleasure when I touched his dick—I was all in. Game over.

I just wasn't sure how to convince Julian that this wasn't an overreaction to being jilted and that I wasn't using him as a safety blanket the way Erin had done with me.

A knock on the door startled me out of my rumination. I tried to remember if I'd locked the door behind Julian or if he was simply giving me a warning so I wouldn't be surprised by his return.

I stumbled out of bed and grabbed my hoodie before opening the door. Instead of Jules, another stranger stood on the front porch. He was a small guy with perfect hair and a too-perfect smile.

"Are you Jay?" he asked, giving me a thorough up-down with dark-lined eyes. He must have liked what he saw because he muttered under his breath. "Baby Jesus, please, if you care about me at all, and if you want to make up for my shitty-ass childhood in Baton Rouge, you will give me this beautiful man."

"No. I'm sorry. He's not here, and there's been some kind of mistake."

He bit his knuckle. "I have some ideas on how we can take advantage of his absence."

"I don't..." How did I tell him I wasn't interested without offending him? It had been one thing when I was straight, but now that I knew I was... not-straight... I wasn't sure of the etiquette. In fact, I could really use some gay advice. "Want to come in?" I asked instead of sending him away.

He looked up at the roof of the porch. "Thanks, Big Guy. I owe you one."

He followed me inside and introduced himself as BJ. "But not the kind you think. It stands for Baby Jeremiah. My dad is Jeremiah Senior. Ask me how it was growing up gay in Louisiana with the name BJ. Go ahead. Ask me."

"Why didn't you change it?"

He leveled a faux patient look at me. "I did. I spent years trying to get people to call me by my middle name, but it never took. Then I moved to California, became a yoga instructor, stopped giving a shit about other people's opinions, and decided my name was a feature, not a bug, so I embraced it. Besides, once guys hear I'm a yoga instructor, they tend to forget my name entirely anyway." He wiggled his eyebrows. "I'm very, *very* bendy... as you'll soon find out."

"I don't want sex," I blurted. "But, ah, I could use some advice."

BJ froze in the act of removing his parka and then continued in slow motion. "Okayyy... advice about what? And I'm going to assume you're just being shy about the sex. We'll ease you into it."

I had to admit he was cute, charming in an easy way. But I didn't need that right now. I needed another not-straight man's perspective, and I needed it before Julian came back.

After offering him a soda and settling him on the small sofa closest to the fire, I took the seat across from him and rested my forearms on my knees to clasp my hands together. "Here's the deal. I think I have feelings for my best friend. Sexual feelings. Love feelings. Forever feelings. All of it."

BJ had already left his boots by the door, so he pulled up his socked feet and wrapped his arms around his knees. "M'kay. And? What's the problem?"

"He thinks I'm straight."

BJ's sculpted eyebrows shot up. "Your best friend doesn't know you're gay?"

I squeezed my hands tighter. "I'm not gay. I don't think. I'm... I don't know what I am. But I like women... sometimes. And I like Julian. Always. I like him most of all."

"Why not just tell him that?"

"I did. I tried to. I will. I want to." I felt like I couldn't catch my breath. There were so many words and thoughts rocketing through my mind, I had a hard time focusing on just one. "But how can I explain what I'm feeling when I don't have the right vocabulary? I don't know how I identify. I just know how I feel."

"Oh, my god! You are so freakin' adorable right now, I don't even care that you're not going to fuck me." He pursed his lips like he was pondering this. "Or, okay, I *almost* don't care. I think you need to tell your friend exactly what you told me. Like, 'Bestie, I have real feelings for you. Sexual feelings and big love feelings. What say we give it a try?' Like that."

I couldn't sit still, so I stood up and selected another log for the fire before grabbing the poker to arrange it just so. "He won't believe me. I know him better than I know myself, and right now, he's thinking this is a rebound thing, that I'm freaking out because of what happened with the wedding."

"Whose wedding?"

I poked the log harder until a chunk of bark flew off and hit the back wall of the fireplace with a *thunk*. "Mine. I was supposed to get married last weekend. But the bride called it off at the last minute, which was the best possible thing she could have done. I'd been going along with the marriage thing because I love her and didn't want to let her down, but I wasn't *in* love with her. And if I'm being honest, looking back, I think I've always been *in* love with my best friend, but I haven't let myself realize it because I thought I was straight and he was gay and there would never be a chance for us."

There was a long silence before BJ's surprised whistle cut through the air. "Oh, honey. You are a hot mess, aren't you?"

I turned to blink at him. Why was he having such a hard time understanding what a shitshow this was? "That's what I'm saying."

BJ took a sip of the raspberry bubble water I'd brought him. The canned beverage was something Julian liked and kept on hand at all times, but I thought it tasted like a faded fruit mirage pressed flat by bald tires.

"Maybe he's right," BJ said, watching for my reaction. "How can you be sure you aren't freaking out post-wedding cancelation? Wait. Wasn't Valentine's last weekend? You got jilted on Valentine's Day?"

"Who cares about Valentine's Day?" I barked. I was sick to death of the Valentine's thing. I'd be happy if I never saw another cartoon heart as long as I lived.

He nodded. "Fair enough. I can see how you'd be a little soured on the holiday. But back to the crux of the thing. I'm not sure the week after a failed wedding is the time to make lifelong declarations to another person regardless of their gender."

"I agree with you, in general. For most people, this would be ridiculous. But for us... it just seems right. *Necessary*." Holding Julian in my arms had been the best, the most natural thing to do. Kissing him, touching him, *pleasing* him had been freeing and mind-blowing at the same time.

I bit my lip before continuing. "He was gonna use this week to get over me, BJ. He's had feelings for me for years, but he stuck by me anyway because he cares about me that much. He was going to watch me marry someone else because he thought I was in love with her. I can't imagine how much it must have hurt. And I don't want him to go another minute without knowing how I really feel."

"How long have you two been best friends?" he asked. BJ's calm demeanor was contagious. I felt myself relaxing now that we were no longer talking about what I did or didn't need to do at this moment.

"Since first grade."

"Wow. That's a long time."

I nodded. "It's always been him. He's my family. He's my... everything."

BJ shifted on the sofa before reaching for the blanket at the other end and spreading it over his legs. "Then how did you end up engaged to the woman?"

I thought back to high school. The homecoming dance. I'd thought about asking Julian to go with me, because he was simply the person I most wanted to hang with at any event like that.

I told BJ about it. "But Erin—who was part of our group of friends—asked me to the dance as her date. And I thought she was cute. I was attracted to her more than I'd been attracted to anyone up to that point, since I was kind of a late bloomer. So I said yes. And we went. We kissed, and it was hot. After that, it was just so easy. When she wanted to suck me off a couple of years later, I was thrilled. And when she wanted to have sex even later still, I was even more ecstatic. I had Jules as my best friend, my forever person, and Erin as my best girl. I wasn't in love with her... or I guess it was more like I thought caring about someone and also enjoying sex with them was what people meant when they talked about being in love."

"Aw. But you were just a kid."

I winced. "I, ah, didn't actually realize the distinction until quite a bit later than that. As in, this morning."

"Ooooh."

"Yeah." I sighed. "You might say I'm *still* a late bloomer."

"So, wait, you dated this girl from high school to now?" He clutched his chest dramatically. "Gurl. No."

I shook my head firmly. "No. For a long time, I was too busy for anything serious. I was on the school ski team in high school and worked my ass off to turn it into a college scholarship. Then I skied for Colorado State, which kept me even busier. I told her all the time that I wasn't in a position to have a relationship, but she said that suited her fine, too. We dated other people. Well, mostly she dated other people. Like I said, I was too busy. And I had a great group of guy friends—especially Julian—who were more fun to hang out with than dealing with dating or hookups or whatever."

"Mmhm. Then what happened?"

"Every time she had a bad experience—a bad breakup, a career setback, whatever—she came to me for comfort, and we'd inevitably end up together again. It was easy and comfortable. Don't get me wrong. I loved her. I love her still. She's a wonderful person, and she's sexy as hell. She's been there for me during some really bad times."

"Whose idea was it to get married? Let me guess, hers."

The wood wasn't stacked quite right in the fireplace, so I crouched down to adjust it again. I felt BJ's searching gaze on the back of my head. It was strange telling this story to an outsider. It made me sound stupid and naive.

I guessed I had been.

"Well, yeah, but I agreed. It sounded nice, finally settling down like that. Her parents are like second parents to me, and her dad is my boss. I pictured us getting a house in Vail and seeing Rod and Lorraine regularly for dinner. Going out to have drinks with my friends from work and their spouses and partners. It sounded really nice."

Why did I sound so defensive?

I glanced over my shoulder to find BJ nodding his head in sympathy. "It does sound nice."

I let out a breath. "Yeah."

"So why didn't you fight for it?" He met my eyes. "When she called off the wedding, what did you do?"

After opening my mouth to tell him how upset I'd been, how I'd tried calling her and texting her, I clamped my jaw closed. It had never occurred to me to go after her. There hadn't been a single wish in my mind to find her and talk her out of leaving me.

"I felt relieved. Like I'd been walking along, not knowing how close I was to the edge of the cliff until Erin pulled us back. So I let her go. After reading her reasons for calling it off—mainly that she wasn't ready to settle down, because she wanted excitement and adventure—I realized she was right. And at first, I felt a little bad that I couldn't be what she wanted, like maybe I should have tried harder. But then I realized that it would never have worked. We wanted different things."

"Hmmm. So how'd you end up here in Aster Valley if you were getting married in Vail?"

"Julian brought me. This is his place." I stood up to put the fireplace poker back in the rack. As I turned to the chair, I noticed a small picture frame set back on the built-in bookshelf next to the fireplace. I stepped closer to see what was in it because it didn't look like a photo.

It was a tiny piece of wrinkled paper with my own familiar handwriting on it.

You and me. Always.

Warmth flooded my chest. I reached out and pulled the frame from its almost-hidden spot deep on the shelf. When I found the chair with my ass, I sat down hard, which must have been why I didn't hear the door open behind me.

"He loves me," I murmured.

"More than anything," Julian's voice replied softly.

I turned to face him, eyes suddenly in danger of betraying me. "Don't leave," I begged in a cracking voice. I stood up and walked over to him, grabbing him and pulling him into my arms so I could hold him tight and never fucking let him go. "Please don't leave me."

Julian turned his face into my neck until I felt the softness of his lips against my skin. I breathed out and inhaled the outdoor scent of him. Along with alcohol.

I pulled back and glared at him. "Tell me right now you did not drive that car after drinking."

Julian's eyes were wide. "N-no. The guys... Declan had one of his deputies bring me back. I wouldn't do that to you."

"If something were to happen to you, Jules..."

"I know. Never. I promise. I'm sorry. I just needed..."

I grabbed the back of his head with my hands and pulled back from him, still holding him close. "I know. I know. I do. I'm sorry, too. I'm so sorry I didn't understand things sooner. Things between us."

He leaned in and pressed a kiss to my cheek, staying there for a long beat and brushing his nose across mine when he pulled back again. "You didn't do anything wrong. We just need to figure some shit out, okay?"

A loud sniff from behind us made Julian jump and try shoving me behind him. He gasped when he realized we weren't alone. "Who are you?"

BJ's hands were pressing his sweater over his heart. "That depends. If you're Jay Thick and you'll agree to a threesome, I'm the luckiest man on Earth. If not, I'm the saddest panda ever."

Julian squeezed his eyes shut. "Another Grindr date."

"Yep. But a really nice one. Didn't you see his car out front?" I asked, turning to peer out of the window.

BJ tossed the blanket aside and stood up. "I walked. My friend and I are in town for a work thing, and we're renting a house a few doors down."

I could tell Julian wasn't happy to discover I hadn't been alone.

His body was suddenly strung tight, and he put on his bitchy fake polite voice. "I'll be happy to walk you back."

BJ grinned. "Sad panda, then. It figures. Well, if you change your mind..."

Julian reached for the door. "We won't."

BJ looked Jules up and down in a way I really didn't appreciate, and then his dancing eyes flashed back to me. "If you need any more advice, honey, don't be a stranger. I'm here all week. It's the red house with the gas lanterns."

Jules's eyes narrowed imperceptibly. "The panda house. Got it."

BJ stepped up to kiss me on the cheek. Since my eyes stayed on Jules, I noticed his hands curl into fists. The sight of his reaction made me feel like I had one of his stupid bubble drinks in my veins.

"Don't let him get away," BJ whispered in my ear. "He loves you, too."

I couldn't hold back my goofy grin. "Thanks. Take care."

Julian made another offer of an escort, but BJ said he needed the time alone to cool off. Once he was gone, Jules closed the front door and made a point of locking it.

"I'm going to kill Mikey," he said, shrugging out of his coat.

I couldn't decide if I wanted to hug him again or strip him naked and explore his body in detail for the first time. The indecision made me feel jittery and strange. I paced around while shaking out my hands.

"You're freaking out," Jules said. "You're panicking just like I knew you would."

I stopped and laughed. "Me? You're the one who bolted. I'm trying to decide whether to strip you down and lick you from head to toe or hold you tight and tell you everything I'm feeling. Which one's less likely to make you light out of here like your ass is on fire?"

But Julian's brain seemed to have stuttered to a halt before he heard the question. "L-lick me?"

"Licking it is, then." I stepped closer to him without touching him. His slightly hitched breath made my fingertips tingle. "This feels right. Kissing you, touching you, making you feel good... all of that feels right. More than right. It feels perfect. It's just you and me here right now. Why can't we try this?"

Julian looked terrified. Even though I wasn't touching him, I could sense his entire body trembling.

"What are you so scared of, sweetheart?" I murmured, reaching out to cup the side of his neck. I leaned my forehead to his. "I will never hurt you. *Ever*. You know that, right?"

Julian slid his face alongside mine until his lips rested near my ear. I waited for him to give me an answer, but he stayed quiet. When I finally slid my arms around him to pull him even closer, he let out a low sound from deep in his chest, but he didn't fight me.

"It's okay," I finally said reluctantly when he didn't speak up or make a move. I tried to hide my disappointment. "No matter what happens, it's still you and me. Always."

I realized we were swaying slightly, a dance with no music. It was enough for now; it had to be.

After several minutes, I considered letting him go, pretending like nothing had changed between us and we were still platonic best friends, bros and nothing more. But then I felt his warm fingertips sneak under my hoodie and press lightly on the bare skin of my back.

I said a silent prayer, begging any higher power to let me have this, to let me pleasure him and see him let go.

The waiting was unnerving. Every muscle coiled in my body, poised to respond as soon as my brain could determine if and when he crossed the line from comforting touch to sexual touch.

It seemed to take forever, but then two things happened at the same time.

His fingertips moved beneath my waistband, and his hard cock brushed against my leg.

That was all I needed, so I pounced.

12

JULIAN

I was crazy to consider this, I knew that. I'd returned home from Mikey and Tiller's determined to be strong and logical, to preserve my friendship with Parker at all costs.

But then I'd seen Parker looking at that note he'd written me a billion years ago, and his whole face had glowed with love and affection, and then he'd called me *sweetheart*, and really, what was I supposed to do with that?

How many people who were presented with everything they'd always wanted had the strength to say, "Nah, I'm good"?

Not me. Not right now. Not when this beautiful soul was overflowing with love and tenderness for me at the same time his perfect, athletic body held me firmly in his sexy grip.

Seeing the Grindr twink snuggled up on my sofa throwing flirtatious glances at my person had turned my nervous energy into lightning bolts of jealousy. Parker was mine. *Mine.* And all I could think was how stupid I'd have to be to let anyone else have him.

There wasn't time to think about Erin and how I'd foolishly "let" *her* have him for the past decade or so. There wasn't time to talk to Parker about the dozens of things we really needed to discuss. There wasn't time for much of anything other than staking my claim however temporary it might be.

And I knew it *would* be temporary. By getting naked again with Parker, I was throwing us both into a thorny bramble that would be nearly impossible to escape without multiple points of pain. But for once, I didn't want to make the logical, considered decision. I wanted to be selfish and spontaneous. I wanted to throw off the heavy shackles of responsibility and expectation I'd clamped around my feelings for Parker in a vain attempt to tame my raw, possessive need and wild longing into something simpler, and safer, and more palatable.

If Parker wanted me, then he was going to get me.

All of me.

God help him.

I found the elastic edge of his boxer briefs and slid my fingers under it. My heart thundered, and my dick hardened enough to make me shift my legs. My brain didn't have the capacity for the words, but my fingers had the capacity to explore, and my mouth had the capacity to taste. I was acutely conscious of the throbbing in my groin, the warm exhales of his breath, the way his back ended in the delicious rounded muscles of an incredible ass.

As soon as I crossed the line, Parker exploded into action. His head turned sharply to seek my lips, and his hands clutched the back of my sweater and began to yank it up. Short curses escaped his mouth that almost made me laugh. "Thank fucking god... holy fuck... thought you... mpfh... taste good. Love you. Love this. Fucking let me... yeah..."

Before I knew it, my chest was bare, my pants were open, and I'd managed to sneak a finger down into the hot cleft between his cheeks. That wasn't how things usually went for me with guys. I'd always been the one in charge. I topped. I controlled.

I dominated.

"Park," I said, gasping for breath between hungry kisses.

"No, no stopping. Don't you dare." He yanked at my pants, mumbling curses when they caught on my boots.

"Not stopping, but —"

"No buts." He leaned over and tossed one of my boots toward the door before grabbing the other. I gripped his bare back to keep from falling over.

He made me so happy. Parker was light and love, fun and exploration. He'd always pierced my darkness with rays of blinding sun. If he wanted to try this, I would give it to him. Obviously, it was no sacrifice on my part since I'd fantasized about it thousands of times, but he didn't know that. He thought I had one foot out the door.

"I'm here," I reassured him. "Not leaving. I want this."

Parker finished pulling off my clothes and stood up to face me again. "You sure?" He looked nervous about my answer, as if I could and would pull the rug right out from under him.

I couldn't bring myself to say the words, but I nodded. After a pause to make sure I wasn't going to say anything more, he leaned in and kissed me. This time, it was soft and sweet. "Thank fuck," he breathed against my lips, running his palms up my chest to my shoulders. His hands had a slight tremble that made my heart hurt for him.

Parker was nervous.

I wondered how he'd feel when he realized who was going to run this show. Would it freak him out? Make him realize he didn't want to be with a man after all?

Was I willing to be less dominant for fear of scaring him off?

The answer to that was a resounding no. I felt deep down that Parker needed someone to take him in hand, lead him through this in a way that left no room for second-guessing.

"Take your clothes off," I said. "And go get on the bed."

Instead of the curl of amused smile Parker usually gave me when I bossed him around about other things, he opened his mouth in a surprised little "o" shape.

I lifted my eyebrows. "Listen to what I'm saying, Parks."

He turned toward the bedroom with a muttered "I've never been this hard in my life and you expect me to walk?"

I bit my tongue against a laugh. "If you want something badly enough..." I teased.

When he got to the bedroom, he pulled off the rest of his clothes and crawled onto the bed, flashing his delectable bare ass at me.

That ass is mine.

I wasn't at all sure what he was up for, but I knew I needed to get my hands on his ass, if nothing else.

He turned around and reached for my wrist to yank me closer. "I want it badly," he said in a rough voice. "Really fucking badly."

I climbed on top of him and reveled in the sensation of sliding my bare body across his. Rough body hair, hard muscular planes, the fat roll of his dick... all of it made me dizzy with indecision. Where the hell was I supposed to begin? I wanted it all.

I started by kissing his freckled shoulder and then moving down to take one of his nipples into my mouth. I kept my eyes on him to watch his reactions, but his eyes were glassy enough to reassure me we were still okay.

My hands couldn't get enough of him. His body was familiar to me — we'd undressed in front of each other many times in locker rooms and at sleepovers, pool parties, and drunken dares — but I'd never been allowed to truly *look*.

And I wasn't about to waste this opportunity.

"You're fucking built," I muttered, moving over to his other nipple. "You live on potato chips and onion dip, and yet you have this incredible body."

Parker's fingers pushed into my hair, and his gaze turned sweetly affectionate. "I love you."

His words made my stomach swoop low and loop around. I swallowed. "I don't want you to be here with me like this just because you love me. I want you to —"

Parker grabbed my face and pulled me forward until our mouths were crushed against each other in a feral kiss with teeth and tongue. The breath rushed out of me, and my head spun.

Okay, this wasn't simple affection. This was raw attraction. Point taken.

I humped against his stomach, pressing hard into the muscular plane of his abs to seek friction for my desperate dick.

"I want to fuck you," I groaned, trying so hard to let go of my hesitation. "I've wanted to fuck you for so long."

Parker wrapped his legs around mine and arched his own dick up into my inner thigh. "Go slow, though?"

I pulled back in surprise. "You'd let me?"

Parker's hands stayed on my face and caressed my cheeks. "I'd let you do anything you want. I trust you, and I want to make you feel good."

"How can you be so cool with this? Why aren't you freaking out?"

He brushed my hair back and continued to sift his fingers through it. "Because it's you. I'm comfortable with you. I don't have secrets from you, Jules. If I don't like something, I'll tell you, and I know you'll listen."

"Yeah, but—"

"I feel like you're waiting for me to be upset about having sex with a man, and I hope to hell that's not the case because it's insulting. My best friends are gay. I've heard many, many graphic stories of gay sex and seen plenty of gay porn. I'm here naked with you, excited to try things and explore this. Stop waiting for the other shoe to drop, and let's enjoy this. Okay?"

Why was he suddenly more mature than I was?

"I just don't understand how you can go from being with women to being attracted to me so quickly."

"Babe. I told you it isn't as sudden as you think. And I am attracted to you *because* I love you so much. Because you're my favorite person in the world and the only person I'd want to try this new thing with. Does that make sense? I trust you. I know you won't judge me if I do things wrong or act weird."

I thought about how good I felt with our bare bodies pressed together. "You can't do things wrong," I admitted with a grin. "Stay naked and touching me, and we're good."

Parker's hands moved around me and down my back to my ass. He squeezed it and got a playful look on his face. "What about me fucking you? We could try that, too, right?"

I leaned in and kissed him. It was still crazy to me that I was allowed to kiss Parker Ellis. After all this time, I could simply lean over and kiss him. Or suck his dick. Or offer him my ass.

"You're breathing fast," he said, pulling back to put a little space between us. "What just went through your head? Was it the fucking you thing, because we don't have to do that. I know you're a t-top."

Talking about this with him was strange enough, but remembering just how much he might know about my sex life made it even weirder.

"No, it wasn't that. I think I'm still trying to convince myself I'm actually allowed to touch and kiss you. Part of me keeps waiting for you to shove me away and say you made a mistake or this is all a joke."

I could see the truth in his eyes. He wanted to be here, and he didn't want me to feel unsure. But there was a difference between my brain knowing it and my gut knowing it.

His voice was gentle. "If you knew I wouldn't say no, what would you want to do to me right now?"

I took a breath and told him the truth. "I'd want to hold you down and suck your dick until you begged for release. I'd want to edge you over and over until you cried. I'd want to tell you to lie still while I ate your ass and fingered you until you realized what you'd been missing all these years by not playing with your prostate, and then I'd want to shove my dick so deep inside you your eyes rolled back in your head."

As I spoke, I felt his cock jump against my inner thigh. One of his hands moved from my ass to the cleft between my cheeks, and an experimental finger ran down the top of it. "You... want all of that? With me?"

His voice was husky and raw in a way I'd never heard before.

"More than you could ever know," I confessed. "Let me have you, Parks. Just this once."

He shook his head, and my heart plummeted. But then he spoke. "Not just this once."

"You don't know how you'll feel," I began, but he cut me off.

"I know exactly how I feel. And this is exactly where I'm supposed to be. So, yes. All of that. I want to try all of that with you." His eyes had turned a little glassy again, and I decided to trust the signs. He wanted me. He was turned on by the thought of being with me.

And that was enough.

For now.

I moved slowly down his body, dropping openmouthed kisses along the way and memorizing the patterns of the freckles I'd always wanted to worship. "Don't move," I warned before running my chin down his hard cock.

He threw his head back on the pillow and groaned. "You haven't even started yet and I'm afraid I'm going to come all over your face."

I waited until he looked back down at me. "Then come all over my face," I said and opened my mouth to begin.

13

PARKER

Didn't he know that wasn't helpful? Even mentioning me coming all over him was enough to make it happen. I forced myself to think of the time I accidentally learned how raspberry flavoring used to be made. Thankfully, that was gross enough to pull me back from the edge.

But as soon as Julian put his hot tongue on my dick, I almost passed out.

I'd had some killer blow jobs over the years, but nothing was hotter than seeing the familiar messy dark waves of my best friend bobbing up and down on my dick. It was forbidden and unexpected, which only served to make it a thousand times sexier.

The man had cherry-red lips. I'd noticed them many, many times over the years, and I'd even wondered what they'd look like stretched around one of his boyfriends' dicks. But seeing them stretched around mine? I didn't even have words to describe it.

I stared at him, too afraid to blink. If I died from raisin eyeballs, it would be worth it. "You're so good at that," I gasped. "So fucking sexy, Jules. Fuck. Christ. Just like that. Oh my fucking god."

I threw my head back again and arched up into his wet heat. This was heaven. Maybe I was dead. If so, I was totally fine with it. Give me more of this death stuff because it was amazing.

My toes curled, and I felt my balls draw up. The release was going to choke him, but I didn't have the ability to give a shit. I clutched his hair with one hand and the bedding with the other. "Jules," I warned.

He pulled off so suddenly, I yelped. "No! What? No."

He ignored me completely and shoved my legs back from under the knees until it was my ass in front of his face instead of my dick. I didn't have time to stress about what he had in mind before his warm tongue was on my hole.

"N-no my god. N-n-n... nghhh." I tightened my grip on his hair and reached out to take one of my knees so he could focus all his attention on whatever the fuck that amazing stuff was.

He was licking my asshole. He was rimming me. I was being rimmed. No fucking wonder this was a thing.

I let out a high-pitched sound of need and desperation. "Jules," I whimpered.

"Stay still."

I shuddered. I wanted to beg him to boss me around again just so I could hear that deep, commanding tone in his voice. "Yes, sir," I teased in a breathless laugh.

He looked up at me with an intensity I'd never seen before. "I mean it, Parks."

Oh. *Ohhh.* Oh god. I reached out and grabbed the base of my dick, squeezing hard to keep from coming. I didn't want this to be over yet, but he was turning me on with every touch, lick, bite, and command.

"Jules," I breathed again.

His tongue continued to press against the tender skin around my hole until I felt the slide of a fingertip join it. My heart ramped up in anticipation, and my entire body tensed.

"Easy," he said. "I'll go slow. Just relax."

He moved over to get something out of a nearby drawer, and when he returned his finger to my hole, I realized he'd been grabbing lube. The slick felt better than the spit, and his fingertip entered me easily.

I squeezed around him instinctively and felt my face ignite. "Sorry," I blurted.

"Shh. It's okay. Just relax and see how it feels. Let me know if you need me to stop."

If he stopped, I would have to strangle him. Instead of worrying about it, though, I tried to relax. I thought about how much I trusted him and how he'd never let me down. I remembered how he'd been there for me from the beginning and had always meant comfort and home to me.

I was all a warm puddle of affectionate and highly turned-on goo until he hit my gland and juiced the goo into straight-up high voltage. "Mother fuck!"

His fingertip pulled across the spot again. And again.

"Jules," I gasped. I'd tried finding my spot before, but it wasn't the same doing it to yourself.

"Hold your legs," he said, moving over to the drawer again and fumbling through it. I kept my knees pulled back, unable to think about anything he was saying, really. I just knew I needed more of him inside me pressing on that spot.

He returned with a foil package and met my eyes. "Can I try?"

He looked flushed and turned on, hopeful and scared at the same time. I nodded and enjoyed in the relief that crossed his face.

Jules leaned in to kiss me on the lips. "I love you. I want to make you feel good."

I nodded and felt like crying with happiness. "I know," I croaked. Because I did. I knew I was the most important person in Jules's world, and he'd rather throw himself in front of a train than let a hair on my head get hurt.

It was one of the reasons I loved him so much.

He rolled on the condom and slicked himself up with lube before pushing some more of it inside me and stretching my hole with his fingers. We both knew his cock was huge, and this was probably not going to work the first time, but I still wanted to try.

The blunt head of his dick pushed against me, and I breathed out slowly. The muscles of his abs tightened, and I couldn't look away. Dark hair trailed down his belly to his dick. The hand holding his shaft was strong and veiny. His other hand held one of my legs before moving to rest on my stomach. I let go of one of my knees to grab his hand and pull it up to my mouth to press it against my lip.

Julian's eyes flicked to mine. "You okay, babe?"

His dick was stretching me open, barely moving but still there, getting me used to the intrusion. I nodded and continued to breathe.

"You're beautiful," he said softly. "You have no idea..."

He didn't finish the sentence. Instead, he squeezed his eyes closed and groaned in a debauched way that brought my flagging dick back to life.

I felt like the outside world had ceased to exist. It was just the other half of me in here, experimenting to see what felt good, what we liked and didn't like.

Together.

I felt my muscles release, and Jules moved forward a little, pushing his fat cock farther in until I felt the burn again. I squeezed his hand. "Stop, *Jesus*. Why is your dick that big? Fuck."

The crease between his eyebrows got deeper, and he began to pull out. I grabbed him. "Stop. Just... just be still."

Jules watched me with a mix of concern and affection that made me want to fall at his feet and thank him for loving me so hard. Instead, I swallowed and told him to try again.

He added more lube and went slowly until the burn turned into less painful pressure. I felt full, so fucking full. It was different and strange, but when I imagined Julian's dick inside of my body, my skin flushed with heat and desire.

This was the most intimate moment I'd ever had with another person, and it made complete sense it was happening with Julian.

"More," I said.

"I decide when you get more," he said roughly, but the edge of his lip turned up, and the crease between his brows eased. He didn't fool me for one minute. I loved the bossy Jules in bed, but deep down, this man would do whatever I needed or wanted.

"More," I said again, teasing him.

He leaned in closer and nipped my earlobe. "I'm in charge here. Got it?"

I turned my face to press my lips against his stubbled cheek. His dick made me almost unable to speak, but I also wanted to tease the hell out of him and tell him how grateful I was to be under him in this bed right now.

"Prove it," I said softly against the damp heat of his skin.

The sound that came out of his chest lit me up, and the look on his face when he pulled back was unexpected. Instead of turning into some kind of dungeon Dom, he grinned at me. "Fuck you. Let me have this. Stop trying to be in charge."

I reached out and tweaked his nipple. "Show me what you got, big boy."

He grabbed my wrist and leaned down again to hold it above my head, taking the opportunity to kiss me hard on the lips. I felt the moment he pushed in deeper. I sucked in a breath and let out a groan as his dick brushed against my gland.

"Oh," I squeaked in a decidedly unmanly way. "Ohhh." At least the second exclamation came out deeper, but I truly didn't care. Whatever the fuck was happening down there was everything. None of the rest mattered. "Fuck me," I urged.

Jules began to pull out and thrust forward again, brushing perfectly across the supersensitive spot that made my skin prickle and my balls tighten. Watching his face flush and his skin dampen with sweat and knowing I was the one who'd turned him on this much, I was the one he was trying so hard to control himself for… it made me want to shout in triumph.

Tendons corded on his neck, his jaw tightened, and that errant curl over his ear stuck hot and wet to the side of his face. I pulled my hand out of his grip and put it around his throat, feeling for his pulse with my thumb. It thrummed strong and steady under my touch.

Julian's eyes locked on mine as he reached for my dick and squeezed it in his grip. When he began to shuttle it in his fist, I realized just how close I was.

"Gonna… Jules…" My breathing veered off-kilter, but it didn't matter. I could see in his eyes he knew exactly what I needed, how I was feeling.

"Let go, Parks," he urged. "Let me have this."

I don't want it to be over. I couldn't say the words aloud, but suddenly, they were all I could hear in my head. What if he freaked out again? What if he left? Even though he'd made promises, I knew he could fall prey to the same fears after this, especially considering how intense it was between us like this.

"Parker. *Come, goddammit,*" he growled.

His command went straight to my balls. My muscles contracted everywhere, and a flood of heat shot through my groin a split second before I spilled on his hand and my stomach with a garbled shout. It wasn't pretty. It wasn't controlled or dignified in any way. I was a hot fucking mess, and if I'd been with anyone other than Julian, I probably would have felt humiliated.

But I *was* with Julian.

And that made all the difference.

He spat out a curse and thrust harder one more time before letting out a roar that startled me. I wanted to laugh, not at him, but simply from the sheer joy and euphoria of this discovery.

I was head over heels in love with Julian Thick. And the sex with him was mind-blowing. Win-win.

My life would never be the same.

As long as he didn't run again.

14

JULIAN

I remembered telling a stranger once about the crush I had on my straight best friend. It was a guy I'd shared a few drinks with in an airport bar after he'd lamented a recent breakup of his own. We'd talked about how the reality of a thing is often not nearly as tantalizing as the fantasy.

What idiots we'd been.

The reality of sex with Parker Ellis was even better than the fantasy. In the fantasy, I'd never seen Parker's eyes widen in discovery. I'd never heard the vulnerability in his pleas for more. And I'd never felt the reverent trace of his fingers across the ink on my chest.

Without removing myself from his body, I leaned in to brush his hair back from his face and press a kiss to his lips. He looked dazed or drunk, and it made me smile. "You good?"

A familiar goofy grin appeared as he reached out to tweak a piece of hair over my ear. "So fucking good."

"We just had sex," I said stupidly. "You and me."

He nodded. "Don't freak out. You promised."

"I didn't promise not to freak out. I only promised not to leave."

He wrapped his legs around me, so I quickly reached to grab the condom and pull out.

"Give me a minute," I said, moving off the bed and to the bathroom. After disposing of the condom and wetting a towel, I returned to help him clean up. This part of sex always seemed more intimate than anything else, and I enjoyed the chance to take care of him this way. Thankfully, he didn't fight me on it and let me wipe him down while he stayed a little dazed on the bed.

When I climbed back in, I shoved him around until he was properly under the covers where I could join him. I propped my head on my hand and studied him. In so many ways, he was the same old Parker—same warm smile, watchful eyes, and incredibly handsome face. But he was also buck naked, with the truth of my attraction to him completely out in the open between us and the smell of sex hanging in the air around us, and all of that was so different that I wasn't quite sure what to say to him or how to act.

I ran a hand over the light hair on his chest, but he grabbed it and pulled it to his mouth, pressing a light kiss on my palm while keeping his eyes on mine. "I'm exactly where I want to be right now," he said, sounding like he truly meant it. It was almost a challenge. He was daring me to say this was wrong.

He would be disappointed.

"Same."

He smiled and kissed my palm again. "Thank fuck."

The word *but* was on the tip of my tongue, but I bit it back. There would be time for *buts* later. Right now was the time to enjoy this. Enjoy him. Enjoy *us*.

"I've never seen your orgasm face," I teased. "It's pretty epic."

His laugh lines crinkled. "I'm sure no one's seen that orgasm face before. The *sex* was epic."

"Keep flattering me," I urged, sliding one of my legs over his until my limp cock brushed his outer thigh. "I don't mind."

Parker reached out to trace the ink on my shoulder, something he'd always done, ever since I'd begun getting the tattoos. My skin craved his touch.

His voice was easy and light. "I remember one time a few years ago when you brought a guy up to Vail for the weekend. He looked at you like you were some kind of god. After two drinks at the bar with me and my work friends, the guy begged you to go back to the hotel room. I could tell he wanted to get you into bed, so I kept finding ways to keep you there in the bar longer."

I huffed out a laugh. "I remember. His name was Thom with an *H*, and he introduced himself that way to everyone he met that night."

Parker's chest vibrated with his laughter. "Yeah. That's right. I remember now. But I also remember wondering how he could possibly be that eager to get you into bed. We were having a good time, throwing darts and listening to good music, and all this guy wanted was to get into your pants." His eyes met mine with a twinkle. "Now I know why."

Before I could say anything, he laughed again and moved his fingers across my skin. "You're getting blotchy. You can't get blotchy with me. It's not allowed."

My skin felt hot and itchy like I was under a spotlight. "I can't believe we just had sex together. It was good? I mean… it was okay? You're okay?"

I'd gone from dominant to unsure in the time it took for a simple wipe-down. But this was Parker, and everything in my world was riding on his answer.

He pulled the hand he was holding until I was sprawled across his naked chest. "I'm okay. I already told you that, but you're obviously still worried. Do you want to talk about it right now?"

I had a million questions. What did this mean for us? What did this mean for Erin? How would it change things between us? What would happen if it didn't turn into the lifelong relationship I so desperately wanted it to be? And if it did—if by some miracle he was all in this with me—what would that look like? Would he want me to move to Vail? What kind of law would I practice?

Parker put his big hand over my face, a move he'd made many times before to annoy me. "Baby," he said. And the word was said with such tenderness, such overwhelming understanding and affection, I got a lump in my throat.

"Maybe not the talking right now," I admitted, shoving his hand aside and leaning my head down on his shoulder. "Not sure I'm ready."

I could tell by his sigh that my words weren't what he wanted to hear, but his hands moved up and down my back soothingly anyway. Being with him like this was incredible. I wanted to savor it.

"I have an idea," he said after a little while. "Let's pretend for tonight that we're boyfriends. We've been together for a long time, and we tell each other everything. We are also two young, fit dudes with voracious sexual appetites, FYI, so the spark is still there in spades even though we've been together a long time."

"Natch," I said with a grin he couldn't see.

"Right, so we hang out, cook dinner, watch movies, and snuggle on the sofa. And when the feeling strikes us, we bone. Little sucking here, little dick fondling there... all the things I've been missing out on. Maybe we stay away from my ass because it was recently rammed with a giant grain silo, but all the rest is good. *Your* ass is fair game, obviously. And we sleep together in the same bed, naked, as long-term boyfriends do. Sound good?"

His fake casual tone made me laugh. I loved him so fucking much. He was my favorite human, and he never failed to put me at ease and help me stop taking things so seriously.

"And tomorrow?" I couldn't help but ask.

"Tomorrow, we're going skiing because I promised Tiller and Mikey I'd help out a friend of theirs on the slopes."

I lifted my head up in surprise. I hadn't known he'd made any plans while he was here. "What friend?"

Parker shrugged. "Don't know the guy's name, but he creates content for one of those fitness apps. He's doing a series of downhill runs and needs someone to help capture some of the footage. Tiller's not supposed to be skiing because of the injury risk, and Mikey isn't good enough to help this guy on the steeper runs. They agreed to give him access to the slopes if he'd promote Aster Valley skiing in the videos."

He moved his hand up to trace my eyebrows with a fingertip. "I was hoping you'd want to join us, but you don't have to. Or you could come hang at the mid-mountain restaurant and have lunch with us. Mikey said they're serving lunch now because they're hosting various athletes and media personnel to help create buzz about Aster Valley opening back up to skiers."

"I'll bring my skis, but while you're doing your lessons, I'll get some work done in the restaurant. After you're done with your student, I'll join you for some runs."

After seeing Parker's smile of approval, I laid my head back down on his shoulder and tried not to think about petty things. Like how he would introduce me to his ski student. Whether or not we'd hold hands on the lift. How long I would play it cool after returning to the cabin tomorrow before begging him for just one more night of playing pretend boyfriends.

Meanwhile, I went shopping on the fantasy aisle of my memories, tossing every hot idea I'd ever had of him into my cart and wondering how we'd fit all these sex acts into the short sixteen-hour period I had left with him as my boyfriend.

"Your dick is getting hard," he said, moving his hands down to cup my ass and squeeze it. When he pulled my cheeks slightly apart, my dick got even harder. "What's going on in that big brain of yours?"

"So many fucking things," I admitted, shifting into a more comfortable position. "I wouldn't know where to begin."

Parker suddenly rolled us until I was under him, and he loomed above me. "Have you ever fantasized about taking a shower with me?"

I rolled my eyes. "That's like me asking you if you ever fantasized about taking a shower with Natalie Freeman."

Natalie had been one of Hazel's friends growing up, and she'd also been, hands down, the hottest girl in school.

I continued. "And if I feel your dick even thinking about twitching right now..."

As soon as I said the word "dick," I felt the movement on my leg and laughed. "You're a teenager."

He smirked. "A teenager with a crush on the hottest dude in school. A dude I want to bang in the shower."

I steered my mental shopping cart to the bath products aisle and grabbed a sudsy hand job off the shelf.

Parker had a lot to learn about the joys of sex with another man, and I was happy to take one for the team to help him along on his journey.

The following day was bright and clear, with almost no wind and plenty of sun. After a hearty breakfast, we headed to the base of the mountain to hop on the lift. I'd brought a backpack with my laptop in it with hopes I'd get a little work done on a contract my dad wanted me to look over.

When we skied off the lift mid-mountain, we headed over to the sprawling wood-sided building that housed the restaurant and ski patrol office. Parker recognized one of the guys wearing a red ski patrol parka out front by the ski stands and went over to greet him with a big hug.

"Jules, come meet Dallas," he said with a big smile and beckoning wave. "He's the one I did that commercial with in Sun Valley, remember?"

I popped out of my skis and leaned them against the stand before reaching out to shake his hand. "Hi, yeah, it's great to meet you. Parker has told me so much about you. Said you blew him away on the moguls that day."

The guy was as tall and muscular as I remembered from the commercial, with sun-streaked hair and a friendly smile. When he pulled down his sunglasses, I could see the same little laugh lines formed by the sun that Parker had from spending so much time on the slopes. "He's a flatterer. What the heck are you doing here, Parker? I thought I heard you were getting married this week."

I knew from Parker that the Colorado professional skiing world was a small community where everyone knew everyone, but it still surprised me sometimes. They were notorious gossipers.

"I was," he said with a self-deprecating shrug. "But it didn't work out. Julian brought me to Aster Valley instead. I didn't know you worked here. How do you like it?"

"It's killer. Love it. I found a great deal on a rental over on Sunrise Trail. You wouldn't believe the views. Best part? I can ski to work." He glanced over at me and seemed to put some pieces together. "Wait. Wait. Are you *the* Julian? Parker's Julian?"

It wasn't the first time someone had called me "Parker's Julian," but it struck me very differently, coming from this guy. Before I could answer, Parker threw his arm around my shoulders and pulled me close, almost knocking us both over in our clunky ski boots.

"Yeah, this is Jules. He's cute, right? And smart as hell. He's a lawyer. He's also —"

"Ha!" I burst in, trying to stop him before he said something else that might embarrass me or, worse, embarrass him. "I sound like a prime steer at auction."

It was enough that he'd just had to tell his friend about calling off his wedding. I didn't want to be the rebound relationship he'd have to try to explain next time he and Dallas met up. I wanted to protect Parker from everything that could hurt him, including himself.

The mischievous look on Parker's face warned me a split second too late that I'd left myself wide open. "That would make you a nice, juicy piece of —"

I clapped a glove over his face and turned a cheerful grin at Dallas. "How long have you been in Aster Valley? You must know our friends Tiller and Mikey. Oh, and Sam and Truman, too."

He laughed. "Yeah, they're great. Mikey and Sam had their hands full through the holidays, but Tiller's been here since the end of football season. Just in time for the skiing to ramp up. Can't wait to see what it's like next year when the lifts are open to the public and the runs are full of even more skiers."

We chatted for a few more minutes before the radio clipped to Dallas's jacket squawked. "Duty calls. Let me know if you guys need anything, and have fun today. Great to finally meet you, Julian."

After he took off down the slope, we headed inside to find the skier Parker would be helping. We removed our gloves and unzipped our jackets, then headed to the enormous corner booth by the window, where Tiller and Mikey had asked us to meet them. But as we crossed the large, open restaurant, I realized that the third man at their table looked very familiar.

"Wait, *that* is the fitness app guy?" Parker grumbled under his breath as we approached. "Really? Tiller didn't mention I'd be helping the dude from the bar and the… the *Grindr*."

"What's the problem?" I asked. As far as I could tell, Rocco had been nice both times he'd interacted with Parker.

"The problem is, the dude wanted to get in your pants, Jules," he hissed. "Twice."

I felt my chest expand with warmth and maybe a tiny bit of smug possessiveness… which was why I didn't immediately notice when Parker's cool, dry hand wrapped around my own and he threaded our fingers together like holding hands was a thing we did.

Unfortunately, I was the *only* one who didn't immediately notice. Three heads turned as we approached the table, and three pairs of eyes zeroed in on our clasped palms.

I blushed and yanked my hand away almost guiltily, but judging by their reactions, it had been way too late to pretend the hand-holding had been anything but what it was. Tiller looked surprised but thoughtful. Mikey looked surprised and concerned. And Rocco didn't look surprised at all. His lips twitched up in a knowing little smirk that might have been sexy if I weren't still drunk off the scent of my best friend.

"You must be Parker." Rocco stretched out a hand to shake. "Seems kind of unbelievable that we've never been formally introduced, doesn't it? I'm Rocco Valentine."

"I remember," Parker grumbled, shaking the man's hand half-heartedly. He muttered something under his breath that sounded like, "Still sounds like a porn star name."

I was pretty sure Rocco heard him, but if anything, his smile only deepened.

"You're one to talk, *Shortbread*," I whispered.

"Can it, Peanut," he shot back.

"Rocco, this is Parker Ellis," Tiller cut in smoothly. "World Cup champion, former Olympian, and all-around downhill badass." He recited Parker's accomplishments like he thought that might make us behave ourselves. "And this is Rockley Lodge's beloved attorney…"

"Julian Thick," Rocco finished, aiming a broad smile at me. "Parker's man."

"*Best* man." I laughed nervously. "You mean *best* man."

"Ah, obviously. My mistake."

Parker scowled at me, but I quickly pushed him onto one side of the booth beside Tiller, while I sat on the other end, beside Rocco.

"So, Peanut and Shortbread." Rocco raised an eyebrow. "I feel like there's a story there."

"Oh, not a good one," I assured him. "Unless you enjoy stories about ten-year-olds left unsupervised with an entire case of Girl Scout cookies my sister was supposed to sell door-to-door." Hazel still brought that up from time to time.

Rocco laughed quietly. "Actually, that's better than how one of my brothers got his nickname." He winked. "There may have been a citation for public indecency involved."

Maybe I was nervous from the WTF looks Mikey kept leaning around Rocco to give me, or feeling antsy because Rocco was being flirtatious, or just giddy because every time I saw Parker's grumpy glare I remembered being inside him, but either way, I started laughing at Rocco's comment and couldn't stop. Between snorts, I tried explaining myself until I could barely catch my breath.

Rocco asked, "Is he okay?"

As Parker watched me giggle uncontrollably, his face softened, and then he began laughing, too. "He's fine. He's remembering the time I was literally arrested for public indecency."

"Time?" I squeaked. "Try time*s*. With an *ess*."

When I finally calmed down, I had to tell at least part of the story. "He was at a ski thing, and he… and he…" The laughter came back harder than ever. Thankfully, Tiller was able to continue the story.

"So Parker was on the pro tour—which, let me just point out, we're talking about his third arrest for indecent exposure—and he needed to take a piss before his next run."

Parker cut in. "To be fair, skiers always pee off to the side somewhere instead of trying to fight our way to the portables or figure out where the athlete bathrooms are. Takes too long."

Tiller flapped his hand to shut him up. "I'm telling it. Anyway, so he wanders over past the crowd to where there's one of those arc-cut flaps in the crowd-control fencing. It's like a printed fabric with sponsor stuff on it. It has cuts in it to let the wind through. So he whips himself out and pees through the flap."

Parker cut in again. "I knew the drill. Don't let the crowd see your goods. Hence, sticking it through the fabric so no one could see."

I snorted and nearly choked. Thankfully, Tiller continued the story. "What he didn't know was that the other side of the fence was the place one of the sports channels had set up their on-air correspondent, out of the way of the crowds. The correspondent was reporting live when a shriveled-up micro peen appeared—"

"Hey! I think you mean a mighty claymore that made all who looked upon it tremble in *fear*."

I howled, only this time I wasn't alone. Mikey was giggling, Rocco was laughing, and two of the servers had stopped to listen.

"Tell them, Julian!" Parker demanded, his eyes dancing. "Tell them about the Claymore."

Ah, shit.

"Yes," Mikey said, lifting one eyebrow. "Please tell us exactly what you know, Jules. And *how*."

Damn it. Why was Parker so determined to be reckless? Why couldn't he at least admit the possibility that this, *us*, was a temporary madness we didn't need to share with our friends? Hadn't he realized how awkward it would make things once Erin came back around?

I kept my smile firmly in place. "Parker, there are very few limits to our friendship, but referring to your penis as the Claymore is one of them."

Tiller snickered.

"I will say, though, that two lube companies offered you a sponsorship after that." I studied my nails fake casually. "And that adult film company wouldn't stop harassing you until 'your lawyer' wrote to them. So make of that what you will, *Claymore*."

Everyone collapsed into laughter again. In the middle of it all, Parker shot me a wink and mouthed the words "You're my favorite."

I placed a hand on my chest and closed my eyes. *Please let me hold this feeling as long as I live.*

The sound of laughter continued around me as Tiller continued the story, embellishing it the way he liked to do for maximum crowd entertainment. I opened my eyes and watched Parker's smile, easy and open as always, as he added to the story here and there.

This was one of the things I loved about Parker Ellis. He thrived on making people happy. He was friendly and funny, kind and welcoming, and he attracted people to him like he was a tennis ball coated in peanut butter and tossed into a golden retriever parade.

When the laughter died down, Rocco said, "Let me tell you what we need help with today."

I offered to give everyone privacy, but Rocco urged me to stay. When he began telling us about the content he created for the fitness app, Parker and I were riveted, though Parker tried not to show it. Even Mikey and Tiller, who'd clearly heard all this before, seemed impressed.

"How did you get into this?" Parker asked.

Rocco sat back and took a sip of his coffee. "My brothers and I own an outfitter shop in a small town in Alaska. We run all kinds of tours. Fishing, hiking, glacier sightseeing, hunting, and cross-country skiing, depending on the season and the clients. We grew up there, and we all know the area well enough to make our own way. Beautiful out-of-the-way spots are kind of our bread and butter. The problem is, the winter is long and dark. Tourists dry up, and money gets tight."

Parker nodded. "You should come down here where it's sunny year-round." He shot a sideways look at me and clarified, "I mean, not *here*-here. Not Aster Valley. Obviously. But Colorado."

Rocco's smile made it obvious he was attached to his home state. "Nah. But it makes you have to get creative. I was trying to stay fit with the app, using it for some weight lifting and simple circuits, but

I kept wishing some of the classes were outdoors just so I could at least get some fresh air. I started coming up with ways someone could do it, and I finally decided to make a class of my own just to get it out of my head."

I'd heard of SocialAdrenaline. Most everyone had by now. It was like Peloton, YouTube, and TikTok had birthed a social media–based fitness app. Several of the most popular content creators were making a killing on it, not only from the app itself, but from the sponsorships and influencer income that came along with the social media following itself.

Parker was obviously as fascinated as I was. We listened while Rocco explained how the class had gone viral because of the unique settings in Alaska. What had seemed like his same old "crappy view" of the snow-covered dock and ice-coated lake was really a fantasy destination for many people stuck inside working out in a home gym.

So he created more and more classes under the pseudonym Rock Valentine. When the seasons changed, he added cardio classes on trails, cross-country skiing runs, obstacle courses through the woods. He recorded nature walks where he captured footage of wild animals and even frigid swims across sections of the lake at home.

"My brothers don't know about any of this," he admitted with a shrug. "I've been doing it for a year and a half now. They're going to kick my ass when I tell them."

"Where do they think the money's coming from?" I couldn't help but ask. "Or do they not know?"

"I've been paying stuff off without them knowing, but they're going to find out soon. It's hard to travel to Colorado to work with an actual Super Bowl MVP and not tell your brothers about it."

Parker let out a laugh. "No shit. Tiller probably loaded you up with merch, too. He's always trying to pawn that cheap shit off on people."

Tiller flicked Parker on the head. "Cheap shit, my ass. That merch costs me blood, sweat, and tears."

Parker leaned over the table to stage-whisper to Rocco. "The tears are from being away from his hot fiancé."

Tiller nodded. "True story." He glanced down at a notification on his phone. "Okay, the ski patrol has closed off Sky Shadow and Serpentine Cross for you for the next three hours. One is a nice wide blue run, and the other is a black diamond with moguls. If you decide you want something different, just text me." He turned to me. "You going to join them?"

Rocco glanced at me with a genuine smile. "Please do. Parker mentioned the other night that you were a great skier." He lowered his voice. "He also mentioned something incredibly intriguing about tattoos that I'd love to know more about, if you'd like to share."

"Oh. *Ha*." I licked my lips. "Sharing. That's, ah... that's not..."

Across the table, Parker clenched his jaw like he was waiting for me to tell Rocco that I wasn't Parker's best man, I was his *man*, and that my tattoos were none of Rocco's damn business. I wanted that too, so badly it hurt. But Tiller and Mikey were sitting right there, watching the whole exchange like they'd stumbled into a reality TV show, reminding me of all the logical reasons why Parker needed to slow his roll.

I cleared my throat. "About the skiing. I'm afraid I have to, um..." I tried to think up a work assignment urgent enough to skip out on skiing *and* the inquisition I knew Mikey and Tiller would stage if I stuck around.

But before I could come up with one, the cute Grindr guy who'd been hanging with Parker in my living room the other day suddenly appeared at my side of the table, dangling a set of keys toward Rocco.

"M'kay, got your backup battery, and I am prepared to be your director of cinematography. Just remember I have my own classes to film tomorrow, so I'm gonna leave the moguls to you and the professi — *Ohmigod*, no way!" His smile warmed by a thousand degrees when he noticed my best friend. "Parker? Baby, how *are* you?"

Baby?

He dropped into the empty seat at Parker's side and leaned up to kiss Parker's cheek in the same spot where I'd kissed Parker that morning. Not that I noticed or anything.

I also did not notice that his hair was perfectly styled, his dark eyes were ringed with black liner, and he was dressed to ski, like some sort of twinky Goth-jock hybrid—which was way sexier than I would have imagined that combination being.

"BJ!" Parker grinned back, because he was Parker, and Parker's only two speeds were friendly and asleep... well, unless you were Rocco, who seemed to be the sole exception. "I'm doing great."

"Yeah?" BJ tilted his head toward me and then back in a meaningful sort of way, like they were passing secret coded messages.

Parker's face softened, the way it usually only did for me. "Yeah," Parker confirmed with that same meaningful undertone. "You?"

"Ehhhh." BJ waved a hand and gave a self-deprecating smile. "Still in sad panda territory, but I swear I'm almost getting used to that. It's gorgeous here in Aster Valley, though, and work is going well, and I forgot how much I enjoy skiing when I'm not falling on my ass." He gave Parker a wink that made me want to hit something. Or some*one*. "Still bendy, you know? That helps."

"Yeah." Parker's grin deepened. "I remember."

He remembered that BJ was bendy? What exactly had I missed yesterday?

A wave of jealousy swamped me, powerful enough to make my stomach lurch.

I'd figured I was more or less immune to the emotion by now, given that I'd had to push it down a dozen or more times over the years whenever Erin had waltzed back into Parker's life. But it turned out there was a whole other half of the population I hadn't known I could be jealous of, and my stupid heart hadn't gotten the message that we were supposed to proceed with caution here.

Lucky me.

"Sorry, back up. BJ, you and Parker are friends?" Rocco demanded. "How'd that happen?"

Exactly what I wanted to know.

"Yeah. We met yesterday because of a weird mix-up with a, um..." BJ paused and glanced around the table like he wasn't sure whether he should drop the word "Grindr" in front of everyone. "Address? But Parker invited me in. We, you know... chatted." He gave Parker a happy grin, and I ground my molars together.

"You chatted." Mikey's suspicious gaze bounced from Parker to

BJ to Rocco to me, and then down to his own phone. His eyes widened, like maybe he'd made the Grindr connection on his own. "Wait. BJ came by, and you *chatted*? You and... and *BJ*?"

"Sure." Parker shrugged. "I chat with lots of people. And BJ was great." He gave Emo Ski Boy a fond look. "Patient."

"Aww." BJ tilted his head down onto Parker's shoulder for a second. "And I found you *inspiring*, Parker. Truly. I'm so glad things worked out the way they did."

Mikey's jaw dropped. "But I thought... I mean, I got the impression, Parker, that you had been *chatting* with Jules."

Parker frowned, clearly confused. "Well, sure, but Julian went to your place. And I was at the cabin alone. Remember?"

I stared at Parker for a moment as the truth of that hit home. Parker and I had kissed and frotted, and it had been *magnificent*. It had been his first sexual experience with a man, because I was *so* not counting that nothing of a kiss with Tiller. And what had his best friend, the guy who loved him most in all the world, done to make sure Parker felt loved and supported after exploring his sexuality?

I'd freaked out and left, even though he'd begged me to stay. I'd gone to discuss the situation with our friends, to get their moral support, and left Parker alone with no one but BJ to talk to about any of it.

And while I knew I had a right to my feelings and that Parker didn't seem angry about it at all, I also knew deep down that Parker never would have treated a friend that way. He was selfless and loyal to the core.

So if he said that this—*us*—was what he wanted right now, who was I trying to protect by pretending it wasn't happening? And who would I ultimately be hurting?

But god, it was still scary as fuck.

"I'm really sorry, Parks," I whispered.

"Huh?" His confused green eyes met mine. "Sorry for what?"

I shook my head. "For not being there to chat when you needed me. I—"

"Okay, hold up." Tiller extended a palm. "Just to clarify, when you guys are talking about chatting, you're using it as a code word for sex, right?"

"Yes," Mikey and Rocco said at the same time.

"God, no!" Parker exclaimed, straightening in his seat. "What? I mean actual chatting. As in, talking. Discussing. *Conversing.* Jesus, you guys."

"Oh! Oh, shit." Mikey laughed shakily. "Okay, for a second there, I was thinking you and Julian were—" He motioned between Parker and me. "And then I thought maybe BJ..." He snorted. "Never mind."

"But Parker and Julian *are*..." BJ said, sounding bewildered. "Wait, aren't they?"

Rocco shrugged.

"Oh." BJ looked almost comically bewildered.

"We are..." I began, but I hesitated.

Parker's gaze met mine for a second, and some emotion flickered over his face, but he looked away before I could identify it. "*We are...* gonna lose the best light if we sit around here gossiping all day. Excellent point, Julian. Time to ski, people." He nudged BJ to stand, then stood and stretched himself, displaying a tiny sliver of the skin I'd caressed with my tongue the night before.

"Sure you don't want to come out with us?"

I blinked away from the magnetic sexuality that was Parker Ellis to find Rocco giving me a friendly smile. "I'd love it if you did."

I slid out of the booth. "It's nice of you to ask—"

"But Jules has other stuff to do," Mikey finished, sliding out of the booth after Rocco while flashing me concerned eyeballs. "Right, Jules?"

I knew Mikey meant well. He was curious about what was going on, sure, but he was also a natural caretaker who wanted to make sure that Parker and I were doing okay. Still, I couldn't think of anything less appealing than rehashing things with Mikey when Parker was the one I needed to speak to.

"Two minutes, boys. Gotta go freshen up." BJ gripped Parker's bicep excitedly. "We're gonna have *so* much fun out there. Feel free to correct my form, okay? I'm great at taking direction."

He winked as he hurried away, and I tried very hard to repress my growl.

Well, would you look at that? Apparently there *was* something less appealing than talking to Mikey, and that was the idea of Parker spending the afternoon with BJ while I waited behind and stewed in my own jealousy.

"You know what? I *will* come skiing." I folded my arms over my chest. "I *adore* moguls."

"You do? Since when?" Tiller asked.

A little smile twitched over Parker's lips, but he didn't call me on my lie. Instead, he gestured with his hand for Rocco to precede him out of the restaurant and left me to follow.

We hadn't gotten more than two steps, though, before he turned around to face me so quickly, I almost smacked into him. Within seconds, his hands gripped either side of my face, and his mouth landed on mine with a possessive crush. I vaguely heard Mikey gasp and Tiller say, "Well, damn," in an admiring tone, but I had no brain cells left to process it. Parker kissed me like he was seeking the Holy Grail and it was located slightly south of my vocal cords. Like the very last thing he cared about was what our friends thought or how he could preserve an out for himself. Like he'd meant every single word he'd said to me last night, and he was pissed off that I wasn't getting the message.

I lost a little time assessing how critical oxygen really was in the grand scheme of things, and then I lost a little more when I realized his lips and his cool, dry hands now pretty much owned me. Forever.

When Parker finally pulled back, straight-faced and determined as if he hadn't just forced someone to second-guess the meaning of life, I almost tipped over onto a tray stand. Instead, I merely knocked the tray on its edge, upending it into a slow-motion rollover that took three half-empty drinks glasses with it.

And I totally would have scrambled to the floor to help pick them up if I hadn't been standing there stupid and brain-tied, wondering why my face felt like radio static as I watched Parker walk away.

"Huh?" I asked, apropos of nothing.

Parker quickly pulled me away from the broken glass before

waving for a server's help. When the server insisted they'd take care of it, Parker thanked them and gestured for me to follow him outside.

"Try to catch up, Jules," he called over his shoulder as he stepped out into the sunshine.

And I was pretty sure he wasn't talking about skiing.

15

PARKER

The four of us made our way out of the restaurant building and into the sunshine. It was a beautiful day to be on the slopes, and I was looking forward to sharing the experience with Julian.

If only he'd stop acting like he was going to jump out of his skin any minute if I so much as looked at him funny.

I didn't appreciate his hesitation in holding my hand or the way he'd refused to acknowledge our relationship in front of our friends because it made it very clear he didn't trust the feelings I had for him. His jealousy was kind of adorable but also kind of annoying for the same reason. I should have insisted on talking things through earlier, regardless of his nerves. Then maybe things wouldn't be so awkward around us today.

But now wasn't the time to keep pushing him. I'd been tasked with hosting Rocco on the mountain and making sure everyone stayed safe while capturing the footage for the fitness project.

"Where to first?" I asked Rocco before reaching for Julian's skis and laying them out for him. "Intermediate or moguls?"

Rocco and BJ found their own skis in the stands and clipped into them before Rocco suggested warming up with the intermediate run. "I'd like to film two workouts if we can. One on each of the two slopes. But it'll mean lots of runs down each one to capture different footage. That okay?"

I agreed and mentioned having been part of many video projects in the past for commercials and documentaries. "We'll get what you need," I assured him.

After everyone had skis on, I pointed us to the smaller lift that continued farther up the mountain. We began making our way over to it as Rocco described the kind of footage he hoped to capture. Since he was still talking when we got on the lift, BJ and Jules ended up on a chair ahead of us, and I was stuck riding the lift with Rocco instead of sneaking a private moment with Jules.

The chair wasn't even out of the terminal when I saw BJ lean closer to Julian to bump his shoulder while they shared a laugh.

"How do you know BJ?" I blurted. "He seems... outgoing."

"We met through the fitness app. Well, more specifically, on a chat for content creators. He makes killer yoga classes and shares tips about lighting and editing, things like that. When I posted about coming down here to make some content, he reached out to see if I wanted to split a place because he was looking for a location to film some outdoor winter classes, too."

I couldn't stop watching BJ's animated charm being slathered all over my best friend. It set my teeth on edge, mostly because I remembered how eager BJ had been to hook up with one or both of us.

"You should chat with him," I said.

"Chat?" Rocco repeated, amused. "In which sense of the word?"

I waved my gloved hand at the chair ahead of us. "I mean the other kind of chat. Like... with your dick. BJ seems like he'd be open to it. Probably. I mean... he uses Grindr."

Rocco's laugh was deep and easy. "BJ wasn't kidding when he said you were 'the world's most adorable newborn baby gay,' was he? You're a hot mess. You really don't know how this shit works."

My back teeth hurt from grinding. "I just know he showed up at our place the same way you did. Since neither Julian nor I are available, it seems like you two..." I gestured again toward BJ. "Should consider each other."

"No, thank you. I have a rule about hooking up with guys I know from SocialAdrenaline. Had a bad experience once with a fan who tried to ruin my reputation rating on the site. Thankfully, I was able to get him banned before he could do too much damage, but I learned a lesson. Don't fuck where you eat. Besides, BJ is a little too eager for me. He seems more like a relationship guy than a hookup, and I sure as shit don't need one of them."

I turned to face him. "Just so we're clear. Julian is a relationship guy, too. So am I."

Did I sound as stupid in real life as I felt in my head? I had to.

Thankfully, Rocco didn't laugh at me. He met my gaze with a serious nod. "Message received, but I already knew that, Parker. You two are clearly into each other."

I blew out a relieved breath and felt my face heat from embarrassment. "It's complicated."

Now he laughed, loudly enough for both BJ and Jules to turn around to see what we were doing. "Having fun back there without us?" BJ called.

Before I could respond, Rocco beat me to it. "Parker was telling me about the time he stuck his tongue on a metal pole because of a dare."

Julian's smile appeared with the memory. While he hadn't been the one who'd dared me—that had been Hazel—he *had* been the one who'd reveled in being able to say, "I told you so," over and over until I wanted to punch him in the face.

I turned to Rocco. "How the hell did you know about that?"

Rocco's face crinkled with a smile. "I didn't. But you seem like the type."

When the lift dumped us out at the terminal, I followed Jules down a short slope to the top of Sky Shadow. It was a nice, wide run, which meant plenty of room to film in the sun.

BJ eyed me while Rocco began unpacking some equipment. "Why don't you have ski poles?"

"I figured I'd want my hands free to hold stuff," I explained, moving over to adjust Julian's helmet strap. "This thing is no good if it's loose. You know that," I murmured as I moved the webbing through the fitting.

His body tensed. "I..." His voice trailed off as I deliberately brushed my nose against his and gave a tug to the chin strap.

"Better," I said softly.

"Mm," he breathed.

I stepped back as if nothing had happened. "Besides, I don't use poles when I'm teaching, so I'm used to skiing without them."

After Rocco set me up with a lavalier mic and a video camera, he clipped a GoPro to his helmet and attached a second one to a harness on his chest. He was very familiar with the equipment and gave me a quick rundown on what to do.

"Most of the class is shown from my POV so the student is in my shoes, right? But if I can cut in some distance shots of me on the slopes, it helps place the student in the environment and gives them that destination feel. They want to see the vistas and know what it would look like if they were actually the person skiing down the mountain."

"You have a calm, deep voice," I said. "I can see why your videos would be popular."

BJ chuckled. "That and he's hot as fuck."

I nodded and grinned. "Good looks certainly don't hurt."

Julian seemed to bristle. But then again, I'd been getting awkward vibes from him all morning. I tried to brush it off and do the best I could for Rocco.

"So I'll go down first and ski backward. I'll get as much distant footage as I can on this run while you do your thing. On the next run, you can tell me what to correct. Sound good?"

"This first pass will be just for the distance shots and whatever I can capture with these while I figure out how I want to structure the run for the narrated version."

"How can I help?" Julian asked.

Rocco nodded. "Yeah, so I was hoping you could keep an eye on BJ. He's going to get some distance shots, too, but he's not a very experienced skier." He handed Julian his cell phone. "Also, if you want to take video or stills with this, I can always use more footage."

It took a few more minutes to get situated. BJ asked me to adjust his helmet strap the way I'd done Julian's, and then he'd asked me to check to see if his boots were adjusted properly. I shoved the camera into my pocket before crouching down to help him with his boots.

As soon as he put his hands on my shoulders to brace himself, he hummed. "My, my, you have big strong shoulders. How does a ski instructor wind up with such big, broad shoulders?"

"Oh, ah… I swim? My gym has a great indoor pool, which is my excuse for going there. The real reason, though, is the sauna so I can get warm in the winter." I noticed that his boots were already adjusted perfectly and gave him an encouraging smile. "You're all set."

I moved away and pulled the camera back out, making sure it was ready to go. When I looked up to check on Jules, he was glaring at BJ. I looked back and forth between them to determine what I'd missed. Before I could figure it out, Rocco was ready.

"Lead us off," he said, gesturing ahead of him.

I glanced once more at Jules to make sure he didn't need help with anything and then tipped my skis over the small lip of the run. The snow conditions were great, and it was a treat to be the only ones in the entire area. I turned around, testing the twin-tip skis Sam had found for me. Once I knew my own gear was good to go, I began filming.

BJ and Jules rode out wide to the sides when Rocco began his run. All of us captured the run as well as we could, but the first pass was definitely a learning experience. This time when we got in line to ride the lift back up, I made sure I was paired with Julian.

Once the chair was out of the terminal, I put my arm through his and held him close. "Hi."

He was still nervous, and his body language was sending me mixed messages. "Hi."

I leaned my head on his shoulder. "What can I say to get you to relax?"

His head automatically tipped down on top of mine, our helmets clacking uncomfortably. Jules pulled away with a laugh. "Invent lower-profile ski helmets."

I blew out a breath. As long as he was laughing, things were okay. "It was hard keeping my camera focused on Rocco when my eyes were following you," I said, looking out to catch a peek of town through a break in the trees. "But then again, I always have that problem when you and I ski together."

"You worry too much," Jules said. "You don't need to look out for me. I'm an experienced skier, Parks."

I looked back over at him in surprise. "I don't watch you because I'm worried. I watch you because you're a very graceful skier. You relax and trust your body in a way I'm always trying to explain to my students. Part of the reason I watch you is to figure out how to teach it. I don't think it's possible. Some people simply come by it naturally."

He didn't say anything for a minute. Finally, he met my eyes. "Thank you."

I barked out a laugh. "That killed you, didn't it?"

Jules grinned. "Yes. It did. Thank you for recognizing my sacrifice."

"What did you really want to say?"

"That you're a liar or that you don't recognize a ski potato when you see one."

I pulled my arm out of his to slide it around his shoulders. "I have taught literally hundreds if not thousands of ski potatoes, Jules. Trust me. You're not one of them."

He leaned a little closer to me. "BJ seems awfully flirty with you today. What happened when you met him at the cabin?"

The little errant curl over Julian's ear was sticking out from the bottom edge of his helmet. It made my heart rate spike. "Who?"

Jules elbowed me in the ribs. Thankfully, our parkas kept it from hurting. "You know who. The yoga instructor. The *super-bendy* yoga instructor," he muttered.

I wanted to laugh, but I also knew this was coming from a real place of fear, and I tried to be patient. "Babe. I talked to him about *you*. About being in love with you and you freaking out."

Julian's eyes flashed to me. "*In* love?"

He wasn't paying attention when the chair approached the ramp, and he almost caught his ski tip on the edge of it. I quickly lifted the safety bar and grabbed his elbow to keep him steady as he overcorrected and nearly toppled off the chair.

Once we were safely off the lift and at the top of the slope waiting for Rocco and BJ, Julian shot me a red-faced grimace. "Sorry," he said.

I reached for his shoulders to keep from putting my cold gloves on his face and leaned in to kiss him on the lips. It was quick and chaste but important.

"Yes. *In* love," I said carefully. "And I don't care about anyone else out here. Now or ever. I know you're having a hard time believing it. I know it's new and scary. But it's real. And we're going to talk about it—and also *chat* about it—until you find a way to trust me. Okay?"

Rocco and BJ interrupted before he could respond. I got the sense Jules was grateful for my words, and he wanted to believe them but still didn't fully.

We got right back on the slope and did three more runs before taking a break in the restaurant for hot drinks and a snack. BJ continued to flirt with me, even going so far as to beat Jules to the spot beside me in the booth, but I decided it was harmless. The man had a bubbly personality. He also flirted with our server, the man in the booth next to ours, and the woman who gave him directions to the men's room.

Through it all, Julian's temper simmered under the surface. Thankfully, he was an attorney with plenty of experience keeping his cool in tense contract negotiations. So, when Julian finally snapped at BJ a little while later at the top of the first moguls run, I nearly dropped the video camera into the snow.

"If you don't keep your fucking hands off my... *Parker*... we're going to have words," he barked.

BJ pulled his hands off my chest in slow motion. The edge of his mouth turned up in a knowing grin, but Jules probably couldn't see it. "Jules, darling, I was only trying to keep myself from wiping out. Like I said earlier, I'm not very experienced on moguls."

"We're on a powdery, flat meadow." Jules's sunglasses hid what I knew had to be a familiar, murderous glare. "But if you can't handle the next run, maybe you should take Pinecone Ramble back down to the restaurant and wait for us."

BJ propped his gloved fist under his chin like he was deep in thought. "I think not. If anything happens to me, surely I'm in good hands with your... Parker. He'll come to my rescue if I get in over my head."

Jules lunged forward as if he was actually going to tussle with BJ. I grabbed his wrist just in time to pull him off to the side, where he tripped over his skis and landed on one knee in the powder. I grabbed him under the arms to haul him back up. Unfortunately, I couldn't hold back my laughter, and the sound of it made him mad enough to fight me. The two of us wound up in a snowy tangle on the ground.

Jules tried to shove me away from him while I tried to pull him closer. "Stop fighting me," I said through a snort. "Jules, cut it out. This isn't—"

A glove full of snow went into my mouth and up my nose.

Julian's face was red with a combination of cold, embarrassment, and anger. What I should have done was calm him down with soothing, reassuring words and help him up.

What I did instead was force my snowy face into his previously warm neck. He yelped and tried to shove me away, but I used my legs to keep him pinned, legs that were considerably strong from years of professional skiing.

He had no chance.

"Dammit, Parks!"

BJ and Rocco were laughing their asses off but staying far enough away to keep from being dragged into the fray. We wrestled again like we had the other day, only this time I was hard for him, and I knew exactly what it meant. My heart thundered in my chest as I tried to get close enough to his ear to say something the others wouldn't hear.

"Just you and me, Peanut. Just you. And me. *Always.*"

He suddenly stopped and met my eyes. His breath panted out of him in faint white puffs.

"*Only* you," I added in a soft but firm voice. "Hear me and stop being stupid."

I could tell he wanted to argue with me, to tell me all the reasons I couldn't possibly know my own heart. But he also knew this wasn't the time or place for further discussion.

"Okay." His grip on the back of my parka changed to a quick hug and then a smack on my ass. "Now get off me, asshole."

We stood up and shook ourselves off before clipping into our skis again to prepare for the moguls run. Julian knew to help me keep an eye on BJ without my having to say a word. The first pass down the bumpy slope went fine. The second was even better. It wasn't pretty, but BJ managed to make it down without too much trouble.

It was at the end of the third run when things changed. I should have been paying closer attention. The responsibility was on me to keep the four of us strong and safe on the slopes, but with my attention split between Julian's emotions and Rocco's filming needs, I failed to identify when BJ's legs began to tire.

We were halfway down the black diamond slope when BJ suddenly cut a mogul wrong, lost control of his balance, and went careening off the side of the trail.

16

JULIAN

Thankfully, BJ's wild momentum was stopped by a thick snowbank before he hit something worse like a tree. It was clear from the way he landed he'd hurt himself. He pushed himself up but winced in pain. Parker got to him first, but I was behind him by only seconds. I slid to a stop beside him and popped out of my skis before crouching down to help.

After a quick assessment, we both decided he'd most likely injured his knee. It was bad enough Parker didn't feel comfortable moving him but not nearly bad enough for him to be howling in agony.

"I don't think you tore your ACL," Parker said, letting out a breath of relief. "Or you'd be writhing in pain. Hopefully, it's just a sprain or something, but let's keep it stable regardless. You wouldn't believe some of the injuries I've seen."

BJ's energetic personality was subdued by the pain and fear of his fall. "I'll bet."

I reached out to hold his hand in mine. "It probably helped that you're in such good shape and flexible. They say flexibility and stretching is a critical component of avoiding injury. Parker learned that from several trainers when he was an athlete." I knew I sounded stupid, but I remembered Parker telling me the key to keeping injured skiers calm is to stay calm yourself and talk to them.

Since I could see tears spilling out of the edges of his eyes, I knew he was in plenty of pain.

While Rocco helped BJ into a more comfortable position, Parker contacted his ski patrol friend, who promised to bring help quickly. Within moments, the engine buzz of a snowmobile greeted us as the ski patrol approached.

Parker's friend Dallas hopped off the machine and raced over to assess BJ. I knew BJ must have been more hurt than he was letting on because he didn't spare a single sideways glance or flirty comment for the sexy, broad-shouldered man in the red parka. When Dallas indicated he'd need to take BJ down the hill on the litter attached to the back of his snowmobile, Parker offered to help.

"Nah, no need. Ambulance won't let anyone ride along. But he'll want some company at the hospital later," he said, looking between us.

Rocco lifted his hand to volunteer. "I'll come. I'm his friend, and I'm staying with him." He leaned down to speak quietly to BJ.

Rocco thanked us for our help and gathered up the remaining camera equipment before following the snowmobile down the mountain.

I wasn't used to this much skiing anymore, so I sheepishly admitted to Parker that maybe this would be a good time for us to collect my stuff from the mid-mountain restaurant and go home ourselves. "I'd hate to wind up with a similar injury," I admitted.

Parker stepped over to me and pressed a cold kiss to my lips. "If you hadn't said it, I would have. I feel awful I didn't notice him tiring sooner."

We made our way back to the cabin, remembering partway there we'd promised to join our friends at the lodge for dinner.

When we finally arrived at Mikey and Tiller's place later, I was jelly-legged and half-asleep. If it hadn't been for Parker manhandling me into the shower back at my cabin, I would have still been stinky and half-frozen from the day on the slopes.

There hadn't been anything sexual about our joint shower, but just seeing his hands on my body taking care of me had been a breathtaking turn-on. But it had also felt bittersweet, like being told I could add as many toppings as I wanted to my ice cream sundae but knowing I'd wind up sick if I actually ate them all. I'd almost been glad of the excuse to postpone the conversation I knew we needed to have.

When I stumbled on the lodge's front step, Parker quickly slid an arm around my waist. "Easy."

"How do you spend all day on the slopes?" I asked, already knowing he was used to it. "My legs are no longer functional."

"Meth and cocaine," he said casually. "Sometimes I even add a chocolate bar midafternoon."

I elbowed him, causing him to make an exaggerated *oof* sound before reaching out to ring the doorbell. It had been days since Parker had been nervous enough to try to deflect things with a silly joke, but clearly, he was as hesitant to face our friends as I was.

We stood there side by side and stared at the closed door.

"We could let ourselves in," I suggested. "They're actually really good friends of ours."

"It's going to be bad, isn't it? They're going to grill us for details and try to get us to define this thing between us."

I nodded without looking at him. "Really bad. Horrific."

He dropped the arm he had around me and clasped my hand instead. I loved the feel of his strong hand in mine.

We continued to stare at the door.

Parker sighed. "They're probably expecting us to let ourselves in."

I nodded again. "Probably."

"What do you want to tell them? We're together. That's all they need to know, right?"

I turned to look at him. "What do you mean, we're togeth—"

"*Hi!*" Parker squawked nervously as the door flew open, revealing both Mikey and Tiller. Parker pulled me forward so quickly, I almost tripped again. "We're here. Here we are. We have come. Here. To have dinner. With you. Here."

Parker's smile was maniacal, and for some reason, that calmed me down. We'd had an unspoken rule in our relationship for years.

Only one of us could be unhinged at a time.

And he was pretty fucking unhinged right now.

"Here," I said, pulling the fancy wedge of cheese we'd brought them out of my pocket and slapping it into Tiller's palm. "Cheese. For you. Well, for all of us, really. It's just... cheese."

Parker tilted his head at me and widened his eyes as if to say, *Remember the unhinged pact?*

I blew breath out between my lips and offered a sheepish grin. "Act normal. Everyone, just be cool. We're cool, right? Everyone here is casual and cool."

Mikey and Tiller stared at us like they'd just wandered into the most fascinating shitshow on Earth. But it was fine, because we were going to be cool about everything and talk about it later.

Parker let out a strange kind of distorted laugh. "It's fine. I'm cool and you're cool. They're always cool, so..."

Sam's voice came from the kitchen. "What the fuck is taking you so long, and why do I keep hearing the word 'cool'?"

Tiller didn't take his eyes off us when he shouted back. "Replace that wine with whiskey, Sam. Quickly."

I flapped a hand in the air and kicked my boots off on the wide tray next to the door. "No, it's really very fine. Nothing is happening. It's all very normal. We're normal. Everything is normal. See?" I gestured to my... solar plexus. "Totally normal."

Parker's eyebrows folded together as his boots joined mine on the tray. "Baby... I have some concerns about your definition of normal because, like I told you before, that sweater isn't my favorite. I wanted you to wear the navy cashmere again, but—"

I cut him off. "And I told you, it needs to go to the dry cleaner because of the marshmallow you got on me when I was wearing it. When I have it on, you can't ever stop petting me. Sometimes it makes things... awkward around other people."

"But I like petting you."

Mikey's voice took on an odd high pitch. "It's happening. Oh my god, it's happening." He turned and shouted toward the kitchen while shoving us forward. "Sam, Truman, code red. I repeat, code red. *It's happening.*"

I leaned over to Parker and whispered, "What's happening?"

Parker shrugged. "Maybe they're excited about the cheese."

We followed them into the kitchen, where every gay, pan, and bi man I knew in Aster Valley seemed to be waiting with eager anticipation.

"Hey, everyone," Parker said, reaching for a shot glass full of amber liquid and passing it to me. I tossed it back without thinking.

Mikey nudged us over to the giant wooden table by the windows. Most everyone else was already seated around the table enjoying a couple of trays of appetizers and predinner drinks. Music was playing in the background, and a security light in the backyard illuminated a light flurry of snowflakes falling outside.

A fire blazed in the kitchen fireplace, and the smell of garlic and other savory treats filled the room. I let my shoulders relax—or maybe it was the whiskey—now that we were among friends.

"Sit," Mikey said, indicating two empty chairs next to each other. At least they weren't planning on using a divide-and-conquer strategy to grill us.

Or were they?

Before Parker could follow me into the empty seat, Tiller grabbed his elbow and turned him toward the pantry door. "Come with me for a second. I need help with something."

I stared after them. Parker turned to look at me over his shoulder. His eyes were wide.

Stay strong, I thought with a silent but near hysterical giggle.

Mikey took the empty seat next to me and lulled me into a false sense of security. "I'm so glad you're here because I need some advice."

I blinked at him and looked around at the other guys who seemed to be listening in also. "O-okay…"

"It's this friend of mine from Texas. Do you remember me telling you about Shannon from Hilltop Cafe?"

I searched my brain but found nothing, so I shook my head.

"Doesn't matter," he said, waving his hand through the air. "She's the one who's been flirting with this regular customer for like a year. Every day, he brings his laptop after the breakfast rush and proceeds to work in a corner booth with breakfast and coffee refills until the lunch rush starts. He tips her like crazy and makes great conversation when she's free to chat."

I relaxed into the story. "That's sweet."

"Yeah, so he finally asked her out, and she said no, can you believe it?"

I glanced around the table to see if I could figure out why I was the one he was asking about this, but all I saw were blank faces. "That sucks. Did she say why? And why are you asking me?"

Mikey's forehead crinkled for a second before smoothing out. "Oh. He's a lawyer like you. I figured you know how lawyers are. Anyway, I asked her what she was so afraid of and said she'd rather live with the fantasy than the reality. It just... I don't know. It just seems sad to me."

I agreed. "Lonely, too. Has she had disappointments in relationships in the past?"

"Not really. But she's definitely romantic. She wants to be adored and taken care of, and this guy seems to be perfect. He's so freaking into her. He really listens when she talks, and he remembers important things she's said. He takes care of her, like when she... dropped a tray of drinks, he pulled her out of the way so she wouldn't cut herself."

"He sounds like a good guy." I wasn't sure what he wanted me to say.

"He is. I've met him several times. He's a really, really good guy." Mikey's eyes had an intensity to them that unnerved me. "Can you imagine preferring a fictional fantasy to a good, devoted guy in real life?"

I opened my mouth to respond when the pieces finally fell into place with a loud and obnoxious snap. "It's safer to cling to the fantasy," I said, trying to act casual. "Real life is much messier. The fantasy can't break your heart."

Truman spoke up from his spot halfway sprawled across Sam's lap. "But it can't reach something on the high shelf for you either."

"Or rub your feet after a long day," Darius said, glancing at Miller.

"Or arrest overly aggressive paparazzi to keep you safe," added Finn.

"Or suck cock until you accidentally alert the people in the stalls next to you," Tiller said, returning from the pantry with a tall stack of plates.

Mikey shot him the bird. "It wasn't *people*, asshole. It was your father and uncle."

Parker followed Tiller with his own armload of dishes. His were thick soup bowls, which he set down with a clatter next to a tall pot of something simmering on the stove.

Tiller winked at me. "And that's why they send him tulips now on his birthday."

Thankfully, the subject changed as Mikey got up to continue working on getting dinner on the table. Parker fixed me a drink from the supplies on the kitchen island and brought it over.

"Go easy. I made it strong," he warned.

The vodka cranberry looked like a dream come true, and I gulped down a healthy swig before thanking him. "Bless you. You're my favorite."

He leaned over to press a kiss to the top of my head before returning to the counter to get his own soda. I didn't think much of it since it was the kind of affectionate gesture he'd always made with me. Even before this weirdness between us, we'd been unusually physically affectionate. I probably wouldn't have even noticed it if Truman hadn't sighed happily.

I glanced up at him.

"For me, it's the forehead kiss," he said, leaning his head on Sam's shoulder. "Gets me every time."

Sam dipped his chin to rest his lips on Truman's forehead. "Love you," he murmured softly.

It hit me hard in the chest. Apparently, I'd been lying my ass off when I'd implied the fantasy was better than reality.

Because I wanted that. And I wanted it with Parker Ellis.

I glanced over at the counter in time to meet Parker's gaze. He lifted a brow in question. *You okay?* his expression asked.

How the hell was I supposed to know?

I nodded so he wouldn't worry, but it was a lie. I wasn't truly okay. I was at a major crossroads. This week was supposed to have been my week of mourning the loss of the Parker fantasy once and for all before moving forward to embrace a different path.

But now I was right back in it. The Parker fantasy was alive and well and dipping its toes into becoming reality.

What would happen if I dove in expecting a nice long swim and it turned out Parker only wanted a quick, refreshing dip?

The soup course passed in comfortable company. Conversation was easy, and Parker seemed to enjoy several of the Aster Valley men he hadn't gotten to meet yet.

It wasn't until Mikey and Tiller had served us all the next course, heaping plates of gorgeous artisan salad, that the interrogation began in earnest.

It came from an unexpected quarter. Declan pinned Parker with his cool sheriff's gaze. "Since no one else seems to have the balls to put it out there, I'm going to go ahead and ask. How can you go from getting ready to marry a woman on Saturday to publicly claiming Julian with that kiss today?"

Silence descended. Only the clink of forks hitting plates broke through. I rushed to defend him. "He's understandably upset. He's been through a lot. He didn't know what he was—"

Parker's hand gripped my thigh and squeezed. "Stop," he said softly. "Because your words are upsetting me more than his right now."

I looked anywhere but at him. He was right. I knew how much it upset him for me to blame this connection, *our* connection, on his "confusion" or disappointment over Erin. It wasn't fair of me.

"I'm sorry," I said just as softly.

Parker found my hand where it was gripping the edge of the table. He took it to his lips and kissed it gently, reverently. "Because I'm an idiot," he said to the table. "Because all this time, I've had the best thing I could have ever possibly dreamed up right in front of me. And I failed to see it for what it was."

His voice was firm and solid. Sure.

I wanted to lean into him for comfort because I was terrified of his words, and he was the place I went when I was scared. But that was too much to take from him right now.

Parker turned to me with a tender smile. "But I see it now. And I want it. I want you. And I'm going to do what it takes to convince you I mean it, even if that includes waiting a very long time."

I looked around at this table full of men who knew what I knew. It wasn't that easy. You couldn't just say you were in love with another man and have everything turn out to be a bucketful of roses and wildflowers. Parker had no idea what it was truly like telling friends and family, coworkers and bosses, that his partner wasn't sweet, pretty Erin Rokas, but instead, ornery, opinionated, tattooed, semi-bearded, and completely male Julian Thick.

But did I really want to scare him off with tales of reality right now? Not one single bit.

I leaned in and pressed a kiss to his face right next to his lips and stayed there long enough to inhale the familiar and provoking scent of him. "I love you. Thank you for saying those things. You're the best man I know."

Those things were true.

But so were lots of other things left unsaid. We both knew it. And it was time to finally say them out loud.

Thankfully, our friends allowed the subject to change, and we were able to enjoy the rest of the meal and evening with them. Parker seemed to have a new sense of calm after saying his piece, and he relaxed into the various conversations happening around him at the table.

By the time we left, he was happily exchanging contact information with Finn to coordinate skiing lessons in the future.

Stepping outside into the freezing night air wasn't easy after such a warm evening by the fire in the lodge's kitchen.

"Fuck, it's cold," I said with a shudder, pressing the button on my key fob to start the engine before we even opened the doors.

"Sometimes you act like you're not from Colorado," he said, following me past several other vehicles to the SUV. He grabbed the key fob out of my hand and walked to the driver's side. "Designated driver," he reminded me.

I hadn't had much to drink, and I knew I'd be okay to drive, but I didn't argue with him. Not when I knew how fanatical he was about this. Instead, I made myself comfortable in the passenger seat of my own vehicle and closed my eyes.

The drive back to my place wasn't long. We didn't say anything while Parker focused on getting us home safely, but it wasn't awkward or tense at all. Things with Parker rarely were.

When we got inside, Parker pulled my coat off before removing his own. We kicked off our boots and locked up the cabin before taking turns brushing our teeth in the bathroom. After sliding into bed in only boxer briefs, we immediately snuggled together.

I was too tired to think about sex, and my head was spinning with everything that had happened today. We lay there together in silence for a while before he spoke.

"I meant what I said tonight. I know you're having a hard time trusting it, but I'm not going anywhere." There was enough light from the moon to illuminate the outline of his profile but not much more. "We don't have to talk about it right now, but I just wanted you to know I'm here, and I'm all in."

I swallowed and tried to figure out what I wanted to say. "I don't want to be someone's second choice."

My own words took me by surprise, but as soon as they were out, I realized the truth of them.

Parker covered my eyes with one hand while reaching over to turn on the bedside lamp with the other. After my eyes adjusted to the brightness, I realized his face was a combination of hurt and anger.

"Julian, you have never, ever been my second choice, and you know it. Every single time I got together with Erin, you were always still my person, my heart." His hand clutched at his chest. "Maybe that wasn't fair to Erin. I see that now, but you and I both know it was still true."

He was right. I did know that. But I still felt prickly and defensive.

And hurt.

"Then why did you choose her?" My question came out heavy with emotion, much more than I'd wanted to reveal to him. But then again, this was Parker. And I told him everything.

Parker reached for my face, holding it gently but firmly in his grip. "Because I was a stupid kid. Because it was the easy path. Because I wanted to be loved. If I could take it back, I would. You need to know that. I was so stupid. But... but also..." He hesitated. "Jules, we couldn't have gotten together when we were fourteen or sixteen or even twenty. How would we have made it through what we did? If I'd followed you to law school, I would have had to stop skiing. If you'd followed me on the circuit, you wouldn't have developed your own career. It wouldn't have worked if we'd gotten together sooner."

He was right, but it still hurt.

Parker's lips landed on each of my cheeks in turn, the smooth skin just under each eye. The touch of his lips made me shiver. He was so damned sexy, and the amount of affection he gave me was incredible. I'd worried that Erin would have eventually discouraged him from being so demonstrative with me.

"What would it look like?" I asked.

His forehead crinkled. "What would what look like?"

I shifted until our legs were tangled together. "You and me. What if... what if we actually tried being together. What... what would that look like, do you think?"

His face relaxed into a big smile. "Whatever you want it to look like. I go where you go."

I shook my head. "It's not that easy, Parks. You have a job in Vail. I work in Denver. I'm considering a move to Aster Valley. You don't do well with change. You find safety in your comfort zone. You crave stability. I don't want to disturb that."

Parker moved one of his hands to thread his fingers into my hair. "You're right about me finding safety in my comfort zone, but you're forgetting something important."

"Mm?" I asked, enjoying the impromptu head massage.

"*You're* my comfort zone. You're my stability. None of the rest matters. If I'm with you, I'm happy. Always have been."

It was all too good to be true, but I wanted it enough to be tempted. He could sense my hesitation because he got a teasing grin on his face I recognized.

"Besides, who said you were the only one considering a move to Aster Valley?"

17

PARKER

I rolled him onto his back and kissed him, not giving him a chance to respond to my comment about moving to Aster Valley. There was no rush. But I did feel a sense of urgency to kiss him, to hold him in my arms and show him with my body that I had no hesitation about the new sexual side to our relationship.

My thoughts had been spinning wildly all day, and with them, some memories had flung out of the depths and surprised me. I remembered sneaking a peek of Julian's dick when he changed clothes in front of me after a baseball game in middle school. And then again in the locker room in high school. I remembered sharing a bed with him one night in eleventh grade and getting hard when I realized his hand was slowly stroking his dick under the covers.

And I remembered nearly breaking my hand when I punched a wall after accidentally walking in on him and Kader Zaman making out in the Rokas' pool house during a party after graduation. Kader's hand had been down the front of Julian's swimsuit, and I'd wanted to strangle the guy for his aggressive presumption.

My stomach had hurt so badly, but I'd misinterpreted it as anger and fear. Anger that someone would presume to touch Julian in such a base way and fear that Julian's heart would be broken. My brain knew Julian would have wanted it, was clearly consenting to the hookup if his eyes rolling back in his head was any indication, but my gut screamed that it was in all ways *wrong*.

I'd told myself I was being protective of Julian. That, as his best friend, I simply wanted him to hold out for the right guy—someone who'd recognize how wonderful he was and treat him accordingly.

Now, I realized what I'd been feeling was nothing as civilized as protectiveness. It was pure, primal jealousy.

Because there would never be anyone in the world who was right for Julian... except *me*.

I wanted all of his kisses. All of his attention. All of his passion. I wanted to be the only one who saw his eyes flare with arousal and soften in the afterglow of his orgasm. And I wanted it to be seriously fucking clear to everyone, especially Julian, that the only hand on Julian's dick from now on should be mine.

Now, *finally*, it was my turn to make Julian's eyes roll back. It was my turn to make his knees wobble and his breathing stutter. It was my turn to hear him gasp out my name in a broken curse as he finally let go.

Julian's hands were large and strong against my back. His legs moved against mine, rough with body hair and muscle. The late-night scruff on his face rubbed at my own and pulled at the tender skin of my lips. He smelled like a combination of faded cologne, good wine, and traces of Julian sweat.

It was familiar, but it was newly intoxicating too.

I moved my face down to inhale the skin of his neck, and then I moved further down to bury my nose in his armpit.

"What are you doing?" he asked with a smile in his voice. "I probably smell."

"You do," I said, inhaling again and again. "And it's fucking fantastic." I moved over to swipe my tongue over his nipple before taking it gently between my teeth. Julian's hiss made my cock pulse, so I added the pressure of my tongue and began to suck.

He arched up into me, moving his hands down to clutch my ass. "You're acting like a guy right now."

"I am a guy."

"No, but *oh god*..."

I latched onto his other nipple and sucked hard before pulling off and sucking a hickey into the ink on the side of his neck. He let out a yelp that turned into a lurid groan of pleasure.

"Fantasies," he gasped. "M-my fantasies are coming to life right now."

I moved my tongue along the colorful splotches of ink, remembering the impromptu design that had started as Julian's doodle of our school's grizzly bear mascot on my math notebook our junior year but had become so much more. "You know how obsessed I am with this."

"It's yours." He groaned again as my fingers reached down to push under the elastic band of his boxer briefs. "You... you... *don't stop.*"

I moved my palm over his shaft as I continued to rain kisses across his neck and shoulder, claiming the drawing that represented three years of our friendship.

We'd passed the paper back and forth, adding odd touches here and there—a swirling constellation reminiscent of summer nights spent stargazing, the tent Julian had added after a camping trip so muddy and miserable we'd had to laugh our asses off, the flame from the bonfires we lit in the Thicks' backyard firepit every winter night senior year while we discussed our plans for the future. At the bottom, I'd added a pair of cupped hands that cradled the whole scene. Finally, Julian had declared it perfect and locked the page away in his dresser, and I'd forgotten all about it.

Julian hadn't.

He'd shocked the heck out of our friends and me when he'd whipped off his shirt at the lake one summer day and displayed his new ink. I remembered Erin asking Julian what it symbolized and Julian simply saying, "Home." And everyone had thought he'd meant Denver, or Colorado, or the mountains where we'd skied, but looking at it now, I knew exactly what he'd meant.

He'd meant *us.*

Because home was the two of us together.

I lifted my head to meet his eyes as my fingers came up to trace the designs I'd just worshiped. "You inked me into your skin, Julian. This is us right here. It's always been us."

He nodded, eyes filling with tears that I didn't want him to cry. "I know," he said in a broken voice. "But I'm so fucking scared you're going to change your mind."

"Jules—"

Julian tugged gently on my hair, forcing me to look at him. "No, listen. I heard everything you said earlier, and I…" He licked his lips. "I believe that you mean what you're saying. And the last thing I want to do is be needy or piss you off or, god, hurt your feelings because I *love* you. But Parker, you have no idea what it's been like all these years, falling for you a little more every day and then watching you get back together with Erin. I get why you did," he hurried to assure me. "I know you were right earlier, too, when you said that if we'd gotten together at sixteen, we might not be the men we are, so I can't regret the way things have worked out. But as much as I want to just accept this—Christ, as much as I want to *revel* in it—" He ran trembling fingers over my jaw, and his blue eyes blazed hotter. "I'm still scared. I don't know how to make it go away."

Warmth and relief spread through my chest that he'd spoken his fear out loud. As long as we could talk to each other, we could work through this.

I ran a thumb over his bottom lip. "Babe. I'm scared, too. I'm scared I'm not going to be enough for you. Smart enough, rich enough, worldly enough. I'm scared you're going to be bored with a ski instructor who doesn't like to travel very far from home and tells the same corny jokes over and over again."

Julian opened his mouth to reassure me, but I pressed it closed again with my thumb. "But then I remember that you're my Jules. You love me for who I am. And you know me better than anyone else and fell in love with me anyway. At least… well… I don't know about *in* love. But I know you love me."

Jules pressed a kiss on my thumb before moving my hand away from his face. His eyes shone with love and affection. "I have been in love with you most of my life. Having you here like this in my arms is a dream come true. And I want it to last. There's not a world in which you could ever *not* be enough. You're more than enough. And you're never boring. Ever. You're the most fun person I know, and you're also the kindest person I know."

I leaned in to press a soft kiss to his lips. This time was different. The kiss was long and slow, patient and effortless. It was the unspoken agreement between us that we were both here, and we would do our best for each other.

When Julian finally pulled away, he looked freer. "I'm all in, Parks. But you're probably going to need to be patient with me because it's not that easy to go from thinking this was never possible —and that you were lost to me forever with Erin—to suddenly having you here with me like this."

"I know. All I'm asking is that you trust me not to leave. I'm not saying it's going to be easy. I'm going to fuck up, but it's not going to be because I don't love you or don't want you."

Julian's eyes took on an unmistakable glint of mischief. "I might enjoy schooling you on the finer points of pleasing a man in bed."

Blood surged southward. "Mm. I'm pretty sure I'm already an expert. I've been pleasing myself in bed for a long time," I teased, pressing my hardening cock against his.

"Sure, but have you ever sucked yourself off? I think not." Julian's eyes widened when he felt my dick move. "Oh, what do we have here? Someone might want to try something new?"

"Fuck yeah," I breathed, scrambling down under the covers to shuck his underwear off so I could put my mouth on him.

I threw the covers off and yanked the cotton boxer briefs down until his fat cock rolled across his lower belly. Clear, sticky fluid draped from his slit to the dark, tidy curls above. I glanced up at him from between his legs.

"I used to sneak peeks at this, you know," I said, reaching my fingers around his thick shaft. "I was obsessed with finding out what your dick looked like."

Julian's voice was throaty and deeper than normal. "Meanwhile, I spent my time trying to hide my erections whenever you were around." A corner of his mouth ticked up. "I would have whipped it out for you anytime had you just asked."

I grinned at him before sticking my tongue out and teasing him. Watching Julian's face while I put my mouth on him for the first time was the hottest thing ever. His pupils widened, and his lips opened.

He tasted salty at the tip, and it took me a while to figure out what I wanted to try first. What made *me* feel good? What did *I* like? How could I drive him completely crazy?

After licking his cock around the outside, I finally put it in my mouth to suck. Julian's hand moved to my hair and gripped gently but firmly. "That's it," he said. "Little more. You can do it."

Julian's deeper commanding tone made my balls tighten. I shifted the lower half of my body against the bed to get some friction. This was so fucking hot. Being here like this with him was insane.

I accidentally took too much and gagged. My eyes watered, and I convulsed, making my face flood with heat.

"Shh," he said. "You're doing great. Try again. Gagging's good, babe. Show me how much you want my cock."

I groaned around his dick. This dynamic was completely unexpected but so incredibly debauched. My dick throbbed, and my legs tingled.

Julian's feet stretched and his legs trembled as I gave the blow job my best effort. He grunted when the tip of his cock hit my throat, and his hand tightened in my hair. I wasn't sure whether he was aware of the gravelly commands that came out of his mouth.

"Take it. Like that. Good. Good. You like that. So fucking sexy. Look at your lips stretched around my cock. Get it wet. That's it. Good."

I blinked up at him through wet lashes. I *wanted* to be good for him. I *wanted* him to be proud of me and know I'd tried my best to please him. But at the same time, my dick was desperate for relief. I wondered if I could jack myself off while sucking him.

Before I could get my own underwear off, Julian had flipped me over onto my back and yanked my shorts down. When his hot mouth engulfed my hard length, I shouted into the room. "Fucking fuck! Jules, fuck! Oh *god*..."

It was too good. I was a goner. His strong hand gripped one of my thighs, and his other snuck a wet finger to my hole. As soon as the combination of his mouth on my dick and his finger in my ass came together in my brain, it was over.

My entire body contracted in the split second before the orgasm hit, and then I was panting and gasping, cursing and nearly choking on my own spit. I spilled in his mouth, and he swallowed it. I couldn't believe the sight of him there taking everything from me.

When he pulled off, he lunged forward until he was straddling my hips. His hand shuttled over his wet cock as precum dripped from the tip in a long string. After several pumps of his hand, he threw his head back and came with my name on his lips and my cum on his chin.

I reached out to run my fingers through the puddle of warm spunk on my chest. How was it that every sexual encounter with Julian was hotter than the last? It was physical and primal, with nothing held back. With Julian, I felt completely free to be myself without fear of judgment.

Julian caught his breath enough to look down at me. "How is sex with you better than the fantasy?" he murmured under his breath.

I grinned up at him. "I'm incredible in the sack."

He blew out a laugh, and his easy grin was almost as good at relaxing me as the orgasm had been. "You aren't lying."

I ran my hands up and down his thighs. "Take a shower with me?"

He nodded and climbed off me before reaching out to pull me up.

When we stepped under the warm spray, Jules pulled me into his arms. "I like this." He kissed me under the water for several long minutes until reaching for the soap. "What'd you think about sucking cock? Was it weird?"

I brushed his flaccid dick with my fingers, making it swing heavily against his leg. "It was hot. But it was way hotter when you sucked me off and..."

He pinned me with a knowing glance. "And fingered your little desperate hole?"

"Mm. Maybe. That's kind of... something I wouldn't mind exploring more."

He teased me while taking charge of washing my body. I enjoyed watching while his big, capable hands moved confidently across my skin. It made me wonder what he'd been like with other guys in the past. Had he taken charge with them? Was he always bossy in bed, or was he submissive sometimes?

"You're looking at me funny," he said with a laugh. "Get out and grab a towel. It's late."

I stepped out and did as he'd said. "You seem more okay with things now. Are you feeling better about it?"

Julian nodded and stepped onto the bath mat next to me. "Yeah." He grabbed another towel and dried himself. When we climbed back into bed and pulled the covers around us again, he faced me. While we'd shared a bed many times, it was definitely different now. There were fewer barriers between us. Julian found my hand under the covers and threaded our fingers together. "It's weird, though, you know? Thinking about having a future together in a real relationship. There's always been a boundary there, and now that it's gone, I have to keep reminding myself I'm allowed to think and feel and say things I haven't been able to before."

I brought his hand up to press a kiss against his knuckles. "Like what?"

The telltale blotchiness spread across his neck and chest. "Like I can talk about sex things with you. It's still a little weird."

"Are you worried about freaking me out or scaring me off?"

"I guess so. Even though I know you're cool with it, there's a difference between us talking about sex as friends and talking about sex as... partners. You've never been uncomfortable talking about gay sex, but you have been uncomfortable with *me* talking about gay sex. Which means I'm used to avoiding the topic with you. It's something I need to get over."

I kissed his fingers again. "I'm sorry. Maybe this is the right time to admit to being obscenely possessive and jealous."

Jules let out a laugh and fell back on the bed. "Yeah, right. I'm the jealous one of the two of us. You're the most chill boyfriend ever. You never had a problem with Erin dating other people when you were broken up. Hell, you probably told her she could sleep with other people if that would make her happy."

I thought back to the texting we'd done after the breakup letter. "I actually did that," I admitted. "But make no mistake. My lack of jealousy and possessiveness over Erin has nothing to do with how I feel about you. You're in a whole different category."

He turned his head on the pillow to face me again. The little dark curl over his ear that I loved so much drew my attention the way it always did. "How do you mean?" he asked. "Why would it be any different with me?"

I rolled over on top of him and braced my arms around his head to look directly into his eyes. "Everything is different with you. It always has been. Do you remember in third grade when Heather Jamison spilled her fruit punch on you at lunch and told everyone you peed yourself?"

Julian's brows furrowed in confusion. "Uh, no?"

"Well, she did. And when she got sent to the principal's office the following day, you thought it was unrelated. It wasn't. I stole Ms. Trainor's emergency chocolate bar from her top drawer and shoved it in Heather's desk. Then I got Bart what's-his-name to find it and tattletale. I wouldn't commit petty theft for just anyone."

Jules turned his head to kiss my forearm. "Sneaky little shit. You've always had my back. Like the time we were at that bar watching the Broncos game and you almost got in a bar fight with that guy who got in my face."

The memory of that night filled me with rage all over again. Jules had complimented a woman on her dress, and the woman's drunk boyfriend had mistaken Jules's compliment for flirting. I'd found out later Hazel had recently ordered the same dress, so Julian had known that particular item was popular and hard to find.

"Fucking prick," I muttered. "I would have put him down if you hadn't stepped in front of me."

Julian's eyes glimmered. "One good shove was enough, babe.

Anything more would have gotten us both arrested. You for decking the guy and me for busting you out of the patrol vehicle."

"I should have kissed you on the mouth instead," I said, looking down at his plush lips. "Maybe that would have convinced him you weren't interested in his girlfriend."

He grinned. "You've obviously forgotten Erin was with us. Not to mention I was dating Shane at the time, and he was a rabid monogamist, unlike Nolan. He was angry enough when you defended me before he had a chance to."

"Shane," I scoffed. I remembered the man Jules dated that year. He hadn't exactly been the aggressive type. "Did he ever tell you about the time Tiller and I had words with him after a Riggers/Broncos game?"

Julian's eyes widened in surprise. "No?"

I couldn't help but steal a kiss of those full lips before telling him the story. When I finished, they were red and wet. I kissed him again quickly before pulling back. "He told Erin he planned to get you a pair of lovebirds for your birthday as a surprise."

If it was possible for his eyes to widen even farther, they did. "Jesus fuck. His mom had pet birds. I hated them. He knew that. They never shut up, and they live for, like, decades."

"She told him you wouldn't like that and it was never a good idea to get someone a pet without talking to them first. Shane told her he knew you better than we did. I think you'd been dating for maybe six weeks at that point."

Julian's legs came up to wrap around my ass. My cock was already chubbing up between us. Being naked and pressed against him was a new privilege.

"You and Tiller talked him out of it, I assume," he said. "Why didn't you just tell me?"

I leaned in close and dropped my voice. "I didn't like the guy. He thought he knew you better than I did. He didn't."

Julian's hands cupped the sides of my neck. "No. No one ever has," he said softly.

"Tiller and I informed him that surprise birds were a little bit like boomerangs, and he might want to make sure he had all the necessary accouterments in place before receiving his boomerang birds. I may have also mentioned that birds tended to multiply in the process of returning to the original gift giver."

Julian's gorgeous lips widened as his laughter took over. "You're such a meddling asshole," he accused. Thankfully, he didn't seem all that bothered. "How many other times have you gone behind my back as my own personal thug?"

The list of remembered moments fell like Santa's dropped scroll and unrolled across the floor of my brain. "Lots," I said without embellishing. "In my defense, I honestly thought I was being a good friend at the time. I thought that was all it was."

When his laughter died down, he asked, "And Erin? How many times did you meddle in her shit like that?"

I pursed my lips in thought. "One time I had to get between her and Hazel. Your sister can be a menace." I remembered another time. "Oh! And once she almost got attacked by a dog while we were jogging in the park. I got her out of the way just in time."

Julian tilted his head. His eyes were bottomless blue. "Those aren't instances of jealousy."

"No."

We stared at each other as the word sank into the space between us.

I knew I probably should feel guilty. It wasn't fair I hadn't felt those same things for Erin. But then again, I'd told her many times how my love for her was comforting and safe. Familiar. Easy. Like a simple melody I knew by heart. She'd felt the same way.

And that had been the problem.

My love for Julian was also comforting and safe. Familiar. Easy. But Julian was comforting like the sound of my own thumping heart, like the sunrise after a long night that lets you know the world's still turning. Without him in my life, I wouldn't know how to be myself.

And he was more than that, too. He provoked me and challenged me. He made me want to be a better person. He quieted my mind when it was zipping in a million directions and kicked my ass when I needed it in a way I wouldn't tolerate from anyone else. He was the guy standing in front of me, when the world was against me, and the guy right behind me when I was achieving my greatest accomplishments. He was up and down, both the thrill ride and the best friend in the seat next to mine, holding my hand while I rode it.

My everything.

Which was why, even if I *should* feel guilty about not being able to love Erin that much, I couldn't. I was just sorry, like Erin had said, that I hadn't figured shit out before it went as far as it had.

Julian brought my face down to kiss me again softly. "This is real, isn't it? You and me."

"Always," I promised. And I felt it deep in my bones in a place last week's wedding vows never would have seen.

We kissed and caressed and loved and explored and stroked each other off until we were beyond exhausted. As soon as I finished cleaning us up, we fell into a deep sleep wrapped around each other's naked bodies.

When the doorbell woke us up the following morning, I was ready to murder Mikey and every Grindr user in the Aster Valley area. I stormed out to the living room and answered the door buck naked. "We don't want to have sex with you," I shouted.

The guy on the front porch was at least thirty years older than me and wore a paint-stained coverall. He didn't seem particularly startled by my words or my nakedness. "You and my ex-wife have something in common, then. You still looking for someone to fix the broken light over the garage? Pim and Bill said you were looking for a handyman."

Julian came racing out of the bedroom, yanking a hoodie over the sweatpants he'd already put on. He shoved me behind the door. "Oh my god, you must be Tiny. I'm so sorry. Ignore my boyfriend. Yes, of course I still want you to fix the broken light. Let me show you where the ladder is."

Julian shot me a glare over his shoulder that made me want to kiss him until he forgot his own name and drag him back to bed, even if it meant the light never got fixed. But I couldn't lie, hearing him call me his boyfriend so casually was almost enough to make me okay with the early wake-up.

I knew this situation wasn't easy for him. In a way, it had been easier for me to realize the truth of my attraction to Julian than it was for him to accept it, precisely because he'd wanted it so much for so long. I'd only had to open my eyes and see what was right in front of me, while Jules had to make a conscious choice to offer up his heart despite me unknowingly stepping on it so many times in the past.

Fortunately for me, my best friend was incredibly brave.

I knew it would take time for him to truly feel confident, but I was more than happy to reassure him as often as he needed that he was my first and only choice, forever.

And the idea that he was starting to believe in us made my heart soar.

Once they'd left the cabin, I headed back to the bedroom to pull some clothes on, wondering if it was too late to apologize to the repair guy. Probably better that I didn't wind up with a reputation as the local pervert the minute I decided to relocate to Aster Valley.

Before I had a chance to go out and talk to the man, though, my phone rang with a call from Erin, and my stomach somersaulted as I felt the real world begin to intrude on my happy Julian bubble.

Had she heard about me and Julian already? If she had, she was going to have questions, and she might not accept the answers as easily as Tiller and Sam and the others had.

Plus, if Erin knew, did that mean Rod and Lorraine did, too? Rod had been my coach and mentor for so long, he and Lorraine felt more like parents to me, and I cared what they thought. How would they feel when they learned that I'd been in love with Julian, not Erin, all along? What would they think about my plan to quit my job at the store and leave Vail for Aster Valley? Was I ready to risk their rejection?

In my head, I heard Julian calling me his boyfriend, and that gave me the boost of courage I needed. All that mattered was Julian, and if he could be brave, then I could, too.

So I hit Accept, ready to tell my ex-girlfriend about how much everything had changed...

But it turned out some things hadn't changed at all.

18

JULIAN

I showed the repair guy where the ladder was and tried to apologize for Parker's behavior, but it was hard to sound sorry when I couldn't stop smiling.

If you'd asked me two weeks ago whether I was doing okay, I would have told you I was. I had good friends, a great family, the excitement of a new job with Tiller and Mikey. I'd told myself I was reconciled to Parker marrying Erin even though it would change our relationship forever, and I had purchased a wallowing hole where I'd naively thought I'd get over the brunt of my sadness within the span of a week.

It hadn't been until this morning, when I'd leaped out of bed to hear my naked boyfriend yelling at the man he'd thought was another Grindr hookup, that I'd realized how close I'd come to utter disaster.

A life that didn't have Parker Ellis in it every morning and night, making me smile, driving me crazy, grounding me in the constancy of his presence so that I could draw a deep breath... that was no kind of life at all.

Not for me.

I looked back at the house, no longer bothering to restrain my grin, while Tiny got the ladder in place. I made a mental note to ask Parker what he thought about adding a deck area off the kitchen where we could entertain in the summer. Or maybe he'd rather move to a new place entirely. The wallowing hole really wasn't built to entertain friends and family, and I knew Parker would—

My phone rang, and I pulled it out of my sweatshirt pocket to see my sister's face on the screen.

"Hazel?" This early on a Thursday morning, she was usually busy with important meetings at work, so I assumed a legal issue had come up she needed my help with. "What's up?"

Hazel didn't bother to greet me. "Has Parker heard from Erin?"

"Uh." It took me a second to mentally shift gears. "No... at least, I don't think so. Why?"

She hesitated. "Look, I'm not sure exactly what's going on because her texts are all disjointed, like she's consumed every ounce of tequila in Mexico, but from what I've managed to piece together, Nolan realized yesterday that fate was, like, *totally* calling him to go surf in Costa Rica, *brah*. Without Erin."

I winced. "Oof. That sounds like Nolan, yeah. I'm pretty sure the months he spent in Colorado were the longest he's ever stayed anywhere. Did Erin get attached?"

I loved Erin, but given what she'd done to Parker less than a week ago, I was feeling more than a little cold-blooded about her getting dumped.

"Maybe? I think it's always been easier for Erin to do the leaving than to be the one who gets left. But she made some new friends at the resort—you know how she can talk to literally anyone, right?— and they were partying and having fun... until the resort manager came up and asked her how she'd like to pay for the tab Nolan had rung up before he left."

"He left her with his bar tab?" I shook my head. "Classy."

"Not just a bar tab," Hazel corrected. "He also hadn't had any warm-weather gear with him at the wedding, so they'd bought him a whole wardrobe when they got down there and charged it to the room. Then there was the fee for the private catamaran they rented—"

"A *catamaran*?"

"Oh yeah. And some Jet Skis they returned damaged because they'd been drinking."

I squeezed my eyes shut. "Fuck. Parker's gonna lose his mind. Let's not tell him about that part right away."

"Well, that's the problem, though. Erin's freaking out right now. And when she gets like that, she doesn't want me to help her, or her parents..."

"She wants Parker," I said grimly.

"Right. Even when she knows he'll be upset. Remember what happened when she got a DUI a couple of years ago?"

I did. Her parents had lost their minds and come down on her hard. But that had been nothing compared to Parker's reaction after he'd gone to bail her out. After I'd been hit by a drunk driver in graduate school, Parker had gotten militant against driving under the influence. He'd seen Erin's action as a betrayal in many ways. They'd fought about it so much, he'd broken up with her. At the time, he'd sworn that was a permanent deal breaker, but then—just like always —he'd fallen right back in with her when she'd come to her senses and apologized.

At least she hadn't been texting *him* last night. But then again... if she'd been texting Hazel, maybe she'd been texting Parker, too, and he just hadn't had his phone on.

"And Jules, that's not the worst part," Hazel continued. "When Nolan packed up yesterday, he just stuffed his clothes into a backpack he and Erin had used on a hike the day before..."

"Oh, god. Do not tell me—"

"That Erin's wallet and passport are at the bottom of a backpack, which is right now somewhere between the Mexican resort and a tiny Costa Rican surf town, so that she's stuck at a resort with no money and no way to get home? Yeah." Hazel sounded weary. "The thing is, I can't even blame Nolan for all this. I mean, he's a total airhead, but she was right there, signing the receipts, letting it all happen. It's like she forgot that actions have consequences."

Because for Erin, they didn't seem to. Not permanent ones, anyway.

"She's my best friend, Jules, but I can't figure out how to help her anymore or if I should even try."

I waved Tiny down and apologized. "I have to take this call inside. You okay out here?"

He nodded and began to climb down. "I'm going to go get you a new fixture. This one's not rated for this temperature."

I thanked him and returned to my call. "Let me ask Parker if he's heard from her," I told Hazel. "We'll reach out to Rod and Lorraine if not."

"Rod and Lorraine are visiting Erin's uncle Dave in California on a kind of post-wedding golf extravaganza. They were my first call, but I had to leave them a message. I didn't want to bring you or Parker into this unless I had to... but then I realized maybe Erin already had." I could hear the hesitation in her voice. "Jules?"

"Yeah?"

"I'm sorry."

"For what?" I asked. But I knew. She was sorry that, once again, my life was going to turn on Erin's whim. Because when Erin called, Parker answered. And when she needed him, he came running.

And Hazel didn't know how much worse it was going to be this time, because she didn't know that Parker and I were together now.

Parker's selfless friendship was one of the things I loved about him. He was loyal to the people he loved. He'd drop everything to keep his friends from feeling pain. But when he dropped everything for Erin, it usually ended in a new attempt at a relationship with her.

At least, it *had*.

"Let me know what you find out," she said.

I ended the call and opened the front door. Parker was in the kitchen area putting bread in the toaster. The scent of fresh-brewed coffee filled the air.

I wondered if this would be the end of our time together here in Aster Valley. Would we come back here? Would this all disappear like a popped soap bubble once Parker realized Erin needed him?

I walked over and put my arms around him from behind, tucking my nose into the side of his neck to inhale the Parker scent of him.

He grabbed one of my hands and pulled it up to kiss it. "Hey.

You want jam on your toast? There's some strawberry left, but we'll need to get more. I may have snuck eight or ten pieces of toast yesterday before you woke up."

I moved around to grab the coffee he'd already fixed for me. "Yes, please." After taking a sip to fortify myself, I asked him if he'd heard from Erin.

"You heard, huh?" Parker rolled his eyes as he slathered jam on the bread. "Yeah, Erin called right after you stepped out. Nolan left with her money and her passport." He slurped a blob of strawberry off the side of his finger and somehow managed to make it sexy. "Not to beat a dead horse, baby, but your choice in boyfriends has improved. Like, exponentially."

He was not wrong about that. But also...

"Nolan was never my boyfriend," I repeated for the billionth time.

"Right. Because you loved me even then." He pressed a quick, satisfied kiss to my lips, then shoved a piece of toast between my teeth. "Hey, you want eggs, too? I'm not that hungry after everything I ate last night, but I can make you some —"

"No, I don't want eggs," I said around my mouthful of toast. "I wanna know what's happening now. With Erin."

"Well." Parker shrugged, but his eyes didn't meet mine. He took the plate with a stack of toast over to the small table and gestured for me to sit and eat, then returned to grab his coffee. "I told her to ask the resort people the best way to get her some cash so she can at least get to an embassy and start the process of getting her passport reissued. She's gonna text me back when she finds out. But other than that, I told her she's gonna have to swallow her pride and ask her parents to help her pay the bill." He huffed out a laugh as he took his seat. "I have no idea how she racked up twelve thousand dollars of charges when the trip was already paid for in advance."

"Probably the Jet Ski," I said without thinking.

"The what?"

So much for not telling Parker right away. I blurted out the whole story that I'd heard from Hazel and watched his green eyes darken with anger and disappointment.

"What the fuck was she thinking?" he demanded when I finished. "Running off to Mexico for a week of sun and adventure was one thing, but you'd think after watching everything you went through recovering from the accident, after all the times I told her how dangerous it was to operate any kind of vehicle while drinking..." He cut himself off with a shake of his head and forced a smile. "Whatever. Anyway. What's on the agenda today? Planning session with Mikey and Tiller about the big financing meeting tomorrow? I promised Tiller I'd follow up with Rocco and see if he had all the footage he needed—"

I laid my hand over his. "Parker. Don't pretend you're not worried."

Parker took another sip of coffee and shrugged. "Of course I'm worried. But Rod will help her. They have more than enough money to cover the damages. They'll probably fly down once someone gets in touch with them. They'll probably read her the riot act, too, because somebody needs to."

I wasn't sure which of us he was trying harder to convince.

"Haven't they read her the riot act in the past?" I asked gently. "Did it work?"

Parker made a helpless noise. We both knew the only person who ever got through to our headstrong friend even temporarily was Parker.

"You want to go down and help her, don't you?" I prompted.

"Pfft. No."

I lifted an eyebrow, and he deflated.

"Okay, yeah, maybe I have that impulse, but it's partly force of habit." Parker admitted. "And also, she's my friend, and I care about her. I can't help feeling like there's something going on with her that I should have seen... that I *would* have seen if I hadn't been so busy trying not to freak out about the wedding. Especially now that you and I are together and I realize why marrying Erin never felt right in the first place."

Oh. *Wow.*

Parker turned his hand underneath mine, threaded our fingers together, and yanked me over to straddle him on his chair. "But I'm not going. It's not my place. You're my priority, Jules. You always were, and you always will be. I told you that last night, and I'm going to keep telling you *every* night. I'm staying here with you." His hand coasted up my back, tangled in my hair, and pulled my head back so he could drop a butterfly kiss on my nose. "Because I love you. Okay?"

Fuck, I loved this man and his generous heart so much. And the selfish part of me wanted nothing more than to keep Parker with me every minute of every day.

But I didn't want him to stay in order to prove something to me either. He thrived on being a rock for the people he loved, and Erin and the Rokas were at the top of that list, along with me. I didn't want him to feel like he had to hold back because he was worried about my insecurities. I didn't want to be selfish.

Besides, I trusted Parker. So I could be mature about this.

"You should go, baby." I patted his chest lightly.

"What?" He scowled. "Heck no."

"No, listen. You're not going to sleep tonight if you think Erin is down in Mexico, alone and friendless, with no way to come home."

"Well, but—"

"And we don't know if Rod and Lorraine are even checking their voicemail. It could be tomorrow or the next day before they get down there. Meanwhile, Erin is... I mean, she could sell ice to a polar bear, Parks, and there's no one I'd rather bungee jump with, but dealing with paperwork?" I shook my head. "She gets over-whelmed. She's not like Hazel."

"So why can't Hazel go down?" But even as he asked the question, Parker sighed. "She's working on a deal for your dad, isn't she?"

"As usual. Besides, you know Hazel doesn't have the patience for this." I kissed a small, white scar on Parker's chin from a long-ago ski injury and tried to savor the casual intimacy of the moment. "It's gonna be fine, Parks, I promise. I'll book your flight. You text Rod with an update and tell Erin you're coming. "

He grabbed my wrist before I turned away. "Wait." When I turned back to face him, I could tell he was trying to read my thoughts. "Are you saying I should do this because you think it's the right thing to do or because you think it's what I want to do?"

I stepped into his embrace and held on to him. "Uh... both? You're a good man, so you always want to do the right thing." I thumbed through my phone, eager to start making arrangements before I gave in to the clawing desire to keep my boyfriend within kissing distance. "I don't want Erin to feel alone or abandoned." And more than that, I wanted Parker to know I supported him. Always.

Parker stood up and pulled the phone out of my hand before setting it down on the table. "The fact that you still believe Erin's a good person after everything that's happened says a lot about the man you are. You're a good friend, Jules."

I was trying. I was really trying.

"You taught me everything I know," I reminded him. "Okay, so there's a flight leaving in three hours. I'm getting you a return flight in two days. You can change it without penalty if you need to. And I'll be waiting for you at the airport when you get back, okay?"

Parker kissed me in lieu of agreeing. Then he dragged me away from the table, abandoning our breakfast, so he could take me to the shower and show me on his knees how much my ability to book a flight turned him on.

Who said maturity didn't pay off?

Later, though, after Parker had left for the airport—alone, because we both knew airport goodbyes sucked—I wandered around my empty cabin and decided maturity was highly overrated. Even after five minutes of solitude, my ears rang from the silence. The air in the cabin was colder without Parker to warm it. Even the sight of his half-eaten toast made my stomach lurch unpleasantly. I wasn't sure how I could miss him so badly when he'd barely left.

After forcing myself to do the dishes and make the bed, I texted Mikey about the meeting later. Then I flopped down on the couch and called my sister back to update her on the situation.

"He's got a quick layover, but he should get there in around five hours," I concluded after a quick check of the time. "And he'll get things figured out. And it'll be... great." I thought my cheerful voice sounded fairly believable.

"You're an idiot," Hazel said flatly, proving me wrong.

"Me? What?"

"You should know that you weren't the only person I called this morning. I called Tiller, too."

"Oh?" I asked innocently.

"Yeah. *Oh.* And he assumed that I knew about your new relationship status. With *Parker.*"

I rubbed a hand over my forehead. "Hazel, I was going to tell you—"

"Once you'd run all the calculations and dotted the i's and crossed the t's? Which might have happened sometime before you two got matching nursing home assignments?"

"It's been a matter of *days.* Like, *two.*"

"And you've been waiting for it for *decades.* Like, *two,*" she retorted. "And now it's finally, finally happened. He loves you back, Jules. Which brings me back to my original point. You're an idiot."

"Parker going to Mexico has nothing to do with me and him," I insisted. "He still loves Erin. Of course he does. They've been friends nearly as long as he and I have. So he's going to help her out as a friend. And I support him."

"Liar."

"What?" I sputtered, caught. "Look, I trust Parker, okay? He says he's in love with me, so he is."

"I believe that. I believe the hell out of that," Hazel agreed. "Parker Ellis has thought you personally hung the North Star since you were a first grader, and he's steered his ship by you ever since. There was only ever the sexual attraction component that prevented you two from being the world's most scorching couple, and from what Tiller said, Parks managed to wrap his head allllll the way around that little obstacle."

I felt my face go hot. "Tiller's a damn gossip."

"Tiller also said he's never seen either one of you look as happy, as *settled*, as you did the other night."

"Really?" I swallowed hard, chest tight.

"Really. So I'm wondering, Julian, how the hell you got handed the future you dreamed of and just... waved it off to Mexico."

"Because that's who Parker is, Hazel. Helping his friends is what he does. And since I love him for all the parts of him, I don't want to hold him back. So I told him he should go."

"Oh, god," she groaned. "And why didn't you offer to go with him?"

"I... Well, I..." I gripped one of the throw pillows so hard the fabric probably imprinted on my palm. "I have an important meeting at the lodge later about acquiring some property nearby, and I can't miss it."

"Not even for a family emergency? Tiller and Mikey wouldn't understand? Weird."

I opened my mouth to correct her—remind her that Parker wasn't family, exactly—but then I shut it again immediately. Parker *was* my family. Always had been.

Why hadn't I offered to go? Why had the idea never even occurred to me?

"Julian, you do this all the time, and it's got to stop. I get that you've always done it to protect yourself, but if you and Parker are together now, you've got to work on better coping mechanisms and stop pushing Parker to rescue Erin."

"Pushing—? Me? Oh, no. *No.* I have never."

I hated that he always ran off to rescue her. Loathed it.

"You do, though. You always urge him to help her out when she gets into trouble. Honestly, there have been times I wish you'd left her to suffer the consequences of her actions. Maybe that's mean, but it's true. I remember one of the times, specifically, when Parker showed up to help move you into your apartment, and Erin called saying she needed to retrieve her exercise bike up in Cheyenne when that guy broke up with her and took it in his move. Parker said no, because he was busy with you. And you were all, 'Don't worry, Parks. I've got Hazel and some guys from work here. We'll be fine. Erin needs you.'"

"I... I..." I remembered that. I'd been so annoyed with her constant intrusions, calling and complaining about needing help while I was trying to move my shit on a very tight schedule, that I'd finally thrown my hands up and told him to go. It was inevitable that

Parker would go eventually, and I hadn't wanted him to feel bad about it.

I also hadn't wanted to force the issue and make him choose because I'd been afraid he'd choose her.

"Erin's family owns a chain of sporting goods stores, Julian. She could have had a new bike the next day," Hazel continued. "But instead, she and Parker fetched her bike from Cheyenne only to find that it wouldn't fit at Erin's, so they had to take it to Parker's place in Vail. And once the bike was at his place, of course she had to come over and use it. And voilà, they'd gotten back together again, and Erin had felt safe. At least temporarily. But you were the one who prompted him to do it, babe."

I sat in silence for a second, processing all of this. Was it possible that I'd misread things all along? That him choosing her hadn't been inevitable until I'd *made* it inevitable?

"Look, I'm not blaming you for all of their shit," Hazel went on when the silence had drawn out. "Not at all. It's just that Erin grew up a little too safe—she craves stability and hates it at the same time, you know? That's why working for her dad is not a great fit for her. She doesn't get to stretch her wings, and she never suffers the consequences of her actions. Meanwhile, Parker grew up with *no* stability, so he never wants to abandon anyone. He always wants to do the right thing, even when he hates it. Even when he doesn't know what the right thing is. Which is why he sometimes relies on you to help him find it."

I remembered Parker asking, *"Are you saying I should do this because you think it's the right thing to do or because you think it's what I want to do?"* and that same sick feeling was back in my stomach.

What had I done?

"You're wasting your talents mediating contract disputes," I whispered. "You should either be a telephone psychic or a TV psychiatrist."

"I know, right? And instead, I'm here talking to you. So, Jules, please listen. Who's looking out for Parker right now while he's busy protecting Erin? Who's making sure that he knows he's safe and loved and that he doesn't *have* to run all over the world saving his friends if he'd rather not?"

"I am," I said firmly. "I will."

"Good. You know, you've waited nearly your whole life for him to choose you, Jules. And he has. So now it's time for you to make sure he knows that you choose him. And that he doesn't need to prove himself to you or anyone else."

God. The idea that Parker might feel insecure in our relationship —that he could somehow not be aware, after all these years, that if I was his North Star, he was my fucking *sunlight*—horrified me. My hands shook as I put the phone on speaker and tried to call up the same website I'd used to book Parker's ticket. Somehow, the interface had all gotten way more complicated in the past hour, and I couldn't remember where I was or where I was going.

"Julian," Hazel said with remarkable patience. "At the risk of repeating myself, brother, you're kind of an idiot."

"I know. I'm being ridiculous. But I love him so much, and I... wait, what time is it now?"

She sighed. "Time for me to call Dad and tell him that you need him to arrange that private plane timeshare thing he doesn't use nearly often enough to justify the cost, while you find your passport."

"Hazel, I adore you," I said fervently.

"Back atcha. Just go get your man. Tell him I love him. And tell Erin to fucking call me. Okay?"

I agreed happily, but privately I knew that before I delivered any of Hazel's messages, I was going to deliver my own. I was going to tell Parker that I loved him, and I was going to make sure he knew I chose him, too...come hell or high water.

But it wasn't until I walked into the bar of the exclusive resort a few hours later to find Parker and Erin grinning at one another while Lorraine Rokas embraced them and cried, "I always knew you two belonged together!" that I realized exactly what hell looked like.

19

PARKER

By the time I landed in Mexico, I was hot, sweaty, annoyed, and cursing Julian for encouraging me on this stupid journey. I was tired of helping Erin out of trouble. Yes, I was the kind of friend who'd help someone in need, and yes, I prided myself for being there for my friends, but part of me resented this particular time because it was once again Erin pulling me away from Julian without a care in the world for what I wanted and what *I* needed. Why the hell had I let Julian encourage me to come down here when it felt so wrong to be away from him right now?

One of my flights had been delayed, and then I'd ended up seated next to an airsick toddler on the final leg to Mexico. The small, cramped customs hall had been overheated and understaffed, so when my taxi finally pulled up outside of the exclusive beachfront resort, I heaved a breath of blessed relief.

If only Julian had been there with me. I hadn't asked him to come because I understood the importance of his meeting with Tiller and Mikey, especially if we wanted to pursue our plan to move to Aster Valley full-time. But I missed him. I'd only had Julian as my official boyfriend for a matter of hours, and now I was separated from him by hundreds or thousands of miles.

I'd tried texting him several times but hadn't gotten any response yet.

Me: *I love you. Good luck in the meeting.*

Me: *I resent having to fly through Texas to get to Mexico. But... I did have a decent taco during the layover, so there's that.*

Me: *Don't let that weird handyman guy in the house. I got a creepy vibe off him. And who names an old man Tiny? Lock the doors tonight.*

Me: *What's the name of that guy who was in the movie with the thing?*

Me: *One of the Wilson brothers. Does it really matter which one?*

Me: *If I'm into guys now, do I care which Wilson brother it was?*

Me: *Can I just be into you and not other guys? I don't think I care about any of the Wilson brothers. I mean... I like them in movies, I guess. But I wouldn't want to touch their dicks.*

Me: *A nun just saw me type the word dicks. Pretty sure I'm on Jesus's shit list now.*

Me: *Why didn't you remind me to wear flip flops? My feet are sweating in these boots.*

Me: *img90478.jpg*

Me: *That was a picture of the inside of my pocket. Sorry.*

Me: *I love you. Text me back or I'm getting on the next flight back to Denver.*

Me: *Okay, that was a lie. I need a few hours away from airports and airplanes. But text me anyway.*

Me: *I wish you were here.*

I hated not hearing back from him. Julian and I had the kind of relationship where we told each other everything. If I didn't tell Julian something, it was like it hadn't happened at all.

So not hearing from him made me even testier. I entered the wide, open-air lobby of the resort and felt the sea breeze hit my skin. Okay, that was nice. I took a deep breath and tried to shake off the travel stress. I'd never been an easy traveler. It was one of the reasons I'd quit skiing professionally.

A young woman in a crisp white cotton blouse and floral skirt approached with a tray of fruity drinks and a cheerful welcome to the resort.

"Bless you," I said with a smile, taking the glass and enjoying the icy, sweet drink. It went down way too easy.

After taking a second quick sip, I asked her to point me in the direction of the bar where Erin had told me to meet her. I followed the woman down a set of wide stone steps and out of the building on the beach side. The place was a massive resort for adults only set way off the beaten path on its own long stretch of pristine sandy beachfront. The water was an impossible aquamarine sparkling in the tropical sun, so different from the frigid Colorado winter I'd left earlier this morning.

Erin was sitting at a table under the large palapa that covered the bar. She looked beautiful as always, with her blond hair swept off her neck and a tan already warming her skin. But the dark smudges under her eyes showed she hadn't been sleeping well, and the salad in front of her had barely been picked over.

I texted Jules one more time.

Me: *I'm here. She looks really sad. Wish me luck.*

"Hey," I said, sliding the phone into my pocket.

When she noticed me, Erin let out a sound that was a combination of happy, relieved, and surprised before launching herself out of the chair and hugging me tight. My arms came around her automatically, lifting her off the floor the way we'd done a million times before.

"Thank god you're here," she said against my ear. "Ugh, what a cluster."

Her body was so familiar to me, soft and warm, clean-smelling and light. But my reaction was very different. I held her close as a beloved friend, someone I knew well and cherished, just like I always had, but she was *not Julian*, so I no longer tried to make myself believe that my feelings for her were more than friendship or to wonder why I couldn't feel more passion for the prettiest woman in the room.

It all seemed so obvious, in retrospect.

I gently pulled away and took the chair next to hers, raising my hand to a nearby server and ordering a large bottle of water as well as another rum punch.

"How are you holding up?" I asked when she settled back into her own seat.

Her chin began to wobble before she spoke. "Oh, Parks. I made a huge mistake."

"You did," I agreed. "Driving a Jet Ski while you were drinking? Fuck's sake, Erin. You know better."

She sniffed. "Not that. I—I mean, *yes*, that too, obviously," she added quickly once she caught sight of the look on my face. "But even before."

I figured she was talking about Nolan. Part of me wanted to put my arm around her and make her feel better, because god knew that I had done some stupid shit for people I'd dated—like agreeing to marry Erin in the first place—but the other part of me knew she needed something besides sympathy.

"I think you're lucky you only ended up losing a few thousand bucks and your passport," I said severely. "You could've gotten seriously injured, like Julian did. Remember how awful that was, Erin? Remember how close we came to losing him? One driver made a stupid choice and almost destroyed my whole world."

Her eyes filled with tears, and I felt like an asshole. I couldn't comfort her the way I had in the past, with kisses and sex and easy promises. I no longer had any desire to. So I was at a loss.

I sighed and patted her arm gently. "Look, it'll be okay. We'll sort everything out." I made a mental note to ask the desk clerk for an itemized bill, along with a recommendation on where to get passport photos. "But please promise me you'll be more careful in the future, okay? And maybe avoid guys who can't use your full name."

"I swear I will." She reached out to grab my hand and hold it between her own. They were small and light, strange to hold after the strong grip of Julian's larger ones. "I'm ready to come home."

"I bet. We'll go to the embassy and get you a new passport first thing in the morning. As soon as we have it, we can hop on a plane."

She gave me a tremulous smile. "And you'll forgive me? And we'll be okay?"

"There's nothing to forgive. You did the right thing by calling off the wedding. And you and I will always be friends. Promise." I'd meant to reassure her, but as soon as I'd spoken the words, her chin wobble returned.

"But what about our wedding?"

"Our…" I shook my head blankly, sure I'd heard wrong. "What?"

"See, I spent all last night thinking about you and me," she said in a rush. "I've taken you for granted, Parker. I've been so unfair to you. Talking about searching for enlightenment and trying to expand my consciousness. God, you must think I'm so stupid. I keep pushing you away when you're the best thing that ever happened to me. But I get that now. And when we go home, things will be different. We'll get married for real this time, no more cold feet. And we'll settle down in Vail or Denver or wherever, and we'll start our new life. It will all be perfect."

I wasn't sure exactly what to say.

I'd spent a lot of time on my endless flights thinking about Erin and me also. But my conclusions could not have been more drastically different than hers.

Our friends figured I was able to get through to Erin better than anyone because she and I were so in love. I'd thought that, too. But even after two days with Jules, I knew better.

Realizing I was in love with Julian had been like tuning the channel on an old radio just a tiny bit so that the song came in clear. He'd always been my best friend, my other half, and now I knew that all along he'd had the potential to be so much more than that, I just hadn't been able to understand it properly.

What I had with Erin had never been like that, even on our best days. We liked each other. We *loved* each other. We were incredibly good at distracting each other. But the reason we kept coming back to each other was because what we shared had never been serious enough to threaten my relationship with Julian… and had never forced Erin to make a decision about what she wanted her life to look like. Maybe what kept Erin coming back to me time after time was the fact that I cared enough to ride to her rescue but not enough to make demands of her when I got there.

It was hilarious that Julian and I in *two days* had already decided

where we'd live and started putting down roots in our new town…
but Erin couldn't tell me where our "perfect life" was going to take
place once our honeymoon was over.

Erin tilted her head. "You're smiling. Does that mean we're
okay? Because I was thinking… maybe we could get married here.
Arrive back home with it already behind us. Mom and Dad would be
relieved, and that way, we don't have to go through the whole
wedding weekend thing again."

I picked up her hands and kissed the back of them before
squeezing them and setting them back on the table. "I love you, so
very much. But we're not meant to be together like that. I know that
now. And I think you do, too, but you're scared. You're scared of the
unknown and of being alone. But you're not alone. You still have me.
You still have your parents, who love you, and all of our friends who
think the world of you."

A tiny crinkle appeared above her eyebrows. "No. Don't say that.
You're the one for me. You always have been. Even when I've fallen
for other guys, it's always been you."

I shook my head and gave her a soft smile. "You wouldn't have
fallen for those other guys if it was meant to be me. You wouldn't
have kept looking for something better. And right now, you're
looking for safety and comfort. I get it, believe me, I do. But you can
have the safety and comfort of our friendship without us marrying."

She pulled her hands away from mine. "You're mad at me."

"Not one single bit. I'm grateful to you. Canceling the wedding
was brave, braver than I could have ever been. But it was one of the
best things that could have happened to me because it made me
realize something important. All this time, I already had a life partner. I just didn't see it for what it was."

I took a breath and continued, not wanting to upset her but
needing her to understand why the two of us wouldn't end up
together. "But I see it now. And I want it. Erin… I'm in love with
Julian."

She blinked at me uncomprehendingly for a beat before her forehead crinkled even more. "Julian?"

The server delivered my drinks, and I took a long slug of the cocktail before offering it to Erin. She shook her head. "I don't understand. You and Julian? Like... dating?"

That word was very small for something so big, so incredibly monumental and life-changing. But it was accurate. I nodded. "Yes. And I don't want to cause you any pain, but loving him has helped me to see that what you and I had wasn't enough. For either of us. You have a big love out there somewhere, Erin. Someone who's going to take your breath away, and you'll wonder how you ever thought this—" I gestured between us. "—could be love. It never was, which is why we kept breaking up and trying again."

"But Jules... is a guy. And you're..." She seemed to realize what she was saying. "Are you attracted to him? Like that?"

I nodded, trying not to look like a bobblehead. "Very much so. And I have been attracted to him like that in the past, too. I just pushed it aside because I was scared to mess up the friendship we had. I kept going back to the status quo whenever things started to get too real."

She hesitated. It was clear she was trying to come to terms with it and was having a hard time. I didn't blame her. "How could you go from marrying me to dating *Jules* in less than a week?"

"Okay, first, I know you're upset, but you don't get to say his name like that," I warned her. "Julian loves the hell out of you. He punched me when he thought I'd been the one to break up with you on our wedding day." I pointed to the mostly faded bruise on my jaw. "And I'm pretty sure he's jealous as fuck right now, but he encouraged me to fly down here and save you because he wanted me to do the right thing."

Erin toyed with her fingers, eyes on the table, and said in a small voice, "I love him, too. I didn't mean it like that."

"Yeah, I figured. But to answer your question... when you left me the way you did, hours before the ceremony, at that fancy hotel, with all our guests waiting—"

She groaned quietly, clearly embarrassed.

"—it was a huge shock. Like, not even a surprise, although it was that, too, at first. I mean, it shocked my system like a lightning bolt. It woke me up. I decided that no matter how much I loved you, you and I were really, truly done for good after that, which meant I had to take a long, hard look at my life and what I really wanted from it. The truth is, I was a little sad when I read your note. And I was a little scared. But I was also relieved." I gave her a half-smile. "Which I'm guessing is probably how you felt when you wrote it."

"I... I was wrong then, though," she repeated, like she was trying to make herself believe it.

"You weren't. We were wrong when we decided to get married. I thought by marrying you, I was getting to have my cake and eat it, too. I'd have Julian as my best friend and you as my wife. But I had it wrong." I licked my lips and tried to make her understand. "You and I, we've always been there for each other during the hard times, but then during the easy times, we've gone our separate ways to pursue other things. That's because you and I are about safety and comfort. About having a soft place to land. But you can't know how high you'll go if you keep tying yourself to your safety net. And with Jules, I..."

"You want him during the hard times and the easy times," she finished for me.

"So much," I admitted softly. "He's always been the person I've gone to first. I've never made a secret about that to you."

She sighed. "No, I know. And I thought that was great. I loved that you had such a close best friend. And you know I love Jules. But I guess I just thought you had Jules like I had Hazel."

"Yes, but now I also want to share my life with him." I didn't add that I wanted to have lots of sex with him, but I assumed she got the message.

Silent tears escaped her eyes, and I reached out to thumb them away.

"He gives you that romance novel heroine kind of love, huh?" she asked. "The butterfly feeling?"

I smiled softly, thinking of Julian's face on the pillow beside mine in the night. How just seeing him there made me want to gently stroke his cheek, and bite his lip to mark him, and wake him up to talk to him, and memorize the precise curve of that errant curl, all at the same time.

"Better," I told her.

Erin pulled herself out of her chair and climbed into my lap, wrapping her arms around my neck and burying her face in my collar. Neither of us spoke, but I felt the transition between us like an odd kind of changing of the guards. Things would never be the same between us again.

I held on to her for a long time before she pulled away and met my eyes. "Do you think Julian would be okay if I was your new Jules?"

No one could ever be like Jules to me, but I knew that wasn't really what she was asking. "I think he'd expect nothing else."

She smiled. "He's a good egg."

I dipped my chin. "The best."

She sighed and returned to her chair before reaching across and taking a swig of my cocktail. "Now I need to figure out what I'm going to do with myself, I guess. My parents were already unhappy with the way I treated you, but they're going to be livid now. And so much for my goal of becoming head buyer for the store. My dad won't trust me after this."

"Was head buyer really your goal, though?" I wondered. "Or another safety net?"

She frowned, and I shrugged. "You love traveling and adventure, and you've never met a stranger. In the right job, those traits would be prized. And if you didn't feel stuck in your job anymore..."

"Then maybe I wouldn't blow off my friends and family for a week of revelry?"

"Then maybe you'd be able to find happiness in other places, too," I corrected. Then I grinned and quoted my own words to her from long ago. "So your talent's not sewing, babe. You'll figure it out."

She laughed out loud—a bright, genuine sound—then sighed. "Maybe you can help me explain it to my parents."

"You know your parents want you to be happy more than anything," I began.

A deep, familiar voice responded from behind me. "They certainly do."

I turned to see Erin's parents. She flew into her dad's arms and hugged him tightly. "I thought you were in California at Uncle Dave's place."

Lorraine nudged Rod out of the way so she could hug her daughter. "The phones work just as well in California, dear. Or they would have if your father had remembered to plug the charging thingamajig into the wall last night."

Rod reached out a hand for me to shake. "Thank you for coming. Hazel told us you were on your way here, but I wanted to make sure you didn't feel obligated to help."

"You know me better than that," I said, clasping his hand. He pulled me in for a hug. I thought about the hundreds if not thousands of times he'd been there for me, encouraging me as a fledgling competitive skier, celebrating my wins through college and beyond, and finally offering me a job doing what I loved. This man was like a father to me, and I'd do anything to keep from disappointing him.

Anything but deny my relationship with Julian.

"Join us," I said, moving over so they could get to the other two chairs around the square table. "Would you like a cocktail? The rum punch is good, but I'm sure they have margaritas, too."

Lorraine gave me a quick hug and kiss on the cheek as she moved past me to take her seat. "Lord, yes. Margarita for me."

I found the server and ordered drinks as well as a few appetizers for the table. When I returned to my spot, I saw Rod had pulled out some papers.

"I brought a photocopy of your passport, your birth certificate, and anything else I thought we might need to get your passport replaced."

Lorraine looked between Erin and me with hesitation. "Honey, your message mentioned wanting to get married down here, but I don't think—"

Erin cut her off. "We're not doing that. That was… that was a bad idea." Her face flushed, and she reached out to take my hand in hers again. "Parker and I agreed we're better off as friends."

"Really?" Lorraine's eyes went wide.

I nodded and took a centering breath. "Because I'm, um…
I'm…"

Erin's face softened in understanding empathy. "Mom and Dad…
Parker is with Julian. They're together."

Hearing her say it out loud somehow gave me the confidence to
speak. "She's right. I'm in love with Julian. I'm sorry for…"

While I searched for the right words, words meant to apologize
for taking us all down the wrong path, which included an expensive
wedding cancelation, Lorraine hurried around the table, wrapped
one arm around Erin's neck and the other around mine while we
were still seated, and dragged us over the corner of the table into the
world's most awkward—but loving—group hug. "Thank heavens!"
she cried. "Oh, I'm so proud. I have the best kids ever."

Rod chuckled. "Good lord, woman. Don't strangle them."

Erin and I caught each other's gazes. She winked and smiled, and
I couldn't help grinning back in joy and relief. Lorraine could
squeeze me as tight as she liked. I was so damn glad that I got to
have Julian and keep this, too. It was beyond anything I'd imagined.

Lorraine sniffed loudly and shook my shoulder. "Ah, Parker, I'm
so happy for you. I always knew you two belonged together!"

"You did?" I wished someone would have clued me in.

"Oh my gosh, Julian!" she exclaimed in surprise.

"Yeah." I was grinning goofily, but I couldn't stop. "Julian. He
and I—"

"No, I mean, *Julian*." She gave me a brilliant smile, then turned
my head toward the man whose long strides ate up the tile floor
between us. Julian—my Julian—was here in Mexico, looking upset
but determined, his blue eyes never wavering from mine.

I jumped to my feet and pushed my chair away, heart thundering
in my chest.

"Baby," I began as he came closer, then broke off as my thoughts
began tripping over themselves. I wanted to make sure he was okay,
and to ask why he'd come, and to tell him that I loved him so, so
much.

But in the end, I didn't get to do any of those things, because
Julian didn't pause and he didn't hesitate. He didn't stop to greet

Erin or her parents or to even say hello to me. Without breaking stride, his hands came up to cup my jaw, fingers sliding over my stubbled cheeks to grab my thick hair and pull my mouth to his.

My breath came out in a soft *mmmph* that was all acceptance, no protest, and I slid my arms around his back to hold him more firmly against me. It didn't matter how he'd gotten there; it mattered that he was in my arms where he belonged, claiming me with lips and tongue in a kiss I probably would have found way too raw and hungry for public consumption… if I'd been capable of thinking, which I wasn't.

After a long, grounding moment, he pulled back just far enough to meet my eyes. His lips were kiss-swollen and wet, and his thumbs stroked the hair at my temples, like he couldn't bring himself to stop touching me.

"I love you, Parker Ellis," he said, possession ringing loud and clear in his voice. "There is no one in this whole world who will ever love you as much as I do. No one will ever be more committed to you or more devoted to your happiness. No one will work harder to be the sort of person that an amazing man like you deserves. And I—"

"Oh my gosh!" Lorraine exclaimed in an excited whisper.

Julian blinked like he was coming out of a trance, and his eyes darted from side to side like he'd only just realized where we were and who was around us.

He cleared his throat, dropped his hands, and took a half step back. "And I thought that was something you should know," he concluded lamely. Splotchy red stained his neck and climbed up his beautiful face.

I had never loved him more.

I took a half step forward, keeping us locked together, not caring one iota whether anyone saw us, but pitching my words low so only he could hear them. "So you flew all the way to Mexico to tell me that, huh?"

"I flew here because I realized I'm an idiot," Julian said just as softly. His reddened lips tilted up in a half-smile. "Because all this time, I've had the best thing I could have ever possibly dreamed up right in front of me. And I almost let my fears hold me back from claiming it."

I recognized the words I'd spoken in front of our friends the night before, and my chest squeezed.

"I thought you already claimed me," I whispered. "I seem to recall a conversation in bed last night…"

Julian nodded. "Yeah, but when the real world intruded, I got scared. I told myself not to cling to you too hard, to let you make your own choices, that I didn't want to hold you back from doing what you wanted to do." He pulled one of my hands from behind him so he could thread our fingers together, like we were slow dancing right there in the bar. "It didn't occur to me until after you left that holding you isn't the same as holding you back. And that trusting you means being honest about what I'm feeling, even when I know I'm being ridiculous. And that maybe you need someone to tell you that you don't have to go jetting off to Mexico to save your friends if you don't want to, because you're loved unconditionally anyway."

"Baby," I whispered, touching my forehead to his. Nobody had ever spoken to me like that. I'd known that Julian loved me unconditionally — I'd felt it, but hearing it spoken aloud hit differently.

Julian's eyes were bright, filled with unshed tears. "So I came here to tell you that I'm going to try to get over my insecurities —"

"It's been two days, Julian. It's new."

"—but I might always have them, Parks. I might always be a little jealous —"

"I'm very okay with that."

"—I might push you away because I want to pull you close so badly. But I love you. And I trust you. And… I'm not giving you up. You're it for me, forever."

"Thank fuck." This man was my life, my past and my future. He was everything to me. "I love you. I'm so fucking glad you're here."

He hiccuped. "Really?"

Instead of answering him with words, I leaned in to kiss him again, only this time, I kissed him with the kind of tender adoration no one around us could mistake as anything other than the deepest love and devotion.

The vulnerable whimper sound Jules let out was too soft for

anyone else to hear, but it shot straight into my heart and lodged there forever. I would take care of him with my whole self and make sure he never doubted me again ever.

"Oh, god." Lorraine sniffled into Erin's shoulder while Rod patted her back comfortingly. "That's true love, right there. And it's so beautiful. That's what I want for you, my girl."

"Yeah?" Erin gave Jules and me a small smile. "I don't know. True love looks a little terrifying."

Julian tucked me against his side and lifted his arm for Erin to step into his embrace also. "But you have an adventurous spirit, right? Present circumstances excluded."

Erin's grin widened, and she moved forward to hug him. "I do."

"So you'll be fine," Jules whispered into her hair.

"And you have friends who'll have your back," I promised, my eyes meeting Julian's over her head. "That's one thing that won't change."

But as Julian's gaze burned into mine, I knew that lots of things *would* change.

And I was more than ready to put some of those changes into motion.

20

JULIAN

If I could get through Parker's public displays of affection in front of the Rokas family without dying of embarrassment, I could do anything. While we'd spent time with Erin and her family, Parker had been incredibly attentive to me and made sure I felt secure in the knowledge that he wasn't going to hide his feelings for me in front of anyone.

Including his almost-wife and his almost-in-laws.

He'd even told Rod that he was planning to relocate from Vail to Aster Valley so he could head up the ski school for Tiller and Mikey.

While it was incredibly endearing, it was also nerve-racking. I didn't want anyone to feel awkward around us, and I'd hoped Rod wouldn't be angry that Parker was leaving the Vail store. I knew Parker thought of him as a surrogate father.

Thankfully, Rod and Lorraine turned out to be surprisingly supportive, and Erin was gracious and kind. It was clear she felt the loss of Parker keenly, but hopefully she'd find someone or some*thing* someday soon to help her realize Parker wasn't the right future for her. Rod had even gone so far as to shake Parker's hand and tell him this was just the excuse he'd been looking for to expand Rokas Sports into Aster Valley.

"You'll manage the new Aster Valley location, of course, son," he told Parker. "I'll call you in a week or two, and we'll start scouting properties for the storefront, alright?"

Parker had nodded and said that was very alright.

Eventually, we'd split up to arrange a room for Parker and me. I'd been looking forward to spending a few hours alone with my guy and maybe a couple of those alcoholic beverages that came in coconuts. But after he let us into our private oceanfront suite, I hadn't had time to do more than push him up against the wall and kiss him before he'd turned me toward the enormous bathroom and told me to have a soak in the tub that overlooked the water.

"I've got a few things to take care of," he said mysteriously, kissing my cheek. "I'll be back in time for dinner."

An hour later, a tuxedo-clad waiter had knocked on the door with a fruity coconut drink and a note in Parker's handwriting that said "Drink Me"... but Parker still hadn't arrived.

I'd ended up drinking on the private balcony, wrapped up in a resort robe.

Half an hour after that, the concierge brought me a linen shirt and pants from the store in the main lobby—an outfit that was perfectly my style and not at all Parker's—with a note that said "Wear Me."

I'd chuckled to myself as I got dressed, thinking this was probably the first time Parks had ever dressed me before, but I could definitely get used to it.

But by the time the third knock came ten minutes after that, I'd gotten a little impatient. I didn't need more presents; I needed my boyfriend.

I threw open the door. "Yes?" I snapped.

Parker lounged against the doorframe, wearing a light green shirt that made his eyes glow... or maybe that was just the loving look he'd fixed on me.

"Get it right, baby. In this family, we answer the door with 'We don't want to have sex with you,'" he teased.

"But what if I *do* want to have sex with you?" I bit my lip.

Parker stared at my mouth for a beat, then swallowed hard and shook his head to clear it. "In that case, you're going to have to be patient. We have dinner plans."

"I take it that's what you were arranging all afternoon?" I stifled a groan. "I'd imagined that flying to Mexico to surprise my boyfriend and tell him I love him would involve some reward nookie. I'd hoped you were just running down to the gift shop for lube."

"Oh, I got that, too," Parker assured me, taking my hand as he led me down the path toward the main resort building. He pulled me close so his words were a breath in my ear. "And you will be rewarded, Julian, I promise. All in good time."

I shivered and tried to call up even a shred of the self-control that had let me hide my feelings for Parker for nigh on two decades... but it all seemed to have evaporated in mere days.

I was possessive as fuck when it came to my boyfriend. I didn't want to hide anything anymore.

When Parker had said we had dinner plans, I'd assumed he'd meant that we would be meeting up with Erin and her parents, but when Parker gave our name to the hostess and she led us to a private table for two at the edge of the sand, I realized Parker had something else in mind.

"Is Erin's family joining us?" I asked, looking around.

He shook his head. "Nope. They already left for Cancún so they could replace her passport first thing in the morning. It's just us tonight."

The warm breeze from the ocean was a nice change from the cold winter night air in Aster Valley. Glass-covered candles flickered on the restaurant tables around us, and faint sounds of crystal and table-ware clinking mixed with the rhythmic rumbling of the waves at the edge of the surf.

I paused beside the little table. "This is... it's like... a date." It sounded silly to say it out loud, but my brain was having trouble putting things together.

Parker laughed, and the little crinkles next to his eyes caught the light. "Yes. That's exactly what it is." He pulled my chair out for me and gestured for me to sit down.

"Oh," I said, feeling my face go hot. "Wow."

Parker nuzzled my neck briefly before taking his own seat. "Babe, one of these days, you're not going to be so surprised when I do something romantic for you. I can't wait for the day when you start to rely on it."

"It's not just you, it's..." My voice trailed off as I wondered how to describe my feelings. "I've never had this with anyone, you know? Even when I've dated other people, there was always you in my mind. In my heart. So in some ways, all of this is new to me, too."

"Then I'm really glad I get to be your first." He winked and reached for my hand on the table, then looked down at the menu and began predicting which dish I would probably order.

I couldn't believe he was so comfortable holding another man's hand in public that he didn't even look around first.

"You think you know me so well," I teased, squeezing his fingers. "Maybe I should get something completely unexpected, just to prove you wrong."

Parker leaned toward me and said in a confiding whisper, "I knew you were gonna say that," and I burst out laughing.

Parker Ellis had been my sunshine for the past twenty years, and there was no one I relied on more.

When the server came, Parker ordered a bottle of wine and an appetizer. I let the fact of the Rokas family's departure sink in.

"It's just us here?" I asked.

"You and me, on my honeymoon," he said with a smirk. "The way it always should have been. I did invite you originally, if you'll recall. See what you would have missed out on?"

I stared at Parker's handsome face in the flickering candlelight and nodded. "Oh, yeah," I whispered. "I see."

The server came and presented the wine, allowing Parker to taste and approve it. Once we were alone again, I savored the first sip.

Parker eyed me over his glass. "This afternoon, while we were talking with Erin and her parents, I couldn't stop thinking about everything you'd gone through so you could fly down here to be with me—"

I blushed. "It actually wasn't that hard. When I told Mikey and Tiller what was happening, they insisted that we reschedule the meeting so I could be here with you. And my dad lent me the family plane. So, really—"

"I don't mean the logistics, babe. I mean the emotions."

Oh.

"You deserve to be my number one priority without having to give it away to someone else, even for a little while," he concluded.

Parker was sexy as hell sitting there in the candlelight with the sea breeze lifting strands of his hair. His shirt collar was open, revealing a hint of light chest hair. I knew how that chest hair tasted, how it felt against my cheek when his skin was sweat-slick and flushed with lust.

My eyes flicked up to meet his.

"Hmm," he said with a knowing grin spreading across his face. "I know that look."

He did. I fucking *loved* that he knew that look.

"I was thinking about being selfish," I admitted. "I want to stay here with you a little longer and take advantage of the rest of our vacation week."

He pretended to consider my words, tapping his fingers on the side of his wineglass. "You know... I had the exact same thought. In fact, we could take all of next week, too. What are our bosses going to do if we don't show up on Monday? Fire us? We're quitting to go work for Tiller and Mikey anyway, aren't we?"

Parker's challenging gaze made me feel a kind of nervous excitement.

I nodded. "We are."

He leaned over and pressed a kiss to the side of my face before speaking in a low voice in my ear. "I'm going to force you to relax, Peanut. Even if it takes days and days of my mouth on your hard cock."

My eyes slid closed. "You're tempting me, Shortbread."

"You going to teach me how to please you, Julian?" His strong fingers trailed lightly over the back of my hand and traced the outline of my middle finger. "Show me again how good it can be with a man?"

"No." The possessive fire I'd tried to bank earlier flared back to life as I opened my eyes. "I'm going to show you how good it can be with *me*. Because there's never going to be anyone else. Not for either of us."

"Exactly," he breathed. He moved his lips over to brush across mine. "Finally, you understand."

What I understood was that it was time for us to go back to our suite. But when he bit his lip hesitantly, I realized there was more on his mind... and for Parker, I could be patient.

"I've been thinking," he finally said. "Didn't you tell me about a friend of yours from college who was only sexually attracted to people after she'd formed a strong emotional connection to them?"

"Oh, right." I nodded, trying to clear my head from the sexual haze. "Ingrid. I met her at a queer student mixer, and we ended up living next to each other the year we graduated. You met her when you visited for that ski competition, and we watched movies all night. She identifies as demisexual."

"I think that makes the most sense. For me, I mean." He took another sip of wine. I could tell he was processing important thoughts, so I stayed quiet. "I never wanted random hookups. I wasn't attracted to people that way. But I like... I like taking our close relationship further. It was sort of like that with Erin, too. I think I had the wrong idea about demisexuality before—like, if I was demi, I should also have been attracted to Tiller or Hazel, or anyone else I considered a close friend. But I never was."

"None of it is black or white, babe," I reminded him. "I identify as gay, but that doesn't mean I haven't gotten hard for a woman before. It's not that cut-and-dried. Just because demi means you need a closer relationship before feeling sexual attraction doesn't mean you'll be sexually attracted to everyone you have a close relationship with."

I could tell he was ready to move on from the heavy discussion when his eyes got a teasing glint in them. "Tell me what woman made you pop wood. And how have I not heard about this before?"

I rolled my eyes. "Never mind."

"Spill. I demand it. As your best friend and boyfriend, I have certain rights. Full disclosure is one of them. We keep no secrets in this relationship, Julian."

I kicked his leg under the table, causing him to make an exaggerated *oof* sound. "Fine, but if you use this against me later, I'm going to get my Sharpie out in the middle of the night and make you sorry."

He gave me a quicksilver grin. "Oh, I don't know. I think I might like wearing your ink the way you wear mine."

I barely restrained a growl.

Or, actually, maybe I didn't restrain it entirely, because Parker's hold on me tightened, and his head tilted back with the force of his laughter.

Answering happiness bubbled up in my chest, leaving me feeling light and relaxed for the first time in a long time.

"Fine, I'll tell you. Remember when we went to that strip club for John Tolliver's bachelor thing?"

Parker nodded.

"There was a woman dressed in a red sparkly thong and lacy bra that did it for me for some reason. Don't ask me why."

Parker's jaw dropped. "I *know* why. Oh my fucking god, you're an idiot. You follow that guy on Instagram who does burlesque and dresses in that kind of thing all the time. She reminded you of *him*. A *guy*. You're so gay. Even when you pop wood for a chick, it's because of a dude."

I stared at him for a beat before remembering exactly who he was talking about. My face heated. "Wait, how do you know I follow him?"

Now it was Parker's turn to blush. "I... I pay attention."

He was totally lying. "What happened to the no secrets in this relationship thing, Parks? Full disclosure is sacrosanct in our new paradigm, right?" I crossed my legs and leaned back, taking another sip of wine and studying his reaction. He was adorably flustered.

He groaned and buried his face in his hands. "I may or may not have kept an eye on who you follow on social media, *but*... and before you freak out, just listen... it's because you follow a bunch of really cool people like the woman who shuffle dances and the guy who rides the unicycle. And the family who sings sea shanties and the little cat who always cuddles with that giant dog."

"And the gay burlesque dancer and the gay bodybuilders and the gay influencers and the LGBTQ activists and the—"

He cut me off. "And the Unofficial Parker Ellis fan page! So who's the real stalker here, hm?"

"Still you," I said with a laugh. "Still totally my creeper bestie."

"I think you mean your creeper *boyfriend*," he corrected with a little puff to his chest.

"*Mine*," I agreed, my hand tightening on my wineglass.

Parker grinned. "You're growling again."

"Am not."

"Super are. Full disclosure," he reminded me.

"You want to know what's going on in my brain?" I challenged. "Fine. I'm thinking I want to take you back to our room and absolutely ruin you for anyone else, man or woman. I want you to sob and beg. I want to tear you apart and put you back together until you can't remember a time when you wanted anyone but me, because I'm jealous as fuck where you're concerned. I always have been, but now…"

Parker's green eyes were wide and his pupils blown, like I'd overwhelmed him.

I forced myself to let out a shaky breath and shrug like I hadn't meant what I said word for word. "Don't worry, babe. I'm not going to jump you at the table. I can control myself until—"

Parker leaped to his feet and summoned our waiter. "Would you excuse us?" He grabbed my hand and yanked me to my feet, still stammering apologies. "So sorry. Unexpected… emergency… thank you so much, we'd love to have our dinner sent over. Maybe in sixty—" He glanced back at me. "—make that ninety minutes? Thank you so much." He rattled off our room number over his shoulder.

We ran down the path to our suite in the moonlight, Parker pulling me along in his wake. But before we got to our building, I tugged on his hand and pushed him up against a shadowed palm tree. Faint strains of music from the bar and the crash of the surf filled the air.

"Baby, I didn't mean to ruin your romantic plans. I really could have—"

Parker put a finger to my lips. "Julian, you *are* the plans. I don't care about the restaurant or the clothes or any of that. I just... I just wanted to show you that I love you. That I want us to have romance, too. And that there are no other people for me. Not like this. Not like what we have. I promised you that when we were fourteen, remember?"

Of course I remembered. Though I'd spent the last six months thinking he'd forgotten. Or at least that it hadn't been as important to him as it had to me.

"But you know what? I think you should sell me on it anyway," he whispered. "Do exactly what you said you were going to. Show me all the best things about having sex with another man. Take me apart. Prove to yourself that I'm yours."

When we got back to our room, I decided to go for it, push his limits with the kind of sex that was as far from what I imagined he and Erin had done as possible.

I stripped him down and pulled him into the large glass-enclosed shower. "Hands on the wall. Don't move."

I proceeded to wash every inch of him with soapy hands, hot water, and my tongue. When I knelt behind him with the handheld sprayer, he was already panting. "Want you," he begged. "Now. Now's good."

"Mm, no. Not yet." I spread his cheeks and teased the delicate skin of his hole with the hot spray before using soapy fingers to clean him inside and out. His begging increased, and when I found his gland, he pounded the side of his fist against the tiles.

"Fucking Christ, Jules. Fuck! More." His words ended in a hot whimper. He was so delicious like this, vulnerable and needy, open and willing to let me do anything to him.

I turned the spray off and leaned in to taste him. The debauched groan he let out when he felt my tongue on his hole went straight to my balls.

"New favorite thing," he croaked. "This... this..." He stopped trying to say anything and let out another groan instead. "Oh god, that's good. That's so fucking good."

I held the rounded muscles of his ass in my hands and used my mouth and fingers to bring him to his knees. When he was finally down on all fours in the shower, his hand vaguely flapping back toward me to get on with it while his throat let out broken begging sounds, I fumbled for the lube and slicked both of us up.

"Still good with no condom, babe?" I asked. We'd talked about it earlier, about our statuses and our shared desire to go bare.

"Please, Jules."

I leaned over him and pressed a kiss behind his ear. "Gonna rail your ass," I said in a low voice. "Going to fuck you so hard, you scream for me to stop."

He twisted his head so his eyes met mine. "That's *never* gonna happen."

He slid down from being propped on his hands to his forearms. His ass pressed against my groin, and my hard dick moved slickly through his channel. I reached out a hand to grip his wet hair.

It was rough and physical, and I wanted him to know from his feet to the top of his head he was being owned and fucked by a man. There would never be another person allowed into his body like this. There would never be another person to see him at his most vulnerable.

"Only me," I gritted as I pushed into him. "You understand that?"

"Jules," he whimpered. His tight heat gripped me and sent stars winging through my vision. "Only you."

It was wet and messy, hot and feral. I thrust into him like I was punishing him for all the years he'd gone without me. Or maybe I was trying to make up for lost time. I was the one desperate and needy. I needed inside him, I needed to own him, and I needed to show him he'd never have anything better than this. It was impossible.

Parker's hand flew back to clutch at my hip, pulling me closer as he begged me for more. The tight squeeze around my cock was pushing me closer and closer to the edge, especially now that I was able to know what it felt like being bare inside him. I reached around his slick body and found his dick, hanging hard and heavy toward the shower floor.

"Give it to me," I growled in his ear while I stroked him off. Our bodies stuck together in a hot, damp press, and our loud gasping breaths echoed in the enclosed space.

When Parker finally came, his hot spunk falling to the shower floor, he screamed so loud the hairs came up on my skin. I was finally free to let go, and I shot deep and hard into him with a roar.

The two of us ended up naked and messy on the tile floor with our faces in soapy puddles and our limbs entwined.

It was amazing.

"Holy fuck," Parker said with a hoarse reverence. "Holy fucking fuck." He turned his face to look at me. "I want to do that to you one day."

I grinned at him. "Yes, please."

He reached out and cupped the side of my face. "I never knew it could be like that."

"Physical and rough? Loud and messy?"

Parker shifted closer and used his fingertips to brush wet strands of hair from my face. "Maybe. But also... possessive. Dominant. Overwhelming. Hot as fuck." He met my eyes. "Unrestrained and fearless."

He was right. I could have held back for fear of scaring him off. But if this was going to work, we had to be completely open and honest.

"Sometimes I like it sweet and tender," I admitted. "But other times, I'm going to want you on all fours begging me to fuck you fast and hard."

He let out a tired laugh. "It seems like that's not going to be a problem. Who knew I had a bossy Julian kink?"

I opened my mouth to disagree with him, to say he wasn't into being dominated by me, but that was a lie. He was. He was clearly into it. I thought back over our life together and recognized the same themes. There were so many times he preferred me to take charge.

But the fact he was willing to trust and follow me so easily in the bedroom, too, was everything I could have wanted.

"Thank you for loving me," I said softly. "You're the greatest gift of my life."

He moved over into my arms. It was awkward as hell and uncomfortable as fuck, but as long as Parker Ellis was in my life and in my arms, I was happy.

21

PARKER

Julian woke me up early the next morning by raining hot kisses down the back of my neck and along my shoulder blades. I felt the faint throb of bruising on my knees from the sex we'd had on the shower floor and the twinge in my ass from being owned by his fat cock.

There was no way I was taking him again so soon, but that wasn't what I wanted right now anyway. I wanted inside of him. I wanted to know what it felt like to get close to him like that.

I turned over and moved on top of him, taking over the kissing and moving up to his mouth, his cheeks, his earlobes. My hands wandered lazily over his warm skin, tweaking nipples, exploring rounded muscles under familiar ink, and teasing his balls with my fingertips.

"Want you," he breathed into the semidarkness.

"Mmhm." I moved over to the bedside table to grab a bottle of lube. When I returned, he'd pulled his knees back, already knowing what I wanted.

I felt for his entrance with slick fingers. "Tell me if I do it wrong," I said in a low voice. "Want you to feel good."

The look on his face was tender and affectionate. "I love you."

They were the last words spoken for a long time as I played with him and learned what he liked. When he was finally ready for me, I moved between his legs and slicked myself up before pressing against his hole. His body was strong and firm, and his muscles gripped me tighter than I'd ever felt before despite the prep I'd done.

"Oh god. Jules," I choked, glancing down at the skin of his hole stretched around my shaft. It looked painful but also hot as fuck. I'd never tried anal sex with a woman before, and even though I'd taken Julian's thicker cock, it still seemed an impossible fit. "Does it... are you okay?"

"Yes," he half moaned, half laughed. "Very okay. Keep going."

I pushed farther in until it suddenly became easier. Julian's hands came up to cup my face and bring it close enough to his to kiss. We kissed hungrily while I pulsed in and out of him, slowly enjoying the tug and press of our connection.

"Love you," I breathed against his lips. "Feel so good."

"Mine," he said on a groan. "Mine forever. Just like this."

I pressed my forehead to his, drinking in the vows we were making. "Yes, yours forever. Always."

His hands continued to hold my face as we stared at each other. There would never be anything better than this for me. I knew it without reservation.

Which was why I'd spent yesterday afternoon planning a *bunch* of surprises, and our dinner date had only been the first of those.

When we came within moments of each other, I felt like staying inside of him as long as I could. Eventually, it became impossible, so we both moved off the bed to clean up in the shower.

Even though it was early, we got dressed to head down to the palapa restaurant for breakfast. Before we left the room, I grabbed the purchases I'd made at the hotel store the day before and snuck them into my pockets.

Except I wasn't as sneaky as I thought.

"You think you might need a pen?" Jules asked in amusement, catching the last item before I could hide it. "Just in case there are any downhill skiing fangirls hanging out at the omelet station in the hopes of getting your autograph?"

"I didn't choose this life of endless fame, baby. I just try to be prepared," I said solemnly, and Julian's face creased with laughter.

As we rounded a bend in the path, the sun was coming up over the water, shooting warm pinks and oranges across the palm trees and pool deck.

The restaurant was still setting up the breakfast buffet, but they gave us coffee and suggested a stroll on the beach for a few more minutes before returning to eat.

"This place is gorgeous," Julian admitted into his mug of coffee. "You picked a good honeymoon spot."

I looked away from the peaceful surf long enough to laugh at him. "You picked it."

"Me?"

I nodded. "You don't remember? I asked you to describe your ideal place for a honeymoon. You said a place with a beach, no kids, good food and drink, luxurious rooms, gorgeous views, and a spa."

"Lots of places have that," he said.

"I guess so, but when I was searching through options one night, you pointed to this one and said it was extra perfect because it also offered kitesurfing."

"Oh, right. That's ringing a bell. You've always wanted to try it."

He knew me better than anyone. "Yep. That's why I booked this place."

"Are you going to try it?" he asked, looking out at the water. "This afternoon, maybe?"

Nerves jangled in my stomach, and I knew the time had come. "No. I had something else in mind for today." I reached over and took his mug from him before setting both mugs down on a nearby stone wall.

Then I took his hands and sank to one knee in the warm sand.

"Julian," I began.

The look of shock on his face would stay with me for the rest of my life. I pulled his hands up to my mouth for a quick kiss.

"I was going to make you a prom-posal poster and tell you all the punny ways that I après-ski-ate you and want to look into your lovely blue ice forever. But apparently, 'all-inclusive' doesn't include posterboard and colorful markers. Go figure."

I took a breath. "So I will say it simply. I am yours. Forever. I would consider myself the luckiest person in the world to get to share the rest of my days with you." I swallowed. "I know that this may not be the right place, or even the right time, but I need you to know—to *feel*—that I am in love with you and completely committed to you. In my heart, we are together forever. Will you consider making it official by marrying me?"

Once upon a time, I hadn't imagined myself getting married. And even with Erin, it hadn't felt quite right. Now, with Jules, I couldn't imagine anything better.

His eyes filled with tears as he nodded. "Yes, but—"

"But?" I asked with a huff of laughter. Leave it to Jules to have conditions.

He pulled me up and into his arms, wrapping me up in a tight hold. "But you need to be sure. Because I want it to be you and me forever, but we said that once before, and... things got confused. I'm not going to let you out of it once we're married. No take backs."

I shook my head and grinned. "This is what I get for falling in love with a lawyer. Fortunately, I anticipated this." I withdrew a tiny notebook from my pocket, along with the ballpoint pen Jules had seen earlier, and opened the cover to the first page. "As you can see, I've amended our earlier contract," I said in my best lawyerly voice.

"You and me. *In love.* Always," Julian read in a hushed voice. "Oh. My. God. Parker Ellis, you are the cheesiest, sappiest—" He clapped a hand to his mouth to stifle his half sob as that beautiful blush stole over his features, and his hand gripped the notebook tightly.

"No take backs. Not a shred of doubt or hesitation. Nobody else involved, ever. I'm sure." I brandished the pen and signed the paper right below the words I'd written. Then I offered him the pen.

He shook his head and took it, grinning while tears formed in his eyes.

I pulled back enough to get a hand into my pocket so I could pull out the ring I'd found yesterday when I'd come up with the idea.

Julian's eyes widened comically. "You got me a ring, too? *Parker.*"

"It's a silicone ring that's meant for sports. It's all they had in the hotel shops that wasn't super-cheesy, but we can get something nicer-*mpppff*!"

His lips crashed against mine even though his mouth was moving. "Yes. Fuck yes, yes." He pulled back and scribbled his name below mine on the paper with a trembling hand.

I imagined this paper framed, right beside the other, in our house in Aster Valley. A testament to the way our love had changed and grown but had never faltered... and never would.

I laughed and kissed and held him until I realized his hand holding the ring was crushed between us. "Put it on," I urged. "I want to see my ring on your finger."

Julian's shining eyes looked at me with such love and appreciation, I felt like I could have walked to the moon on my own star power.

He put it on and held it out. His hand was shaking, and his other one was covering his mouth in awe.

"I feel like I can finally breathe," I admitted, staring at my ring on his finger. "I didn't know how much I needed you to be my husband until this week, and now..." My throat felt tight, and my voice came out wobbly. "And now I can't help but think about how close I came to ruining everything."

"Nothing's ruined. We're here. Together." He gripped my hand but managed a teasing smile. "Your life path and my life path? They're one and the same path."

I laughed and sent a quick thought into the universe that I hoped Nolan was doing well, wherever he was. The dumbass had helped ruin my wedding... and inadvertently provided the "enlightenment" that enabled me to find the love of my life. I couldn't help feeling a little grateful, even though I fervently hoped we'd never see him again.

I scraped my bottom teeth over my top lip. "What if something happens to fuck things up again?"

Julian held the front of my shirt in two fists and shook me gently. "We don't let it. Let's get married now. Here. Today."

I bit my lip and offered him a sheepish grin. "I'm glad you said that because I may have already made some arrangements…"

When the resort wedding coordinator led us out to the beach several hours later, after the sensuous couple's massage I'd booked, a flirtfest in the sauna, and a decadent seafood lunch during which we discussed the logistics of making a permanent move to Aster Valley, we were dressed in board shorts and T-shirts, my favorite casual wear, at Julian's insistence. The sun was already slanting at an angle from behind the resort, leaving gold sparkles across the water.

Island music played from the nearby palapa restaurant, but it faded as we moved farther down the beach toward a canopy hung with tropical blossoms. Purple, pink, and white flowers lifted and lowered lazily in the breeze.

Julian squeezed my hand. "I feel a little bad that we're doing this without our friends and family around, but I also don't want to share you right now."

I turned to him as we arrived at the spot where we would pledge ourselves to each other.

"I can't think of a better way for us to do this than just the two of us. We can do another ceremony with our friends when we get home, but it's not about the wedding with us. It's about the marriage." I hadn't realized the difference until Jules. "And I don't want to wait."

"No cold feet, then?" he teased.

"Nope." I wriggled my toes in the sand. "Warm and toasty."

"Because as your best man, I could —"

"Not just my best man," I interrupted, raising his hand to my lips. "My only man."

"Yeah," Julian agreed, because he was sensible that way. "I am."

The officiant was a smiling older man dressed in rolled-up beige linen pants and a guayabera shirt with elaborate black embroidery on either side of the buttons down the front of the white shirt. He welcomed us and introduced himself before beginning the simple service.

When we said our vows to each other, each of us added the line "You and me. In love. Always."

We exchanged rings, including a matching silicone band for me, and held hands as the officiant declared, "I now pronounce you husbands in love, in law, and in name. You may seal your vows with a kiss."

The kiss was simple and chaste, but the gentle press of our lips carried with it years of truth and history behind us and the promise of years of love and new memories ahead of us. A vow we would never break.

When it was all over, when we'd signed the official paperwork and shared a celebratory toast of champagne, we slipped off our clothes until we were down to only the skimpy swimsuits Julian had dared me to wear under our clothes.

I chased him into the surf, tackling him bodily in the water and tangling myself in his limbs until we came up laughing and gasping for air.

And then I spent the rest of the afternoon playing in the sun and surf with my husband, my partner in crime, my Peanut, my person, and my very best friend.

He was mine, and I was his. Forever.

Want to read a free 12k-word short about BJ and Dallas? Click here to download Ski Patrol!

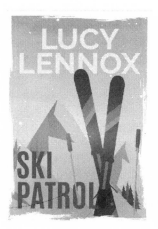

LETTER FROM LUCY

Dear Reader,

Thank you for reading *Thick as Thieves*.

I giant, pink, puffy-heart loved Parker and Julian's story. In fact, I originally began writing this book over two years ago as the first book in my new Aster Valley series. But for some reason, it didn't feel like book one to me, so I set it aside and waited. What an appropriate metaphor for their story!

You'll have noticed I teased several other stories and characters in this book. I can't help myself! Here's what's coming next:

First of all, grab the FREE bonus short story about BJ here: *Ski Patrol.*

Secondly, I'm hoping to start a series set in Knockwood, Alaska, featuring Rocco Valentine and his brothers. The first Knockwood story can be found in the current volume of the *Heart2Heart Charity Anthology* (only available for a limited time). Rocco's story will probably be next in that world, but it wouldn't release until much later this year. Grab Heart2Heart here.

So what am I working on now? Two exciting novels! The first is book two in the Licking Thicket: Horn of Glory series with May Archer. *Hitched* will be out this summer! When an ex-military guy has to pretend to be engaged to his casual fuck buddy in order to trap a villain during a wedding weekend, things don't seem so casual anymore. Pre-order Hitched here.

I've also started a solo standalone story I'm keeping under wraps for now. I expect to release it in early September.

Finally, May Archer and I are releasing an exciting new series later this year called **Honeybridge** and I am already in love with it!

All Lucy Lennox novels can be read on their own so find a story that appeals to you and dive right in.

Please take a moment to write a review of this book on Amazon and Goodreads. Reviews can make all of the difference in helping a book show up in book searches.

Feel free to stop by www.LucyLennox.com and drop me a line or visit me on social media. To see inspiration photographs for all of my novels, visit my Pinterest boards.

Finally, I have a fantastic reader group on Facebook. Come join us for exclusive content, early cover reveals, hot pics, and a whole lotta fun. Lucy's Lair can be found here.

Happy reading!

Lucy

ABOUT THE AUTHOR

Lucy Lennox is a mother of three sarcastic kids. Born and raised in the southeast, she now resides outside of Atlanta finally putting good use to that English Lit degree.

Lucy enjoys naps, pizza, and procrastinating. She is married to someone who is better at math than romance but who makes her laugh every single day and is the best dancer in the history of ever.

She stays up way too late each night reading gay romance because it's simply the best thing ever.

For more information and to stay updated about future releases, please sign up for Lucy's author newsletter here.

Connect with Lucy on social media:
www.LucyLennox.com
Lucy@LucyLennox.com

WANT MORE?

Join Lucy's Lair
Get Lucy's New Release Alerts
Like Lucy on Facebook
Follow Lucy on BookBub
Follow Lucy on Amazon
Follow Lucy on Instagram
Follow Lucy on Pinterest

Other books by Lucy:
Made Marian Series
Forever Wilde Series
Aster Valley Series
Twist of Fate Series with Sloane Kennedy
After Oscar Series with Molly Maddox
Licking Thicket Series with May Archer
Virgin Flyer
Say You'll Be Nine
Hostile Takeover

Visit Lucy's website at www.LucyLennox.com for a comprehensive
list of titles, audio samples, freebies, suggested reading order, and
more!

Made in the USA
Middletown, DE
23 May 2022